Praise for Jorrie Spencer's
The Strength of the Pack

"I loved this story... A real page turner. I, for one, am looking forward to the sequel."

~ *Rites of Romance Recommended Read*

Angels 5 "Jorrie Spencer has written an enthralling story, I started The Strength of the Pack and couldn't put it down until the very end..."

~ *Dana P., Fallen Angels Reviews*

4.5 "THE STRENGTH OF THE PACK is filled with love, sorrow, danger, and thrills. ...I experienced the characters' pains, joys and needs right along with them."

~ *Robin Snodgrass, Romance Junkies*

"Do not miss out on this powerful love story; you won't regret one minute of it! Jorrie Spencer has an incredible way with the written word as she spins and weaves her way into your heart."

~ *Barb, Two Lips Reviews*

5 Roses "Ms. Spencer did an awesome job with STRENGTH OF THE PACK. ...All the pieces of a great read were woven together and I got that great read. ...It's definitely a keeper!"

~ *Robin S., Book Cravings*

"Don't miss THE STRENGTH OF THE PACK, a fabulous read that combines a depth-filled storyline, characters with tremendous physical and emotional chemistry, and the spice of danger."

~ *Lori Ann, Romance Reviews Today*

4.5 "The Strength of the Pack is the first book in the Strength series and a fantastic werewolf paranormal. Ms. Spencer starts off her series with action that will keep readers riveted throughout the story and anxiously awaiting the next installment..."

~ *Water Nymph, Literary Nymphs*

4.5 "The Strength of the Pack is a story where you wonder how can this couple ever be together? ...There is such angst and longing. Jamie is like any woman who loves a man who has a dark secret. ...Seth knows that when the moon is full his shifts into a werewolf. How can he ask Jamie deal with that?"

~ *Janet, Once Upon a Romance*

"I love werewolves and Strength Of The Pack, although gentler than I'm used to in this genre, is a wonderful story. The coming together of Jamie and Seth is at times both beautiful and frustrating. ...Watching these two grow in both love and trust is beautiful."

~ *Lyonene, Joyfully Reviewed*

The Strength of the Pack

Jorrie Spencer

A SAMHAIN PUBLISHING, LTD. publication.

Samhain Publishing, Ltd.
512 Forest Lake Drive
Warner Robins, GA 31093
www.samhainpublishing.com

The Strength of the Pack
Copyright © 2007 by Jorrie Spencer
Print ISBN: 1-59998-656-6
Digital ISBN: 1-59998-512-8

Editing by Sasha Knight
Cover by Dawn Seewer

First Samhain Publishing, Ltd. electronic publication: June 2007
First Samhain Publishing, Ltd. print publication: April 2008

Dedication

To my many critique groups. I wouldn't be here without you. In particular, THL and the great years we had together. Thanks also to Susan and Anna for your hard work on this book.

Prologue

"You look lovely in the moonlight," said Gordon Carver.

Jamie Buchner groaned. Not that she was ugly. She was fine. Whatever.

"And beautiful." Gordon appeared to think generic flattery would affect her, but only the wine had gone to her head.

He touched her shoulder.

"Just leave me alone, will you?" She shrugged off his hand. Her husband might be Gordon's employee but Derek's duties did not include handing over his wife for the evening.

"Jamie," crooned Gordon.

She cringed at his attempt to sound soothing.

"No," she responded firmly, but he had drunk enough that he wasn't going to listen to anything she said.

She sidestepped his next attempt to touch her. Where the hell was her husband? Derek was supposed to be with them in the backyard, admiring Gordon's new gazebo.

Gordon clasped her forearm. She tried to jerk away and his grip tightened. Gordon, who had never done more than talk. Why was he coming on so strong now?

To her horror, he trapped her chin. His mouth fell on hers and she couldn't escape his scotch-soaked tongue.

She swung hard. Her free arm came up, dislodging his grip. Wrenching free, she backed up, spitting in the space between them.

But Gordon backed away from her, too. Jamie's scream lodged in her throat as she watched fear and revulsion play across Gordon's face. She didn't know what to make of his reaction.

She wiped her mouth with the back of her hand. Its trembling annoyed her. She refused to be frightened of this loathsome man. Who wasn't even looking at her now. He stared into the shadows.

A growl, low and angry, made Jamie jump.

"I didn't know you had a pet." She tried to show she wasn't shaken, though her voice was high and breathless. "Good dog."

Without a word, Gordon turned and retreated to the house.

"Not yours then?" she whispered to his back. She rather wished the dog wasn't between her and the house, but mostly she was overcome with relief. Gordon had never been so aggressive that she'd had to *grapple* with him. And to think that Derek, goddamn him, had told her to handle these episodes with his boss diplomatically.

The bushes rustled and she took a deep breath, peering into the shadows. After all, the dog had run Gordon off. He was her savior of sorts.

"Hey there. Great timing. I love you already."

The answering growl sounded affirmative.

"Don't be frightened. Gordon's gone."

Another throat noise, more of a grunt, still affirmative.

"Are you lost?" she asked.

Silence. She wished she could see it better. Maybe it was a toy poodle with a deep chest. She made her way up the path, giving wide berth to the shadows where the dog lurked. She talked in what she hoped was a calm, confident manner, even if it was about stuff that hurt.

"*I'm* lost," she admitted. "I want to go home. Back to Cedartown, Ohio. I miss it. Georgia doesn't suit me."

Jamie wiped away a stray tear. She missed Andreas, too, though she'd tucked him into bed this evening. Her son, who was going to be the child of a broken home.

She sniffled. The maudlin stage of being drunk had arrived.

"Andreas is my son," she told the shadows. She stepped farther up the path, more at ease now that the dog couldn't block her escape to the house. "He'll probably be lonely growing up, but I can't have another child with Derek. Our marriage isn't exactly a success."

She froze as the darkness seemed to move, taking the form of the creature she'd been talking to. Its eyes glowed pale blue in the moonlight. The eyes of a husky.

"Ah, a dog interested in marital problems. Very unusual."

She pegged it as a he—something about the way his large shoulders rolled forward. He moved slowly, tentatively, as if he might bolt. Neither of them, she thought, was feeling confident.

He was darker than husky, his coloring more like shepherd, his build rangier than both. Wolf came to mind.

Despite being mesmerized, she backed away. She didn't believe this creature would hurt her but she was sometimes naive about the good intentions of others, Gordon's unwelcome attentions being a case in point. She rubbed her sore arm.

As if sensing her fear, the dog-wolf whined and crouched low. His ears pointed forward, somewhat at odds with the classic submissive pose. *I won't hurt you*, he seemed to say with great dignity.

He stayed still.

They stared for a few minutes, getting used to each other's presence. The dog-wolf's expression was one of friendly interest—his tail, held high, waved at her. Jamie let out a long breath. He was not in attack mode.

"Well, I won't hurt you either," she said. He'd convinced her the time of danger had passed. "Come here, if you want a pat."

He hesitated.

"Come on. I'll be nice. Promise."

His whole body trembled as he approached. She must have been more affected by the wine than she realized, because she was moved by his seemingly twin emotions of fear and eagerness—wanting the contact, fearing she would hurt him. She felt a real connection with this dog-wolf.

Obviously, she was very lonely.

The wolf inched forward. His slow progress might have been for her sake or his own. He remained low to the ground, his ears at half-mast.

She knelt and held out her hand so he could smell her. His tongue wet her knuckles.

"Aren't you a sweetheart." She raised her arm, brought her hand over his muzzle and slid her palm over his dark head.

"Hey, has someone been hurting you?" His nervousness made her sad. He continued to tremble as she stroked his handsome head.

"I should take you home."

He jerked away, as if in negation.

"Come on, you can't be that smart. Pretend I said you are the most attractive guy I ever met. Come back," she coaxed. "Keep me company. I'm lonely. My husband is having another affair."

The wolf cocked his head in sympathy.

"You are beautiful. Nicely proportioned, though too skinny. Someone should take care of you."

He rose, hackles up. Perhaps he was trying to impress her with his size.

"That wasn't an insult," she protested. Then she heard the angry voice that had caused the wolf to change his demeanor. Of course, the wolf's hearing was more acute than her own.

"Where the hell are you, Jamie?" Her husband.

Growling, the wolf placed himself between her and the voice. She appreciated the gesture but she didn't want the wolf to attack Derek. They'd find and kill the wolf, then.

She laid a hand on his side and felt a tremor run through his body. "Hush, boy, it's my husband. He's decided to watch out for me. A little late and not with great goodwill, mind you."

"Jamie?" Derek hadn't yet noticed her kneeling on the ground.

"I'm here." She felt tired, just seeing Derek.

A big man, too heavy at thirty years of age, his face would be red from drink by now. "What are you doing down there?"

She ignored the question. "I want to go home."

Derek stepped towards her and the wolf's muscles bunched as he growled again. Derek's progress halted. "That thing is huge. Get away from it," he ordered.

She spoke calmly. "Go on, friend. Derek won't grab me like Gordon."

"What are you doing with a damned *wolf?* Gordon says it's been causing problems and someone from animal control needs to come out and shoot it."

Pushing herself up off the ground, Jamie stopped feeling sorry for herself. "That's the kind of lousy, cruel thing Gordon would do. This guy is a sweetheart."

"Yeah, I can tell by the way it growls."

"At you. You're scaring him." Turning to reassure the wolf, she stared at the place he'd been. He was gone, his exit silent, as if he'd dissolved into the night. As if he'd never been there.

Tearing up, she faced her husband. "I didn't even get to tell him goodbye."

"Jesus, you're drunk and crying over a rabid animal you don't know."

"He is not rabid."

"We're calling a taxi. I'm in no shape to drive, either, and you can hardly circulate after kneeling in the mud."

She ignored Derek and gazed into the shadows. *Run away, wolf. Run far away.*

She turned to gaze at her husband. It was time she broke free, too.

Chapter One

Condensation ran down the side of Jamie's mug. At the rate she was drinking, the beer would be flat before she reached bottom. That was fine. She barely touched alcohol since her break-up with Derek. Though when she flashed back to that night two years ago, she thought less about her ex-husband, who hadn't fought her declaration of incompatibility, and more about the wolf that'd come out of the shadows to offer friendship, even protection.

Not that she'd told anyone, because she recognized anthropomorphization. No one was going to be impressed if she waxed sentimental about a wolf she'd encountered while drunk.

"Another beer for you, ma'am."

Jamie jerked her head up. "I didn't order one." She indicated her half-full mug as proof.

The bartender placed the new beer on a coaster beside her old drink. "But your friend did," he informed her.

Jamie squinted down the bar. She'd put away her glasses. The smoke and dim light gave her a fuzzy picture of her fellow drinkers.

Five seats over, a man inclined his head. She was astute enough to guess that he was her "friend". At this distance his features blurred, but he was lean and in her age range, give or take a decade. She returned his gesture with an uncertain

13

smile. She was here to meet people, wasn't she? In theory. After sitting on her own for half an hour, the idea of spending the evening by herself had become an attractive option. Less stressful that way, if pointless.

The man stood and walked towards her. Two women at a table eyed him with interest and, as he came into focus, Jamie could see why—long legs, rangy build, approaching too thin but not quite there, despite powerful shoulders under the white T-shirt. Lifting her gaze to his face, she reacted with a jolt of recognition. He responded with a crooked, almost embarrassed smile.

His face was...perfect. Beautiful. Her stomach flip-flopped, distracting her from the fact she'd seen those eyes before.

Damn. She looked away. One man orders her a drink and she panics. Coming to this bar had been a bad idea, even if she'd secretly hoped to stare at her beer all evening while pretending she was adventurous. She liked playacting. It was quite safe, but only if you did it right.

Which she hadn't because the man stood to the left of her, making it impossible to ignore his presence. His eyes startled her. A pale, unworldly blue. Not marring his perfection, but taking away from his cover model looks some. She'd seen this eye color once, years before, in her kid brother's friend's face. But the Kolski family had disappeared from Cedartown long ago.

He placed a dark hand on the empty stool beside her.

"May I?" The question was tentative and his voice familiar.

"Seth?" she ventured.

He took that as a yes, and sat. "I wondered if you'd remember me." Perhaps pleased by her recognition, his entire face transformed, briefly, with warmth and pleasure.

She was flattered. "I remember you." Always too skinny and pretty as a teenager, poor Seth had not been popular with the boys. Tom had protected him some, when he noticed Seth in trouble, which wasn't often given Tom's penchant for living in his own world.

"You've changed," she added. Okay, not great small talk, but something. He had changed. He'd stopped being too pretty, that's for sure.

"I would hope so. It's been ten years."

"You must be all of twenty-four now."

"Twenty-five. I was a year older than Tom." His mouth curved ironically. "I missed a year of school during one of my parents' many moves." His gaze swept over her in apparent appreciation. "You haven't changed."

"Oh, I think I have." She'd lost the body tone of late adolescence quite a while ago. "But that's gallant of you."

"Gallant, eh? I like that." Seth the teenager hadn't been so charming. "But really, Jamie, you look great."

She would not roll her eyes. Or argue. Biting her tongue, she accepted the compliment and held up her mug. "Thank you for the beer. I'm afraid I'm a slow drinker."

"Slow is good," he drawled.

"Hmmm," she replied less-than-wittily, unsure if that was a double entendre.

Seth might not have been cool when she'd known him, but he was now. White T-shirt, leather pants, well-muscled. She wondered if he was a player. Probably why he was here.

Her idea to pick someone up hadn't been serious, but rather a thought experiment when she needed out of the house for the evening. Summer had been long this year, with the move and Andreas home day in and day out. Single motherhood was better than a bad marriage, but still a slog at times.

"I didn't think you lived in Cedartown anymore." He spoke easily, despite the silence.

"I've been in Atlanta." She'd moved home last month, but didn't want to get into the whole divorce scenario and explain how living close to her workaholic ex had not provided Andreas with father time, while living in Cedartown gave her son grandparents and an uncle on a regular basis. It all sounded, well, needy. And needy was not what would attract Mr. Cool here.

Not that what attracted Seth mattered.

He looked down at her hand, now empty of rings. Would he care that she was available? She wanted him to care. A realization that had her draining her first mug.

Calm down. This wasn't about sex, but whether or not she could carry on a conversation with someone outside her family. She didn't chat with adults these days, unless she was discussing toilet-training, preschools or Pokemon.

Mr. Model-good-looks had no reason to know who Pikachu was.

"Are you back in town for a visit?" He generously ignored her lack of conversational skills.

"It never quite feels like visiting." Truthful, if evasive. She just couldn't talk about Derek right now, or the failure of her marriage.

"I've lived here a couple of years. I enjoy Ohio."

"For the wild nightlife," she suggested.

"I was thinking more about the change of seasons. I missed that in the south."

"Is that where you went after leaving Cedartown?"

"Yup."

"Where?"

He shrugged. "We moved around. You could say my parents were nomads."

She blinked, feeling bad for him. "*Were?*"

"Still are, no doubt." He paused, smile gone, face impassive. "I'm not sure where they are now."

"Oh, I'm sorry." While her parents drove her crazy, she couldn't imagine not knowing where they were.

"Don't be. It's better this way. I have a difficult relationship with my parents."

"I remember." Tom, who did not comment on anyone's personal life, had described Seth's father as cruel.

"Careful there." He indicated her second half-drained mug. "You've sped up since I arrived."

"Well, talking makes me nervous." Geez, what a stupid thing to say. "Unless I'm talking to my five-year-old."

His eyebrows lifted with interest. "You have a five-year-old? That's a nice age."

She assumed this was the stock response of a non-kid-aware guy who wanted to sound positive about children. "Why do you say that?"

"I work with them at an elementary school. I'm a gym teacher." He sounded defensive.

"Oh!" she exclaimed, pleased, though whether by his occupation or his defensiveness, she wasn't sure. One of them made him more accessible. "That's great."

Well, you couldn't get more stock than *that* response, even if she was sincere. In truth, Jamie found men who liked kids attractive.

17

Derek hadn't been one of those men, and since they'd split she suspected some female genes had been activated. They responded to men who interacted well with children, as if proclaiming *good mate material* in their search for a man with whom to continue her family. She thought it wiser to keep this post-feminist observation to herself.

"I'm a stay-at-home mom. It doesn't get more glamorous than that." She tucked a stray hair behind her ear. "Don't get me wrong. That's where I want to be until Andreas is in school full time. He starts half-day kindergarten this fall."

It was a good out. Downing her second mug, she turned to him. "I'm not much of a night person. Part of the motherhood territory, I suppose. I was about to leave when you ordered the beer for me. Which was kind of you. It was great catching up." She took a deep breath, in part because he was watching so attentively. "I think I'll head out now."

"Can I drive you somewhere?" As if he knew she was attracted to him.

"I'll walk," she said without thinking. She'd had her fun, talked to a human being over the age of six about something other than picture books, but she had to end this conversation. She wasn't ready. Why couldn't she have met Seth at a mall? It would be easier to explain she had things to do while shopping with a kid in tow.

"There are no sidewalks around here," he observed. "It's kind of dark on the roads."

True. She'd meant to drive home after nursing one beer all evening, but now she wasn't keen to get behind the wheel. Seth's drink caught her eye.

"Coke," he said. "I don't drink in bars. Gets me in trouble."

There was an edge to his words that softened her urge to get away. Maybe he was someone she could spend time with.

She was out of practice. Not having dated for a decade, she couldn't judge if this was potential date material or pure nostalgia.

"I didn't mean to chase you away." His blue gaze pinned her to the barstool.

"No, no." Her heart beat faster, responding to his interest. "You haven't."

"I'll leave you be."

"Seth." She cast about for an explanation that would make sense to him and ease the sinking sensation in her stomach. If they parted this way, the entire evening, such as it was, would be remembered with disappointment. She was weary of disappointment. "I'm glad I ran into you. It's just, I never come to bars." She winced.

He laughed, but the laughter was generous and she wanted to hear it again. "I do, for what it's worth."

"I've drunk enough that I'm not comfortable driving. I'll call a taxi."

"I'll drive you where you want to go. If you like." His words were careful, almost diffident, as if he expected her to say no. He broke eye contact and sipped his Coke.

She was tempted. The thought of her empty house— Andreas was at her parents' overnight—filled her with despair. "I don't want to drag you away from here."

"Not at all." He smiled, encouraged. "I make a mean cup of coffee, if you'd like to come back to my place." His shrug implied that coffee would suffice. She thought.

She wanted to go with him. The desire, taking hold, surprised her. She wasn't ready to be alone, but she had to warn him. Heat flared on her face. "Just coffee."

He acquiesced with a nod. "Sure. You can tell me what Tom is up to. How your parents are."

Seth the teenager had been a gentle soul and this man's voice was reassuring and humorous. Nothing bad was going to happen.

"Okay," she said.

"Good." He rose from the stool and they stood beside each other.

She looked up at him. "God, I think you've grown a foot since I knew you last."

"Yup. And you haven't."

They stared and Jamie remembered Seth the boy who'd been shorter than her. He'd changed a lot. "You're too handsome now."

He flinched before he could smooth the expression on his face.

She tilted her head, confused by his reaction. "That was a compliment, Seth."

"Thanks," he said without meaning it, looking away. She couldn't make sense of his reaction.

"I'm sorry, but that wasn't an insult," she insisted.

"You're right, it wasn't." He shrugged into his jacket, his good humor apparently restored. "Don't mind me, I wasn't expecting it." He held open the door for her.

"So, I should give advance warning before I compliment you?"

At that, he grinned. "Nah. I'll cope."

Maybe women fawned over him and he was sick of it. The idea intimidated her. What was she doing, going with him?

Don't overthink this.

He touched her on the shoulder, careful not to crowd her. "Jamie, everything okay?"

She didn't like the night nearly as well as the day, but she walked out into it. For this brief moment, she was not alone.

Chapter Two

Really, Seth, if you want to seduce someone, drop the moodiness. He'd almost lost her, with his sharp reaction to her compliment. Maintaining the mask was more difficult than usual because he knew Jamie, even if from childhood.

He shouldn't break rules. But seeing her in the bar alone and a little lost, remembering her from two years ago, her hand soft and voice kind, well, he hadn't been able to resist.

Besides, he had waited too long for physical contact. He knew that, but couldn't get past the little issue of trust, even for an hour of casual sex.

"Allow me." He opened the door on the passenger side and she hesitated, as if she, too, were justifying a broken rule. Perhaps she was. Jamie lived in Atlanta with a husband to whom she would return. But if adultery wasn't the most attractive of betrayals, Derek had already committed his share. Seth shut the car door firmly to emphasize that thought.

Pulling in a long breath of reassuring night air, he rounded the car to the driver's side.

He could trust Jamie for one night and, despite her nervousness, he could get her to trust him. It wouldn't work with a stranger. After two years of celibacy, his choice had narrowed—either bend a rule or give up sex, and he couldn't quite get there.

He had to hide his desperation.

Guilt, he set aside. She was a grown woman. Three years older than he was. Furthermore, she was better off with him than an unknown quantity she picked up. "Only coffee" aside, it was obvious, despite or because of her blushes, she wanted to be persuaded. The idea of her going home with someone else made his stomach clench.

She was naive, in a good way. That's why she'd thought Tom could protect him, way back when.

Time for small talk, if he wanted to make this work. Starting the engine wasn't enough. Now that she was ensconced in his car, she might have second thoughts.

"Tom didn't mention you were back," she said.

"No. I didn't look him up." His last memory of Tom was less than friendly.

She gripped her purse in front of her stomach, as if it protected her. He looked forward to the shedding of her armor, both physical and emotional. He'd been good at seduction not long ago. Surely seduction was like riding a bicycle. You didn't forget how.

No doubt she wondered why, in a small town, he hadn't looked up a childhood friend so he expanded on the topic as he backed out of the parking space. "Your brother never considered me a close friend. Tom didn't have a mean bone in his body so if I wanted to hang around, he wouldn't tell me to go away. I suspect your mother used to urge him to invite me over because she felt sorry for me."

"She thought your parents moved around too much."

"They did." He kept his voice even. "I suppose they didn't have much choice." In truth, his parents were unstable. Not something he aspired to be.

"I think parents make their choices to some extent," she said carefully.

"No doubt."

"Not that I know the specifics in your parents' case."

So she'd heard rumors about his parents and was curious. But she was polite about it and he found himself explaining while he pulled into traffic. "Dad had trouble working for other people. He always wanted to be his own boss, but he didn't have the self-discipline to run a business. He was lucky to pick up the jobs he did." Plumber had been a safe occupation for his father, given their lifestyle, even if it had led to some taunting in the schoolyard. *Eat shit, Kolski, ha ha ha.* Though he saw enough of kids these days to know not only itinerants were picked on.

Why defend his father? Did he think his father's choices made him look bad in Jamie's eyes? Well, maybe they did.

"So, you've decided to change that pattern?" she continued, more chatty, he noted, since they'd left the bar. "Or does teaching lend itself to the nomadic life?"

"I've been in Cedartown two years. We'll see how it goes. Teachers can change jobs but I'd like to stay put." He wanted, more than anything, to be nothing like his father. He'd made his life as different as possible. His parents had moved around. He didn't. His parents didn't take responsibility for children. He did. But there was one aspect of his heritage he would never escape.

Indeed, he lived in a house that sat on two acres of land for that reason. It afforded him more privacy than the various apartments and townhouses his parents had rented during his childhood. He'd bought the house to share with his sister but he did not want to dwell on Veronica's fate tonight.

They turned onto his street in silence. His palms were damp. He hadn't brought a woman home before. But that was okay. Jamie was just visiting Cedartown. And a married woman was not going to talk about their tryst.

What wasn't okay were his nerves. Ironic that the last woman to touch him with any affection was sitting beside him now. And she wasn't going to touch him again if he didn't relax enough to relax her.

He needed a drink. He'd be okay at home with his meager supply of liquor. It was in a bar that he ran into trouble with alcohol, trying to gather his nerve to make a move, and failing. Just getting drunk instead.

The need to touch and the fear that had accompanied it since his sister's disappearance was like a vise grip. And Jamie's tenuous association with Brian Carver did nothing to ease his tension. *Don't think about the Carvers, Gordon or Brian.* He pulled into his driveway.

"Seth? You okay?" Her voice, deep for a woman's, sexy, brought him back into the moment.

"Yeah." He'd been sitting with the ignition off. Pulling up the parking brake, he turned to her. The presence of the girl—though now a woman—he'd worshiped ten years ago pleased him. The clarity of her gaze transformed the fantasy into reality and her sweet mouth charmed him. "The truth is, Jamie, I keep to myself. Hardly anyone comes to my house."

Her eyes widened as he leaned over and kissed her cheek. Her soft skin smelled faintly of wildflower and spice. He couldn't tease out their specific sources. His olfactory senses were not at their monthly peak and they'd been muted by the smoke in the bar. He ducked out of the car and waited for her to follow suit.

She stood up, across the engine from him. Maybe she'd been put off by his confession.

"I'm honored." Her face relaxed into a genuine, if shy, smile.

So, he hadn't forgotten how to do this.

As they walked to the front door, the outside light came on and Jamie really looked at where she was. The bungalow was about the size of her place but set farther back from the road. His house was better maintained too, with a fresh coat of paint and a paved driveway.

"Will you be offended if I compliment your house?"

He slanted a smile down at her. "I guess I deserve that but why don't you wait until you see the inside."

He opened the door and switched on the light, motioning her inside. The foyer was pretty empty, which wasn't so strange, but so was the living room. She gave a short laugh. "And how long have you lived here?"

"Two years." He answered too calmly and she realized she had offended him. Again. "The back of the house is more lived in," he added.

She shouldn't be here if she could so easily, if unwittingly, insult him. On edge, she glanced at the front door. He stepped towards her. Gazing down, standing close, he made thoughts of empty rooms and insults flee. She could smell the leather of his clothes and something Seth underneath. He dipped his head and she quivered when his lips skimmed hers. She almost reached up to hold onto his jacket and keep him there. But she wasn't ready to commit by responding. Yet. Her heart beat high in her throat as he lifted his face from hers.

The kiss brought on a crush of unexpected emotions. She didn't want to appear vulnerable, even if she felt exactly that.

Embarrassed by her burning face, she braced herself to meet Seth's eyes. But he didn't wait for her gaze to lift. Turning her away from their potential embrace, he draped an arm over her shoulders and guided her down the hall. She liked the warmth of his hand on her upper arm. The last time Derek had touched her, they'd both been angry and the sex had been unpleasant. These kisses felt so different—like gifts she hadn't known she wanted. So what if they barely knew each other and the conversation was at times stilted? Her body found it easy to lean into Seth's side.

The kitchen, at least, was furnished. The white counters, cupboards and tile floor might have been spartan without the clutter of dirty dishes and empty bottles.

The sight made her smile. "You do indeed live in the back of the house."

"Sorry for the mess. I wasn't expecting company." That he hadn't meant to bring anyone back, warmed her. As did his expression of being caught out.

"It doesn't matter."

"Good." He squeezed her shoulder and walked over to the coffeepot. "Would you like Mocha Java or French Roast?"

"Since Andreas, I drink instant coffee so either flavor will be great."

"Java it is."

He measured out four spoons of ground coffee and the slight tremor in his hands intrigued her. He was used to bars. He'd said so. But maybe that didn't mean what she thought it meant.

Or, Seth was a sweetie and *cared.*

"Would you like whiskey in your coffee?" he asked over the burble of the coffee machine.

"No, thanks."

He added a dollop to his mug, then stilled. She might not have recognized the tension in his body if she hadn't been watching closely.

"I had a crush on you, you know," he said abruptly.

Her cheeks warmed as she sat on a stool behind the counter, putting a barrier between them. She didn't want to get too emotional, something she was quite capable of, as Derek had pointed out oh so many times.

"I'm flattered." Her words made it past the tightness in her throat as she realized they were going to make love. She was unlikely to back out now.

He hitched a hip on the edge of the counter. "Now you are. You wouldn't have been flattered back then."

"I liked your company." She remembered the skinny, awkward teen. He'd followed her around when Tom was off playing with other friends who didn't want to hang with the unpopular Seth. Derek—they'd just started to date—had teased that she had an admirer and she'd laughed, not wanting Derek to know she enjoyed the attentions of a fifteen-year-old boy. Derek would have given Seth grief.

Other memories were sweeter. "You thought everything I said was wonderful. Pretty heady for an eighteen-year-old girl." With a college boyfriend who made sure she knew who the smart one in the couple was.

"I was obviously devoted." He crossed thick, muscular arms. Despite his leanness, this was a man with a good amount of upper body strength.

"I didn't quite figure that out."

He raised an eyebrow in doubt.

She shrugged. "I didn't think about it like that."

"You didn't think about me much," he corrected. "Understandable. I was young."

"You were Tom's friend and Tom's friends were first and foremost from another planet. Including the nice ones, like you."

"So, I was nice."

"Oh, yeah. Aren't you still?"

He blinked at the question. "I try my best."

"You were nicer by far than my then-boyfriend Derek. Even if I thought he was great at the time." She didn't hide her bitterness.

"I think it's better we don't discuss Derek." His voice was solemn. Part of her wanted to complain about her ex, but it would spoil the mood.

Instead she watched him pour coffee, hands now steady. She, too, felt more at ease. Casual sex scared her, but this no longer felt casual, or at least thoughtless. They didn't have much history, but they had something.

He picked up the two mugs and walked past her. "Come with me." His elbow pointed towards the doorway.

He exited the kitchen. His straight back and strong shoulders mesmerized her, bringing alive a desire that had long been buried deep. She entered a cozy den. A place for friends. Though the thrum of excitement beating through her veins contradicted that thought. Since she'd set eyes on Seth, her body had its own ideas.

He placed the mugs on the coffee table. As he settled into one corner of the couch and she in the other, she was tempted to scoot over and cuddle up to him. She liked his caresses, his firm arms around her. The space between them suddenly seemed daunting.

He held out his hand to her.

She opened her mouth but the word "I" stuck in her throat. Indecision grappled with desire, tangling her words.

"Whatever you want, Jamie." He dropped his arm, eyes pale and watchful. Attentive.

"I don't know what I want. How's that for sophisticated? Though presumably I knew when I accepted your invitation to drink coffee."

"You wanted coffee," he suggested, drinking his. She hadn't thought that eyes twinkled, but Seth's did.

"Truth is, I never drink coffee at night."

"You don't have to drink coffee for my sake." His rapt attention flattered her. It had been years since anyone focused on her like this.

"I know." She set down the mug and he reached over to snag her hand. "I just—"

"You don't have to talk, either." He closed the space between them.

Don't talk.

He pulled her next to him, smelling of musk and male and outside. His fingers ran across the back of her neck and she shivered. The other hand came under her chin and he turned her face towards him, brushing a thumb across her lips. The feather-light touches had her trembling and he'd hardly done a thing.

"I don't usually—"

"Shhh." He brought a thumb back to her lips.

He was right. He didn't want to know she'd left Derek two years ago and their sex life had stuttered to a halt before the split. He might want to know her belly was knotted with desire, but he was going to find out before long.

As his arms came around her, she forked a hand through his dark hair and remembered the buzz cut his father used to insist Seth wear. "You have gorgeous hair."

He stiffened slightly and she wouldn't have noticed if he hadn't just pulled her into his lap. Maybe he feared she saw him as some kind of trophy. He *was* handsome, as well as physically fit. But what drew her were his volatile eyes, his soft, persuasive voice, his frank interest.

"I wouldn't be here." She evaded his lips though she did want to kiss. But she couldn't make love without talking. It wasn't her way. "If I hadn't known you ten years ago."

His mouth explored her neck, giving her goose bumps.

"And you used to rescue frogs the other boys captured. Put them back into the pond where they belonged."

He drew back, his eyes crinkling with humor in a way she hadn't seen before. "My unpopular actions have had long-term benefits, I see."

"I couldn't have gone home with anyone else."

His hold on her tightened. "Be careful, Jamie, if you do go to bars on your own again. Don't go home with a stranger."

She had to laugh. "Are you trying to talk me out of this?"

His serious, somewhat guilty expression puzzled her. She reached up and touched his face, rough from shadow that had formed by the end of the day. "I want to be here, Seth."

"I sure don't want you to be anywhere else," he said roughly.

She grinned. "Maybe it is better if I don't talk."

"Let me think about how I can arrange that." His mouth skimmed hers and her lips parted, wanting more. Which, she suspected, was how he wanted her to feel.

He took her mouth with his.

He'd expected shyness from her, not eagerness, and he shifted to deepen the kiss. The scent of beer lingered on her tongue, in her mouth, and he wanted to taste it all.

He had to keep it slow, the burn might scare her. Two years of celibacy were breaking loose, and he didn't want to make it all about him and his lost restraint. But her hands skimmed under his shirt and over his back, causing his breath to hitch. She smiled into his mouth at that reaction and explored further.

He flipped her leg over his lap so she could straddle him and the kiss broke. Feverishly, he worked on her buttons, wishing he knew her well enough to rip the blouse off, but he never knew his lovers well enough for that.

She started to undo his pants, pressing against his erection which seemed to harden even more, if that was possible.

"Watch that," he warned hoarsely.

"Oh, I will."

Her buttons undone, he pulled down her collar, trapping her arms against her sides.

"Hey," she protested. "I wasn't finished."

His mouth found a cotton-covered nipple and teased. She arched against him and suddenly he needed her naked now. He lifted her up. Her legs wrapped around him as he slid the blouse off her arms.

He reached to undo her bra and found smooth material. "Where's the goddamn clasp?"

In answer, she wriggled down to settle on him, and he groaned.

"Hold me," she said.

"I am."

Crossing her arms over her chest, she pulled her sports bra up and over her head. The lift of her breasts as her arms were raised undid him.

He had her on the floor, ripping off her pants, tearing the foil packet open, covering himself. Regaining some control, he drew back to look at her, beautiful and flushed in the bright light of the den.

Not where he'd planned to have sex.

He opened his mouth and she must have known the word sorry was on his lips because she said, "Seth. I want you *now*."

All thought of restraint fled. He entered her. His chest hurt with emotion he didn't want to feel, but he didn't care. He began to move, hard strokes that blocked out everything but his connection to Jamie who knew where to touch him with her small, caring hands.

He tried to hold on—at one time he'd been good at that—and come back to her. He prided himself on self-control, important when he needed to keep a certain distance. But instead this coupling was becoming all about breaking his long streak of celibacy. He slowed down, in a vain attempt to stop what was building within, but she urged him on and he did what his body longed for—gave himself over. She cried out as he slammed into her, then he was pulsing. Thought fled.

It took him a while to recognize the ragged breathing as his own. Blood pounded in his ears and he gritted his teeth so he didn't say something stupid like, *I love you*, though he'd never uttered such idiocy in his life.

"Seth?" Her voice was breathless, questing, as if she were trying to find him as her hands played with his hair. He blinked twice as he turned to face her. A spear of tenderness unnerved him and he forgot to paste on a smile. He just stared while she smiled at him. She was happy, and a little disoriented.

"You okay, Jamie?" He eased the bulk of his weight off her, thinking he'd been too rough, his foreplay curtailed by urgency. He'd meant to court her.

Next time, he'd keep control and they'd take it slow, and to the bedroom. What had he been thinking, rolling around on the floor of the den like a couple of sex-starved adolescents? Well, once she was in his lap, he hadn't been thinking.

He didn't want to withdraw from the warmth of her body but he rose on his elbows. Her smile faded and now she looked as stunned as he felt. He cradled her face in his hands, marveling at this moment, resisting the passage of time that would let it fade. He hoped the memory would nurture her as much as he needed it to nurture him. The isolation drove him crazy at times. Wolves were made for bonding, touching, mating, and he had to strive against those needs.

Her hand came up to caress his cheek. He didn't like anyone to touch his face but Jamie was different.

"I'm great." Her contralto voice was deeper than usual.

"You are indeed." Stroking the curve of her hip, he examined the rest of her soft, wonderful body. He hadn't had a chance to linger appreciatively. Well, the night was young. He just had to rein in his intensity. Strive for casual. Not act as if they were star-crossed lovers.

Her expression changed from that of satiation to slight unease.

"What?" he asked.

She reached for the blouse that had somehow ended up bunched under her shoulder.

"What do you think you're doing?" he teased. "It's a little soon for modesty to kick in. Me, I still have that after-sex glow."

"Easy for you to say. *You're* pretty much covered."

"I'm covering you."

"And looking at me."

"With great pleasure."

The compliment made her smile. Before she could say more he kissed her, deep and long, and the tension leached out of her again.

"That's better." The return of her sated expression pleased him, as did her swollen lips. "I love your mouth." He kissed her once more. "I always have."

She sighed. "It's impossible to argue when you kiss me."

"That's the idea. But what is there to argue about?"

"Don't get me wrong, it was great, but I'd like you to get naked with me next time."

That he still wore his T-shirt was not an accident. The lights were bright and he wanted a dim bedroom before he undressed.

"Yeah, well things kind of got away from me." He never wanted her to know how much. Still, he claimed her mouth one last time, to remind her of what they'd shared. Then he took care of the condom.

She slipped on her blouse.

"I wouldn't bother doing up those buttons of yours. They'll come undone again." He flapped open one side and kissed her breast.

"Since your pants are on the floor, I'll leave mine there."

"That's fair of you." He picked up the two cups of now cold coffee and padded into the kitchen. "Let's refresh our drinks."

"Is that a useful thing to do?"

"Sure. I might get in a sip or two before I want another taste of you. Would you like a bed next time?"

"That might be nice."

"Come here." He couldn't get enough of her. Knowing this interlude would last only one night pressed down on him. The goodbye had to be final but not, he hoped, wrenching.

As if sensing his thoughts, she went to him. He skimmed his hands over her face, neck and shoulders, ridding himself of his thoughts and her of her questions. He wanted her naked in his bedroom where his night vision saw all. And hers didn't. An unfair advantage and Jamie was probably sensitive enough not to ask intrusive questions, but he didn't want her to examine the scars on his shoulder. Explaining that he'd been ripped up by razor wire would ruin his mood.

She came up for air. "I've never done this before."

He did not want to discuss the fact that this was her first extramarital affair.

"Derek—"

"No." He shook his head. Derek made him see red, with anger that the man didn't appreciate his wife, with jealousy that he could have a normal relationship with Jamie. Exactly what Seth longed for. But Seth wasn't normal. He was a freak.

He took a deep breath. They had to keep things light tonight. The sex had been heavy enough. Scars and adultery discussions were off-limits. "Jamie, talking about Derek is not what's on for tonight."

She winced and backed up, as if he had slapped her. "Sorry. Obviously I didn't read the operating instructions. Please, tell me which topics are allowed."

"I don't discuss husbands with my lovers," he said flatly.

She stared at him long and hard. He shifted, feeling uncomfortable, but held her gaze. After all, she was here, wasn't she?

Though if he didn't do something soon, she wouldn't be here much longer and there wouldn't be a second time. He *really* wanted to make love with Jamie again.

"Let's make tonight just about us," he urged, walking towards her.

She stepped back, expression wary, perhaps angry. "Are all your lovers married?"

"No." Rarely, and before tonight, only when they'd seduced him. But he was not going to defend himself.

"You're right. Not all your lovers are married, Seth. *I'm* not married. The divorce came through a year ago and I left Derek a year before that."

He froze. Dammit. She was available. Strangled elation twisted inside him, potent and useless. He had to discard any hope of something long-term. It was dangerous. Nobody wanted a feral human, especially the mother of a normal child. Because he could never have children, a family, a normal life.

She was in his house. Broken rule number two. He looked back at her.

Her palm was pressed against her forehead, though her gaze didn't leave him. As if observing him would help her, though his surface would reveal nothing right now.

"I can't believe you're disturbed by this news, Seth."

He shrugged, aiming for nonchalance.

Her brown eyes turned liquid with fury. "What the hell was this about?"

He let his own anger form. "What do you think?" he asked, voice rough. He pushed on, ignoring the hurt his words caused. He had to do this right though he could feel a muscle jump in his cheek. "You might have mentioned this little fact about your divorce earlier."

Her stunned, pale face cut him and he gritted his teeth so they wouldn't chatter with emotion.

"You didn't ask," she said, confused. "I didn't realize you wanted me to be married. I thought you were interested in someone single. Like I was." She drew in a long, shaky breath. "I've been lonely, see, though that's stupid to admit."

She lived in Atlanta, not here. Distance was important. She thought she understood his alarm but she didn't. His sister had revealed herself to a normal lover who'd felt disgusted and betrayed. Who had betrayed in turn. Who knew what Jamie's reaction to his real self would be? "When are you going back to Atlanta?" he managed.

"You're scared I'll be around to beg you for another invitation. Don't worry about that." She spun on her bare foot and headed back to the den, almost running into the doorframe.

He followed, observed two spots of color on her cheeks and wished he could ease her wounded pride, her sadness. She shoved her legs into her jeans and wiped a tear from her eye.

"Jamie, look."

"Shut up. I'm not going back to Atlanta. I live here now."

Wariness overrode his guilt. Again. "You lied to me."

Her jaw dropped. "I did not."

"You said you were living in Atlanta."

She shook her head. "It upsets you that I live here? God, Seth, you sure do keep to yourself." That concern flickered in her eyes, made his gut churn. She was too good and this conversation was going from bad to worse. "I didn't tell you I'd moved back because I didn't want to go into how Derek has no time for his son and my parents do. It seemed like too much information, too soon. My mistake, though not my biggest one, I think."

"That was a lie of omission," he insisted.

"Don't make me out to be the bad guy, Seth. If I'd any idea this information was critical, I wouldn't have avoided it."

"And I wouldn't have..." He jammed a hand into his hair, at a loss. Explaining they wouldn't have made love if he'd known she was available was not going to help. "Why would you go to a bar on your own? Not with a friend, at least?" he asked in exasperation. He'd thought she'd wanted to keep her infidelity secret.

"I'm having trouble connecting up with old friends," she replied woodenly. "The two I keep in touch with no longer live here."

He didn't know what to say. "I'm sorry" seemed inadequate.

"I've heard of people like you."

"People like who?" he demanded, instantly alert. She couldn't know he was a werewolf but her contempt made him nervous.

"Players."

"*Players?*" He practically stuttered on the quaint word. Relief. "I've never thought of myself as a player. I'm good to my lovers when they don't lie to me."

"I didn't lie. Stop twisting this."

"I need people to be upfront with me."

"Yeah, like you were with me."

If you only knew. He shut his eyes. "Look, Jamie, stop playing the angel here. Or the prude. You were on the prowl."

"Not really." Her mouth played at the corner. Regret. "I wanted to pretend that I could be wild."

"You wanted good sex. You got it. You should be satisfied."

To his horror, her eyes filled with tears. He crossed to her. "I didn't mean that. You've knocked me for a loop."

She batted his hands away. "Seth. I doubt you understand what single motherhood is like. I needed to get out of the house. I don't know how to pick up men in bars!"

"You managed fine. Stop talking like casual sex is an anathema to you. We enjoyed it."

"It wasn't casual for me."

He couldn't argue. Women, as he bloody well knew, didn't wear sports bras when they wanted to go home with someone from a bar. He spread his hands before him. "Tonight is all I can offer you. I'm sorry."

She was picking up her purse now, grabbing her jacket. He wanted to rewind the scene so they could get back to the sex, the cuddling, the kissing. Of course, he'd made sure to destroy any chance of that. He had to. His sweat smelled of fear and self-loathing. He wondered if she subconsciously picked up his emotions because she was staring at him in consternation and bafflement.

He broke eye contact and pulled on his pants.

"Call me a taxi," she ordered. "Now. I need to get out of here." She stalked across his house. He followed her uselessly as she opened the door and stood in its threshold. He wished he could pull her back in and soothe away that battered look. Instead, he crossed his arms and held his position.

"I'm stupid, that's all. You're the second guy I've had sex with and I'm overreacting." She slammed the door shut and he hunched over, as if she'd punched him in the gut.

Clamping down on his desire to go after her, he dialed the taxi's number. From his window, he watched her pace the driveway, waiting for her ride. He fought the insane urge to run out to her, to explain everything. But he couldn't—the results would be the same, or worse. She would leave. Not hurt, but revolted by him.

The car arrived. She climbed in. He watched her drive away, and that was that. He would never see her again if either of them could help it.

He would have to give up sex after all.

Chapter Three

Seth woke, his body slick with blood, and panic bloomed. It was happening again. Obscene to be caged under the full moon, to be trapped by thick, silver bars. His shoulder ached but Seth's heart was tearing open. Veronica was going to die.

He passed out. Woke and fell into the same pit of terror, surrounded by Brian's precise voice. "I may have overshot the dose, Seth, but I'm sure you wolves need a strong sedative."

The words made Seth gag. His gut was already empty from a previous round. With enormous effort he rose and leapt against the door, leapt into razor wire, as if ripping up his shoulder this time would save his sister.

It never did.

Seth woke in a crouch, man-form, body drenched in sweat. Reflexively, he ran a hand over his scarred shoulder and looked for the telltale darkness of blood. Of course there was none, just his nightmare-induced sweat which nauseated him. He panted, a sign he was about to shift.

Before Veronica's disappearance—he would *not* think death though his dreams sometimes did—he'd never had trouble controlling his shift.

He hadn't had insomnia, either. If he were normal, he would screw up the courage to go to a doctor. Counseling seemed doable, if unpalatable. He'd give a lot to make his thoughts his own again, instead of belonging to the aftermath of terror.

Insomnia had recurred after that episodc with Jamie. *Episode.* He sat on the bed, his mouth curling into a widening grimace of pain that would terrify the only lover he'd taken since his return to Cedartown. He tried not to embrace the bitterness as his body turned fluid, moving in and out of form. His mind retreated from the shift, focused on human thoughts, thoughts that helped him make it through the change.

As a youngster, he used to fear the schism between body and mind would grow so great he'd become lost. It had been his sister, not his parents, who explained this was a normal— werewolf normal—reaction to the strain of shifting.

Today his lightheadedness was buttressed by his longing to see Jamie. Three weeks had passed and he couldn't let go of his desire to phone and apologize. Ask for a second chance. *See, I'm a werewolf. I don't quite trust you normals.*

Oh, she'd say, *I'm so glad we cleared up that little misunderstanding. When can I see you?*

He lost consciousness. When he came to, his body had become solid again, settled to wolf, though the ache of shifting muscles and tendons threatened, as it always did, to overwhelm him. He breathed, gulping air, and the moment passed. Werewolves had to heal quickly and deal with pain often. Physical pain, at least. Seth wished he was better able to deal with emotional pain, like grief, but he hadn't had great role models. His parents had drunk away their emotions.

The moon called him. On all fours, he leapt through the window and onto the grass below, fleeing into the cooling night. Running was a kind of escape, though the only thing he truly left behind was the smell of mowed lawn and forest that mingled in this subdivision at the edge of the city.

Cedartown was a stopping place he'd hoped to share with his sister—wolves weren't meant to be alone. But Veronica was gone and he'd turned to Jamie. He hadn't meant to have sex, just to say hello, but those plans had flown out the window as soon as she'd shyly said his name. One word and his brain went offline, leaving another part of his body to think. Except the sex had been as much about touch as intercourse.

He wondered if part of the attraction lay with Jamie's connection to Veronica, tenuous as it was. Jamie's ex—*ex, why hadn't he thought to ask? Damn it*—worked for Gordon Carver. And Gordon Carver was the father of Brian Carver. Upon whom Seth had wreaked vengeance. But Seth could never undo the damage Brian had wrought, and Veronica's whereabouts remained a mystery.

Seth sped up, as if he could outrun the nightmare of Veronica's fate. He didn't want to even think of Jamie.

The only individual he intended to bond with now was a five-year-old werewolf coping with the burden of his heritage on his slight shoulders. Not that Seth felt much like a wise mentor, but he was all the boy had. Eastward bound, Seth searched for the pup's scent and caught it, too far out. Sanjay shouldn't be out on his own but he didn't always obey his mother, or Seth. The boy was headstrong, as werewolves could be, especially those abandoned by a father.

Seth loped through the forest, towards Sanjay's mansion. Rani was lucky her rich parents could afford to buy her a house in the country to shield Sanjay from curious eyes. Or, Sanjay was lucky to have a mother who loved her werewolf son. Seth ran with Sanjay most nights of the full moon though his stamina was that of a puppy. Seth's inadvertent adoption of Sanjay had ended the worst of his screeching tantrums. Even so, it had taken a few months for Rani to trust a lone werewolf to care for her son.

The pup stood now, stance eager, tail raised, searching for Seth with his eyes more than his nose. Sanjay still hadn't learned to make proper use of the stronger wolf senses and the extent of his vulnerability made Seth uneasy.

It was safe here, Seth reminded himself. Brian was dead and most people didn't believe in werewolves. Still, no harm in inculcating caution in this pup.

In the distance, Sanjay froze. Finally, he'd seen Seth approaching from upwind. They had to work on Sanjay's awareness.

As Seth came near, Sanjay's ears went back and he mock-cowered, knowing Seth was angry at his disobedience. Sanjay had ventured outside the small woods off his backyard. They touched briefly in greeting before Seth pinned Sanjay down, threatening with noise and teeth that Sanjay didn't take seriously. He was too happy to see Seth after the three-week separation.

Sanjay's joy did not mitigate Seth's concern and he nipped the pup's shoulder. Sanjay yelped in protest, as if oblivious to what he'd done wrong. Seth was tempted to teach Sanjay a lesson by leading him straight home without a romp, and the pup knew it. Whining, he groveled and licked Seth urgently. The smell of pup was sweet with youth.

Seth relented, if for no other reason than this was the closest he would get to fatherhood and he treasured his time with Sanjay.

They played Sanjay's favorite game of tag, followed by chase after chase, exhausting the boy so he'd sleep the night before kindergarten began. At Seth's school.

Neither boy nor mother knew Seth's human identity. He couldn't afford the trust, though it was a shame and the secrecy ate away at him. He'd grown attached to the pup who greeted him with such enthusiasm and would play till he dropped unless Seth ordered him back to his mother.

The hour late now, Seth did just that and, ears back, Sanjay gave Seth one last lick before turning away. From the shadows Seth watched Sanjay trot home, big feet and ears hinting at the large wolf to come. Rani waited on the dark veranda, wrapped in a shawl, silent and still. Seth had to wonder what kind of life she led.

He didn't want to care, like he didn't want to care about Jamie and her pleading brown eyes. She'd been hurt, angry and concerned by his strange behavior.

Seth loped over the highway, towards where he knew Jamie's house to be. He would see where she lived. As human, he'd been careful to avoid contact with Jamie but as anonymous wolf he couldn't resist investigating.

She hadn't meant to mislead him about her marital status or her residence. He could see that now, had recognized it during their ugly argument. Breaking it off with Jamie had been a wise decision, but each time he told himself that, the reassurance felt more hollow. He thought of her incessantly. His heart beat with anticipation as he approached her house.

Jamie's lights were on. It was a small bungalow on an acre of land. Not a surprising home for a single mother, though an interesting contrast to Rani's mansion with its four garage doors. Jamie's parents were solid middle class.

Obviously, Jamie was not waiting in darkness for her little werewolf to come home. She roamed a lit house. He could see her shadow move behind the blinds. Smell her, too. She wore flowers again, geranium and chamomile.

Giving in to his simplest desire of the moment, he threw back his head, opening his throat. The howl was a long, lonely plea to the moon, starting low and rising to the sky, for all the good it would do him. At his mournful song, her shadow froze and she was on the porch, under its fluorescent light, face slightly haggard in its harsh yellow light.

"Wolf?" she called out and he remembered how she'd enjoyed talking to his wolf self in Georgia. Her one word implied that she'd missed him.

He could walk into the unforgiving light and his appearance might ease the worries creasing her face. His muscles bunched and he strained a full minute against his desire before he gave way. As he had two years ago, he walked out of the shadows.

He emerged from the woods and trotted through moonlight towards her. Jamie's heart rate picked up. Perhaps this wasn't sleeplessness, but a vivid dream.

"Wolf?" she repeated.

He was silent and dark, his coloring similar to the wolf she'd petted in Atlanta. But he couldn't be one and the same. Georgia was far from Ohio and the chances were nil that he'd show up on her doorstep.

Maybe this one was a German Shepherd mix.

He halted three feet from her. Stared. Those pale blue husky eyes glowed moonlight and her teeth chattered.

Lack of sleep wasn't doing a lot for her grasp of reality.

"Wolf?" She giggled. "You must think I'm a one-word woman."

His tail swished through air, as if he was amused. Well, for a hallucination he seemed real.

"Have we met?" She sat, bare feet on wet grass, butt on the cedar deck. "I know, bad line, but you *do* look familiar."

His throat rumbled affirmation, then he was beside her, licking her hand, arm and face, acting like an old acquaintance who had missed her company.

"Wolf, you're quite assertive this time." In a whisper, she added, "We're going to pretend we know each other."

He placed his head on her lap and his big eyes stared up at her winningly.

She patted and ruffled his fur, happy at the contact. "At least one guy wants to spend time with me."

He stilled.

"That's okay. It's not your fault I have a self-esteem problem." He licked her all over again, making her smile. "You're lovely, do you know that?" She breathed in his pungent, appealing wolf smell and her loneliness receded. She had someone to talk to. Never mind if the conversation was one-sided.

"Do you mind if I unburden myself?" she asked.

His tail thumped against the deck. She took that as a yes.

"Well, I did something stupid." In fact, she had humiliated herself but even a wolf didn't need to hear that.

His muscles tensed beneath her hands.

"Hey, don't take me seriously. I'm trying not to." *And failing.* "I'm sure you have mating issues yourself. Or is it simpler when you're wolf?"

He responded with a low whine that seemed to negate her assumption.

"No? I'm sorry to hear that. We'll commiserate with each other, how about that?" She paused while he lifted a paw onto her lap. "I'll go first, okay? You'll be the first I've told about Seth. Lucky you."

His bark was low and subdued.

She blew out a puff of air, wishing she wanted to chatter about something besides rejection, something light and loving, quixotic, to match this strange meeting with her wolf. "So, I met this guy I knew ten years ago. Really liked him, because he can be sweet and funny. Had sex with him and he blew me off. Three weeks ago. He hasn't called. Not once. Yet I'm still mooning over him. Stupid, eh?"

The licks became urgent and reassuring.

"Ah, you think I'm beautiful and can't understand his actions. But maybe he didn't like my stretch marks. Who knows? I'm no longer eighteen."

The wolf nuzzled her neck again, making her shiver.

She wrapped her arms around him, enjoying his warm, rough body. "I need someone to hug, Wolf, but the trouble is, this guy, well, he's too good-looking."

The wolf tensed again, withdrawing slightly, but she kept talking. "Things get out of balance if someone is too attractive and they think they can treat people badly."

He whined.

"The worst thing is, get this, I'm worried about him. It's like he's in some kind of trouble and he's strangely defensive at times. God, I'm reading too much into the sex. As if—" She stopped herself. Wolf didn't want to hear how Seth's body had reacted to hers. Yet no matter how often she told herself that a hard cock and a wildly beating heart was just about sex, her heart refused the explanation. She laughed at herself. "He's a self-centered jerk, right?"

The wolf sank his head back into her lap, gaze sorrowful.

"Sorry, buddy." He seemed to be taking her confidence quite hard. "I shouldn't dump. Let's talk about you. Is your life carefree and happy? Do you have a girl?" She scratched behind his ears and he closed his eyes. "You must, a handsome, affectionate guy like you, no?" He didn't move. "Or are you one of those beta wolves who don't get the girl? I've never thought your pack dynamics were all that fair."

He barked.

"Right. Life's not fair but let's move away from that idea. You know, I never did thank you properly for scaring Gordon Carver away two years ago. I don't know about you, but I loathe having an unwanted tongue in my mouth. Yech."

He growled.

"Exactly. My skin crawls just thinking about it." The wolf's body vibrated.

"Hey. Sorry, I'm babbling. Strange things come out at night when you meet your wolf in your backyard." Her laughter was high, almost giddy. Though this encounter warmed her, it was bizarre. "Let's talk about good things now, okay?"

He licked her ear with great attention and she gave a muted squeal. "That tickles. You sure are into kisses."

She could have sworn he grinned, in his wolfish manner.

"Can I try to tame you, Wolf? You're too skinny. You need a home."

He barked and backed away, rising up in all his majesty.

She stood. "There you go again, acting like you understand every word I say. I hope not. I'd be mortified. A guy like you—the silent type—listening to all this girl talk."

He barked again, in negation, then reared up, paws on her shoulders, for one final kiss on the cheek before he turned and bounded out of the yard.

"Come again, Wolf," she called, wistful. But she could feel the smile on her face. Some of the emptiness of the last three weeks had been filled by Wolf's companionship.

Not that Wolf could take away what Seth had done, but Wolf had eased her loneliness.

Funny that they both had almost the same color eyes.

ᘓ

"I don't want to go, Mommy."

Minutes before the bus was to arrive, her son dug his heels into their gravel drive. Jamie gathered him in her arms, picking him up, burying her face in his hair. He smelled fresh and boylike, as only Andreas could smell, and she didn't want him to go either.

But she couldn't say that.

"Hey, you're carrying me to the bus," he accused her. "I can walk."

"I know." She plopped him down at the side of the road and took his warm little hand in hers.

"I don't want to go," he repeated. As the bus came into sight, his lower lip began to tremble.

She closed her eyes for a moment. Jitters and sleeplessness made the effort to be calmly firm difficult, but she couldn't mess up Andreas's first day of school. He'd been excited to take the bus around the school's parking lot last week during orientation. Today was different.

"You like Mrs. Sanders," she pointed out.

The teacher had charmed Andreas but he shook his head, refusing to remember.

A little voice in Jamie's head told her to drive him to school. She could, but she fought herself on it. It was important Andreas be independent. If she gave into her own needs, she'd do everything for her son in an effort to bind him to her. As her mother had tried to do with her and Tom.

She grasped him by the shoulders. "Andreas. If you get on the bus this morning, I'll pick you up at school today."

He gazed at her, wide-eyed, considering, while the bus pulled up beside them. The stop sign swung out and the door opened. The stench of exhaust blew past.

Jamie straightened, wondering how far she'd be able to push Andreas, trying to find strength.

"Hi, Andreas." Mandy, the second grader down the road, liked to mother Andreas, to his great annoyance. The bus driver smiled rather distractedly.

It wouldn't be so bad to drive Andreas back and forth every day. Better than dealing with the bus, surely.

No.

"Bye, dear." She kissed her son's cheek. His hand slid out of hers. Shoulders bowed, he trudged up the large steps of the bus and sat beside a solicitous Mandy. Familiarity trumped Andreas's usual irritation, to Jamie's great relief.

"Thanks, Mandy," Jamie called as the accordion door straightened shut. She waved madly to Andreas who stared at her, book bag clutched in his hands.

God, her little boy was growing up. Off to school for the first time. She was so proud of him for getting on that bus and she didn't know how she would get through the rest of the morning.

CB

Jamie started her car. It was finally time to pick up Andreas for lunch. She hadn't been able to think of anything else since she'd put him on the bus and, despite almost three hours on her own, her chores remained undone.

She hoped this separation got easier. It had to.

Rattled, that's what she was. Mostly by Andreas's absence, but last night's chat with Wolf, while reassuring at the time, now seemed downright spooky.

Damn Seth Kolski. She'd been fine before their little dalliance. Okay, fine and lonely, but her heart and hands had been steady. Unlike now.

If only the sex had been mediocre. Or if he'd been technically brilliant but cold. But, despite their awful fight, she could have sworn he had feelings for her. That slight tremor of his hands, or the groan as he entered her—she wished to hell these vivid shards of memory would leave her alone. They inspired a lot of daydreaming about how he'd phone her up, or come by and offer a reasonable explanation for his hurtful behavior.

What that reasonable explanation could be, she didn't know, but she yearned for it.

Andreas prevented her from dropping in on Seth. She'd been absent-minded enough these past three weeks. Imagine what a serious entanglement with someone who messed with her feelings would be like.

She didn't intend to be a nun for the rest of her life—although occasionally she considered it a viable option—but any new relationship would not take away from the care of her son. Andreas came first.

Last week, when her period had started, she'd been foolish enough to feel disappointed. Seth had used protection. Being a single mother of one child was more than enough for her to handle. Crazy maternal instinct.

She sighed as she pulled into the school's parking lot. Too much had changed this past month—a new home, first sex in years, Andreas starting school. No wonder she felt like the earth below her feet had shifted. It had.

And she would deal with it. Andreas wasn't just a responsibility, he was her anchor. He kept her rooted to the ground and for that, she was indebted to him.

She shoved hands into her jean pockets and entered the school. Ten minutes early. Well, she wouldn't hover near the classroom door, trying to catch a glimpse of Andreas. She'd wait in the foyer like a calm and sane mother. Study photos of graduating classes from the last decade. That was always fascinating.

The ten large photos took five minutes of her time.

Another five and she could walk down the hall and collect Andreas. She hoped he hadn't been crying though that concern was baseless. He wasn't a crier. He just became serious.

She turned to look at the clock again as someone exited the office, facing away from her, listening to a parting comment from the cute secretary.

Before he pivoted to walk forward into her, she recognized the line of his body, the thick shoulders, the unruly hair. Her already roiling stomach threatened to make her sick.

A mother's normal separation anxiety over her only child's first day at school was more than enough to deal with. She couldn't face Seth right now. A man whose smile fled upon sight of her, whose countenance became grim.

She frowned. Did Seth have this not very casual reaction to every woman he brought home?

"Jamie?" His voice was low and controlled, as if her presence rocked him back on his heels, though he stood quite still.

She turned away. This was not how she wanted to greet her son, spinning tales in her head about how she meant something to Seth. She marched down the hall to look for Andreas.

Dammit. He'd considered the possibility, of course, even hoped when he was feeling irrational.

Jamie's son was attending Eastdale School.

Running into Jamie was a complication he shouldn't have created when he couldn't move from Cedartown. He was responsible for Sanjay.

Ducking into the men's room, he was thankful that only three other men worked in the school. He needed a moment to compose himself and figure out how to handle the fact he would see Jamie from time to time.

It was odd how he found her a threat *because* he wanted to see her. Jamie was not here to find him. She'd been shocked by his presence. And uncomfortable.

He could keep out of her way—a coward's solution. Perhaps he could ease things between them so that they wouldn't have to brace themselves for uncomfortable run-ins. He owed her that after their tête-à-tête last night under the full moon.

He'd go meet Andreas, who hadn't yet attended gym class. Seth would establish his relationship with Jamie as that of acquaintances. That was the ticket. He ignored that he was eager to talk to her.

Striding down the hall, he rounded the corner to see kindergartners lining up to take the bus home. Except for Andreas and two little girls who stood with their respective mothers.

"Say goodbye to Mrs. Sanders, Andreas." Jamie tilted her head towards young, pretty Gina.

"Goodbye, Mrs. Sanders." Andreas's voice was subdued.

Gina crouched down to give the boy a hug. "He's such a great kid."

Jamie's pale, worried face softened. "Thanks."

"I'm hungry, Mom," Andreas announced.

"Oh, here's Mr. Kolski." Gina directed her big smile his way. Newly and enthusiastically married, Gina was Seth's ideal colleague. Grateful for the welcome, Seth smiled back.

"I'm here to get a preview of my newest charges," explained Seth.

"You're a tad late, but Andreas hasn't left yet. Andreas, this is your gym teacher, Mr. Kolski."

Andreas looked up with watchful eyes. Jamie's eyes, brown and clear, under a blond fringe of hair. Seth wanted to connect with him.

"Are you a soccer player?" Seth bent down to tap the soccer ball on Andreas's T-shirt.

Solemn-faced, the boy nodded.

"Excellent. Soccer is one of my favorite sports."

"Every sport is Mr. Kolski's favorite," said Gina.

"Is that why you're the gym teacher?" asked Andreas.

"Yup."

Jamie stood beside her son, silent and stiff. Seth smiled at her hopefully, a peace offering.

Before Jamie could react, Gina spoke. "Well, I'd better grab lunch. My afternoon kids arrive soon. It was so nice meeting you again, Ms. Buchner. Bye, Andreas. See you tomorrow." Gina nodded goodbye.

"Thank you." Jamie's smile was strained and she no longer looked at Seth.

"Mom," whined Andreas, pulling on her hand.

Unwilling to leave them yet, Seth walked around to the double glass doors and held one open for their exit. "I'll show you to the parking lot."

Jamie eyed him. "I can see the parking lot quite well from here."

"I'll make sure you don't get lost on the way."

"I see our car!" Some of Andreas's gravity dropped away as they left the school.

Jamie's Honda sat on its own, near the end of the row. Seth was glad she had a trustworthy car, even if he was trying not to care. He kept walking with them.

"No need to exert yourself, Mr. Kolski," Jamie said, dismissing him.

"Mr. Kolski, is it?" Even so, it was good to talk to her as human. Last night, communication had been one-sided. She was pissed and wouldn't believe he'd missed her these last three weeks.

"Isn't that your name?" asked Andreas.

"Indeed, it is. But I knew your mother and Uncle Tom when we were kids. She used to call me Seth, back then."

Andreas stopped on a dime and ignored his mother's efforts to urge him forward. "You know Uncle Tom?"

"Yup."

His lower lip pushed out. "I never get to see him."

"I'm sorry to hear that."

"Andreas, that's not true," admonished Jamie. She dragged him by the arm towards the car and talked to him, not Seth. "Uncle Tom took you to your soccer game last week, remember?"

"Last *week*, Mom."

Her son's grasp of time caused a slight smile to play on her lips. She unlocked the car. "Climb into the booster seat, Andreas."

"Bye, Mr. Kolski."

Seth waved and the boy did as he'd been asked. Jamie shut the car door.

She turned and looked straight at Seth. "What are you doing?" she murmured. Direct, but voice low as she no doubt didn't want Andreas to hear their conversation.

"I'm sorry. I'd like us to be comfortable when we meet up at the school."

"That's difficult, given your utter dismay at the sight of me—"

"Jamie—"

"—but I'm game to try." She walked around to the driver's side.

"Say hello to your parents," he said quietly.

She stopped, hand resting on the car handle. "No. I'll feel guilty and strange if I talk about you and it would show."

His chest felt tight with regret. To make matters worse, he took a step closer. "Don't feel guilty. It's my fault. I'm a piece of work, okay?" He indicated Andreas with a jerk of his head. "He's worth your time. I'm not."

Crossing her arms, she looked up at him, eyes flat with anger. "That is such a cop-out."

He broke eye contact. Talking to Jamie had been a bad idea.

"I keep thinking you'll call me, or that I should drop by your place," she admitted.

This wasn't how he'd wanted the conversation to go.

Jamie shook her head. "That flinch of yours should be a huge warning, but it's not the body language of someone who doesn't want to be tied down. You're more complicated than that."

"Forget the analysis, Jamie."

"Right, we'll stick with 'piece of work'. That explains everything."

He flushed.

Andreas opened his door. "Mom, I'm starving."

"Okay, coming." Her hand returned to the door handle and she flung one last gaze at him. "Thanks for the escort. Seth."

He nodded once and left without watching her drive away. His plan had been to lessen the intensity of their reaction to each other, using casual friendliness and some professionalism.

It hadn't worked.

Chapter Four

Say hello to your parents. Seth's words echoed in her head. *Jerk.*

She gripped the steering wheel.

"Mom?"

"Yes, sweetie?"

"Why are you breathing funny?"

She pulled in enough air to calm down. Later, she could become furious again. "Guess what?" She kept her voice from sounding too high and false. "We're going to Oma and Opa's for lunch."

Andreas fairly bounced in his booster seat. "Did Oma make cake?"

"I don't know. We didn't discuss the menu this morning."

"I bet she did!"

Jamie bet she did, too, but just smiled. Her mother didn't spend a lot of time interacting with Andreas. She usually wanted to talk to Jamie about her latest shopping deals at Marks or Target. But she baked for her grandson. Well, there were different ways to show love.

Telling someone to get lost wasn't one of them. Escorting them to the parking lot, however. What was that?

Seth had complicated matters by, first of all, being employed at Andreas's school but, more actively, by accompanying them out the door. Now Jamie would be stuck with another month's worth of daydream scenarios where she and Seth got back together.

Or got together in the first place.

"Do you think Opa will play Pokemon with me?"

No. Opa didn't play with Andreas, either. Tom did, when his wife let him off the leash. Hiss. She was feeling less than generous today.

"You don't have your cards with you, honey."

"Oh, yeah." Silence for two seconds while she pulled into the driveway. "Can I watch TV?"

That's all he did at her parents', though Jamie hoped the routine would change. At least Andreas had grandparents who were there, in person. Unlike his father. Last year, Derek had stopped showing up for his weekly visit. Something a baffled and hurt Andreas didn't understand and she couldn't convince him it wasn't his fault. He nodded as if he understood Daddy worked too hard, but deep down Andreas thought something was wrong with him.

"Let's have lunch first, okay? We're not staying all afternoon. I have chores to do."

"Oh, Mom," said Andreas, disappointed. He constantly wanted her to play or read to him. She felt a pang of guilt. There was no one else around for him with any regularity. Someone like Seth—a man who enjoyed kids—would have been wonderful. If Seth had been interested in a relationship. But he only liked her well enough to walk her to her car.

As she cut the engine, her mother bustled out of the house.

"Hi, Oma!" shouted Andreas. Jamie stepped back so her mother would hug Andreas first. "I went to school today. I took the bus."

Oma enveloped her grandson in her big arms and Jamie felt better.

"Good for you." Her mother straightened and looked at Jamie. "Hi, dear."

"Hi, Mom."

"I bet your mother missed you, Andreas."

"I missed her. Did you make cake, Oma?"

"Plum. Your favorite."

"I want some."

"Andreas," warned Jamie. "Lunch first and don't forget your manners."

"Okay! Where's Opa?"

Jamie could hear the lawnmower going. Her father rode that loud machine every day he could, cigarette in mouth.

"In the back, dear," said Oma, and Andreas raced off.

Her mother patted Jamie's cheek. "You look tired."

Jamie gave a wan smile. "I didn't sleep well last night, first day of school and all."

"Oh, Jamie. It's good for him. And you."

"I know." She and Andreas needed some time apart. It was part of what had driven her to the bar on that ill-fated night. "I'll get used to it."

"Of course you will." Her mother continued to expand on that theme as they went inside, set the table and called Andreas and her father in for lunch.

Andreas decided to have some rye bread with his butter until Jamie took charge of the knife and scraped off an inch of yellow. "Cheese and tomato with the bread, Andreas."

"I don't want them."

"You like cheese and tomato." Jamie kept the exasperation out of her voice.

"No, I don't."

Her father frowned sternly. "If you want your Oma's dessert, Andreas, you'll listen to your mother."

Jamie appreciated the backup, but didn't like the way Andreas sank into his seat, wary eye on his grandfather while she fixed up his sandwich. They'd only been back for a month. Andreas and her parents were getting to know each other better. There hadn't been frequent visits in his first five years.

Jamie broke the silence that followed. "Andreas's teacher seems nice."

"Good," said Oma.

"I like Seth," Andreas piped up.

Damn.

"Is Seth a new friend of yours?" asked Oma.

Jamie gritted her teeth. It didn't matter, it didn't. It just hurt.

"He's my gym teacher," Andreas explained.

"Teachers go by their first names these days?" Her father was all disapproving.

"He's Mom's friend," said Andreas with clear delight. How had Andreas decided he liked Seth so much, given their short time together? "And he likes soccer. Do you think he'll come to my soccer games, Mom?"

Jamie focused on her salad though she couldn't bring herself to eat it. "He's probably busy, Andreas."

"But he *likes* soccer, Mom."

She looked up from her bowl to her mother. "Tom took Andreas to his last soccer game," she told her parents brightly.

"Did he now. At least *you* are allowed to see Tom," said her mother. "Cynthia must have given him a day pass."

"Mom." Jamie indicated Andreas with a tilt of her head. At five years of age, her son did not need to be exposed to the petty family tensions between mother and daughter-in-law.

"Seth and Tom are friends, too," announced Andreas, ignoring his grandmother's no doubt indecipherable comment.

"Oh?" Oma looked at Jamie for an explanation.

Jamie restrained a sigh and tried to sound matter-of-fact. "Andreas's new gym teacher is Seth Kolski. You won't remember him—"

"Seth Kolski, that poor boy? He moved back here?"

The excruciating topic of Seth was not about to be dropped.

"Why's he poor?" asked Andreas.

Oma lifted eyebrows at Jamie. "Andreas, dear, would you like to watch TV while you eat your cake?"

"Yes!"

With alacrity, her mother settled Andreas in front of a show about animals and hurried back to the table, eager to hear the gossip. She pulled herself up short though and frowned at Jamie. "You're flushed, dear. Do you have a fever?"

"No, Mom. I'm tired, not sick."

"Well, well, so Seth Kolski has moved back to Cedartown," mused her father, to Jamie's dismay. She'd thought only her mother would be interested in further discussions of Seth. Now she had two of them to fend off.

"Yes," Jamie admitted.

"I can't say I'm surprised that Seth is an elementary school teacher," drawled her father.

"And what do you mean by that?" demanded her mother.

"You know what I mean. He was always too skinny. Wimpy."

"Oh, for goodness sakes, Karl," said her mother. "He's not just any teacher. He teaches *physical education.*"

Her father snorted.

"I don't know why you never liked him. He was a nice boy, even if his parents were irresponsible. He wouldn't have been skinny if they'd fed him. Look how they left town, skipping out without paying their rent. What kind of people do that?"

"People with funny-looking eyes," declared her father.

Her mother bristled. "That's the kind of thing you would say. They were an attractive family. You make me so mad, judging people by their looks. Jamie, honey?" Her mother shifted her attention back to Jamie, and her tone from bickering to one of concern. "Aren't you feeling well? Why don't you go lie down?" Despite the irritating conversation, her mother's cool hand on Jamie's cheek was a comfort.

"He had a crush on you, Jamie," recalled her father.

She closed her eyes again. *I have a crush on him, Dad. Oh, and I picked him up at a bar and slept with him three weeks ago. Oh, and he hasn't called since.* "I'll rest here while Andreas eats his cake. Then we'll go. He needs a nap after his first day of school."

"Now look what you've done," accused her mother.

"What? What did I do?" Her father was clearly baffled.

"Chased Jamie away. She doesn't like us to argue."

Jamie pushed herself away from the table. "Mom. It's okay. I'm exhausted, that's all."

"Eat some cake," ordered her father. "You're too thin."

She could be a hundred pounds overweight and her father would say the same thing. "I'm not hungry, Dad." The last thing she wanted was something sweet. She glanced into the TV room where, with rapt attention, Andreas was watching a monkey. A few more minutes till the show was over and they could leave.

"Have you heard from Derek?" asked her father.

"Karl." Her mother tried to warn him off the subject.

"Nope," said Jamie.

Her father lit a cigarette, annoying her mother who wanted him to smoke outside. Normally the smoke didn't bother Jamie but today, with her lack of sleep, it made her queasy.

"Is he still working for the guy whose son had his throat ripped open?"

"Oh, Karl, we're eating."

"You're eating. Jamie's not hungry."

"Fine, I'm eating and I don't know why you have to harp on that gory incident."

"It interests me. Never heard the like." It interested her father enough to bring it up once a week. "Damned strange business, losing your throat to a wolf."

"It must have been rabid," said her mother.

Not *her* wolf, her wolf was nothing but gentle. But Jamie didn't speak of him. She just thought of him. A lot.

"What was the victim's name again? Brian Carver?" Her father knew the name. Jamie nodded listlessly, then rubbed her head.

Her mother leapt up. "See what you've done?"

"What? What have I done?"

"Your daughter isn't feeling well."

"She would if she ate and slept. I just don't know how a man gets his throat ripped out by a wolf in his own backyard."

"A wolf?" asked Andreas, big-eyed. He'd come back in quietly, having finished watching his show. "But wolves don't attack people. Wolves are nice."

"Wolves are nice but they're wild animals who need their space." With this little speech, Jamie felt hypocritical, given the cozy and affectionate behavior of her wolf last night.

Her mother clucked in disapproval, while her father continued. "Then the wolf disappeared. No one found it. The wolf must have died in the woods of rabies because if it was healthy and had developed a taste for human blood, it would have attacked again."

"That's what they say about lions, Karl, not wolves," said her mother.

"They're both wild animals that can turn vicious."

Andreas watched his grandfather solemnly.

"Guess what?" Jamie pushed back her chair. "It's time to go."

"Can I have another piece of cake?" asked Andreas.

"No." But they packed up a piece for Andreas to eat later. Then Jamie escaped.

She loved her parents but it didn't always feel like coming home had been quite the right move.

C03

Jamie's grogginess overpowered her, making it difficult to wake. She wouldn't have stirred at all except Andreas was rocking her shoulder, asking if he could have Oma's cake now, he was hungry again. "Mom. *Mom?*"

With great effort, she opened her eyes and shook her head, as if that motion would sharpen her thoughts. "Did you sleep?" she asked.

"Yes. But now I'm awake."

Unlike her. Blearily, she blinked at digital numbers that arranged themselves into a time. Four o'clock in the afternoon. What a long nap. Well, last night's restlessness had caught up with her. It had also ruined her appetite because she wasn't hungry. She'd hardly eaten anything for lunch, either.

And she'd skipped breakfast. She frowned as she rose from bed and stumbled into the kitchen to get Andreas his snack. Once he was happily munching on plum cake, she made herself drink some juice. But it tasted all wrong, too bitter and too sweet, though Andreas was downing his own glass with his usual gusto. She still didn't want to eat anything. The last time food had seemed this unappealing, she'd been pregnant with Andreas.

She almost dropped her glass. With trembling hands, she set it down and orange pulp sloshed over the rim. Gripping the counter's edge, she breathed in, once, twice, trying to still the panic. She couldn't be pregnant. Seth had used a condom. She'd had her period.

Though it had been unusually light.

She sank to the kitchen floor and rested her head between her knees until the dizziness passed. Surely, the possibility of being pregnant would pass, too. She counted to twenty but it remained, as did the nausea that had accompanied her first pregnancy. Oh, God.

"Mom? Mom? Where'd you go?"

She lifted her head. "Right here, Andreas." Shakily, she pushed herself up to standing again. "I don't feel well, honey. Maybe I have the flu."

Please God, let her have the flu. Of course she had the flu. It had only been one time in two years. People didn't get pregnant by one time. Unless they weren't trying.

Andreas got down from his chair to give her a hug, planting crumbs and plum juice on her yellow shirt, but she didn't care. He gripped her waist in a bear hug while she ruffled his hair. "Feel better now?" he asked her stomach.

"You know what?" She smiled down at him, steadied. "I do."

Children were a blessing and even if she were pregnant, which she was not—stress was playing with her—she'd make it work. She'd always wanted children. Four, at least. Of course, she'd wanted a faithful husband around, too.

Maybe she had allergies.

"You should drink lots if you're sick," Andreas said.

"Yes, and I'll make myself eat a bit of cake. I never feel well when I don't eat." She picked up her glass of juice and sat beside her son. "I love you, Andreas."

He beamed at her, making her smile as she nibbled on cake that tasted wrong and was difficult to swallow.

She loved this cake. Her taste buds were out of whack. A quick trip to the drugstore was in order, to get rid of this notion she was pregnant.

"Finish up, Andreas. We're going for a ride."

"Why?"

"Flu medicine," she declared, grateful Andreas couldn't yet read the word pregnancy.

"Good, I want you to feel better, Mom."

"I will." She was determined to feel better.

Her mind flicked back to that evening with Seth and she started calculating dates. Five weeks since her period, three weeks since sex. But she couldn't be *pregnant*. Never mind that with Andreas, the nausea had kicked in during the fifth week of pregnancy.

It had to be a coincidence.

CG

The next morning Jamie opened the pregnancy kit. The sky was faintly gray with the first hint of light. The moon itself was long gone and she thought wistfully of her wolf while she ripped the plastic wrapping off the box. A good listener, he'd be amused to learn she'd been silly enough to buy and use a pregnancy test.

She couldn't be pregnant. It was some desperate fantasy on her part. Single and twenty-eight, she subconsciously feared her biological clock was running out. Her body was tricking her into a fantasy of morning sickness. Stupid body. Most women got fantasies that involved tall, dark, handsome men. She got nausea.

Focus. It was time to face the results of the kit. Waiting under the bright light of the bathroom bulb, hands trembling, she watched the two windows of the pregnancy stick.

As the second blue line formed, she closed her eyes. Despite her denials, she'd known since yesterday that this result would be positive. Early pregnancy was too obvious a state for her.

She pressed a hand to her belly, imagining the tiny life that had taken hold there, against such long odds. Her eyes flew open as she realized a part of her was thrilled. Honored, even. That small life seemed, at this moment, incredibly brave, and she would do all in her power to protect and nurture it. She was its mother.

And Seth was its father.

Seth.

She had to face him again. How humiliating. She breathed in deeply.

Well, she had a knack for picking men who weren't interested in her, or her offspring. But hope sprung eternal. Seth might be different from Derek. Seth might be active in this child's life. He liked kids.

Her face heated up. If only he liked her, too. His rejection was not going to make her news easy to impart. She considered not telling Seth.

No.

She'd seen how Derek's absence had hurt Andreas during his first five years. He latched onto men like Tom and even Seth, an indication of how desperately he wanted a man, a father-figure, to love him.

Still, she had some time to regroup. She didn't have to tell Seth right away. Or her parents. Or, oh God, Derek. Leaning on the bathroom counter, she stared into the mirror, tired eyes and weary mouth. Seth had declared he loved her mouth but that statement's expiration date had run out three weeks ago.

The timing of the revelation would be of her choosing. If she could get to know Seth better, scout out the unfamiliar terrain, say, and then massage the news so he didn't react with utter horror, it would be better for her and the baby. She'd also have to make clear at some point that this was not some ploy on her part, or some desperate attempt to bond with him.

It had been an accident.

Still, despite its less than promising start, this baby had been made with love—well, not love but affection. Jamie was going to hold on to that.

CЗ

"You sure it's Seth Kolski?" Tom asked the following Saturday as he steered his car off the highway and onto the exit ramp.

Startled by the question, Jamie answered sharply. "What do you mean, am I sure?" Tom didn't know she was pregnant. No one could have told him. Yet.

"Are you sure this guy you saw at Andreas's school is Seth Kolski?" Tom spoke with exaggerated patience.

Jamie attempted a playful comeback. "Do I look addled? Befuddled?" She felt it. Panicked, too.

"I don't know. I'm watching the traffic, not you."

Thank God.

"I didn't think Seth would come back to Cedartown," he added.

"Why not?" She looked over at him.

Tom shrugged.

"You're not keen to see him," she said.

"Is that an accusation?"

"Observation. I'm not driving, I can look at you."

"You spent more time with Seth than I did, Jamie."

She straightened. "I did not."

"Sure. Ostensibly, he was my friend because he didn't want the guys to know and bug him more than they already did."

"Bug him about what?"

"You. He was besotted." He pulled up to a stop sign and glanced over. "That's cute, you're blushing."

"Shut up. I thought you weren't watching me."

Tom grinned. "Do I turn right here?"

"Yes. Are you saying you don't want to see him this afternoon?" She hadn't been able to bring herself to visit Seth on her own. Tom, whether he liked it or not, was her pretext to see Seth again. She didn't know what Seth would make of getting reacquainted with an old and not terribly nostalgic schoolmate.

"You've told me that I want to see him, so I do."

"Tom."

"Look, you marched into our house, pale as a ghost, cloistered yourself with Cynthia while I learned about the latest incarnation of Pikachu, and marched back out the door with me in tow, leaving Andreas with Cynthia who doesn't like to baby-sit. That's got to be the strangest set of events since you've come home. I'd be entertained if I weren't dumbfounded."

Silence seemed to be the wisest response.

After Jamie's outburst Cynthia had been surprisingly sympathetic. Jamie hadn't meant to say anything. She'd wanted to demand some brother time and, whoosh, the whole story tumbled out, pregnancy and all. The cool Cynthia had risen to the occasion and actually hugged her before assigning her husband to Jamie's mission—visiting the father of her baby.

That Tom didn't know she was pregnant was just as well. It might put a crimp in the reunion of old school buddies.

"Uh, we're at 37294 Holbrook Drive, Jamie." He switched off the ignition. "Nice enough place, I guess. When's he going to cut his lawn?"

"Ask him."

He peered at her through his thick glasses. He was more shortsighted than she was. "You look awfully pale. Again."

"I'm a little sick," she admitted.

"Yet you want to visit a virtual stranger."

Seth might be many things, but he wasn't a stranger. "I'm getting better." She snapped the seat belt back into its slot beside her.

Tom gave her a measuring stare. "I hadn't thought it was in the cards for you and Cynthia to be chums, given Mom's opinion of my wife—"

"I form my own opinions, Tom."

"—but I assume Cynthia knows more about what's going on than I do."

"Can't you be a little enthusiastic about seeing an old friend? I thought you would be."

"Oh, sure," said Tom neutrally as they walked to the door. "I'm keen."

Jamie rang the doorbell.

They waited.

Tom glanced at Jamie and she thought, *He's not home.* She should have called first but she hadn't wanted to talk to Seth on the phone.

The door opened. Eyes groggy, hair rumpled, face unshaved, Seth stared. His eyes widened and, at the sight of Jamie, a smile began to form before wariness displaced it.

"Seth." Tom held out his hand and went into social mode. "Tom Buchner here. Jamie told me you were back in Cedartown. I dropped by to say hello."

Seth reached out and shook. "Hi. Tom."

"I hear you're teaching my nephew this year."

Seth's face remained blank but the gears seemed to whir beneath the surface. "That's right," he responded slowly, as if it was a trick question.

"Well, Andreas is an active little boy. I'm sure he loves your classes."

After a brief glance at Jamie, who nodded agreement, Seth raked a hand through his hair. "I like having Andreas in my class. Nice kid." He gave his head a shake. "I just woke up. I'm not entirely alert, I'm afraid."

"Sorry about that," said Tom easily and without much sincerity.

Seth took in a deep breath and came to a decision. "Why don't you step in? Though I have to warn you, I'm not prepared for visitors." He looked at Jamie questioningly. "Hi, Jamie."

"Hi, Seth. Nice place," she observed. Tom didn't need to know she'd been here, not until Cynthia told him. She held out her hand and Seth's large hand engulfed hers.

His eyes darkened at the contact. As Tom walked past them, Seth fixed her with a look that said, *What is going on?*

She waited until Tom made his way down the hall. "You said you keep to yourself too much," she murmured. "So, I brought you company."

"I didn't say *too much*."

"Wow." Tom stood in the kitchen. "I can see you don't have a woman around." His smile was sympathetic and smug. One thing about Tom—he didn't let you forget he liked the married life. "I almost miss the days when the state of the kitchen was my affair entirely. Almost, but not quite. No wife, I would hazard?"

"No," said Seth flatly.

"I can't understand that." Jamie entered the kitchen. It was messier than a month ago. "You're quite good-looking, you know."

Seth scowled while Tom looked at her as if she'd sprouted horns.

"But I'm sure you get a lot of compliments," she continued airily. "They must go to your head."

Seth crossed his arms. "Not always."

"Good. Andreas thinks you're wonderful."

"Can I ask a question?" said Seth.

Tom and Jamie nodded.

"What inspired you to drop by?"

Tom looked baffled, and when Jamie didn't answer, Tom shrugged. "Jamie thought it would be a good idea to say hello."

"Yes." Jamie felt the heat rise in her cheeks. She looked out to the backyard. It was mostly grass with a few trees to provide privacy. "You showed Andreas and me to the parking lot the other day and I was touched by your hospitality."

Seth shifted, getting more uncomfortable by the moment. She reminded herself she was here to get better acquainted, not pick fights.

"Would you like some coffee?" he asked.

"Sure," said Tom.

"I won't have any." The thought of hot drinks nauseated Jamie. "Do you have milk?"

"Yeah." Again, he telegraphed her a *What's up?* look and the uncertainty touched her. But she was not going to talk about the pregnancy now. She had to figure out how to best approach him with the news.

"You know what? While that coffee's brewing, I'll take a look at your yard." Tom disappeared through the sliding door and onto the deck.

Jamie snorted in embarrassment.

"What?" demanded a flustered Seth.

"When Tom senses something isn't right, you know you're not subtle." She smiled despite herself.

Seth placed two mugs on the counter with a thud. "Tom doesn't like me, Jamie. We parted badly."

"I didn't know that."

"He never told you?"

"Tom's not much of a talker, Seth. Unlike you, say."

"Jamie—"

"You're so expansive. Really."

He moved stiffly, opening the fridge door, pulling out the milk carton.

"Maybe I should annoy you with unwanted compliments. Then you talk."

"That doesn't annoy me, Jamie. It pisses me off."

"You know, I'm guessing, wildly mind you, that someone used you for your looks or whatever. But everyone gets used at some point in their lives. Including me."

He set his jaw.

"So, I think you should get over it, handsome."

"I think I should get over it, too."

"Good, we agree. Tell me about it."

"No. It's an ugly story." He poured her milk and set the glass before her. "Look, Jamie, I'm sorry."

"I don't want your apology."

"What do you want? And why is your brother here?"

"He's a pretext. Call me strange, but I wanted to see this guy I slept with a few weeks ago. I'm still trying to figure out what that was about."

His face softened. "I can't date anyone now."

"Why?"

His gaze settled somewhere beyond her shoulder.

"Strong, silent, beautiful type, are we? Quite perfect."

"I'm not perfect." The harshness of his words gave her pause.

"No one is, Seth. But your reactions are way outside my admittedly small knowledge base of how men act."

He glared. "You came here to satisfy your curiosity."

She didn't look away. The blue eyes fascinated her. If only she could read them. "You could say that. Mostly, I wanted to see you again." Though she wouldn't have risked her peace of mind if she weren't pregnant.

"Why?"

She laughed. "There's a complicated answer to that but, basically, I like you. And—this is what's stupid—I want you to like me."

Seth blew out air. "For chrissakes, I *like* you, Jamie. That's not the problem. I have things going on in my life that make it impossible to carry on a relationship. That's why I hoped you lived in another city. Now it's awkward for us."

She was amazed at her ability to persevere. Despite everything, Seth, now, did not make her feel rejected. "Awkward can be good."

"Nice lawn," announced Tom, stepping back in.

Seth got busy pouring coffee and handed a full mug to Tom.

"Thanks." Tom glanced from Seth to Jamie. "Are you two involved?"

Jamie waited for Seth's denial. It didn't come, though the silence was strained.

"I see." Tom drained half his coffee and set it aside. He leaned towards Seth. "Look, do you think you can call her next time so I don't have to come along and hang out with your pine trees?" He walked to the front door. "Let's go, Jamie. Andreas's soccer game is in half an hour."

Jamie finished her milk and trailed after Tom.

As they left, Jamie turned back to a bewildered Seth. If he regularly blew off his lovers, she guessed they didn't come knocking on his door asking for coffee weeks later.

"Andreas wondered if you'd come to his soccer game. You've made a great impression on him. The game's at three o'clock at Cedar Lane Park."

Seth opened his mouth.

"No, don't say anything. Show or don't show."

Before he could decline, she walked out of the house and shut the door.

Once she and Tom were in the car again, she felt bereft, her bravado disappearing as abruptly as it had arrived, as if it depended on Seth's presence. A Seth who was uncomfortable around her and would not show up for Andreas's soccer game.

"He won't call me," she said, despite the fact that it was her brother in the car.

"He will." Tom backed up, face turned towards her. "He's smitten."

Chapter Five

When Seth was fifteen years old he announced he had chosen his mate—Jamie Buchner.

His father had laughed at Seth's teenaged infatuation and said the only reason Seth stooped to a human bond was because werewolves weren't available, not that they'd have him anyway. Dad liked to throw out such compliments to boost Seth's ego. Because Dad never accepted Seth as his son. Seth's blue eyes, at odds with the rest of the family's golden color, convinced his father of infidelity on his mate's part. Especially when his father was drunk and his mother was screaming.

Jamie had been a refuge. At eighteen, she'd been sturdy, calm, pretty and kind. Seth didn't think a better person existed. His father used to say she wouldn't be interested in a runt like him. Seth had been late to develop.

Now Jamie was all those things he'd valued, and vulnerable. It was her vulnerability that undid him. He couldn't push her away if she showed up on his doorstep making overtures of friendship.

The hot water drummed against his aching shoulders and ran down his back. The past week's full moon was on the wane. He'd be able to sleep at night and his midnight outings could wait another three weeks. This month, trying to escape his thwarted desire, he'd overexerted himself.

She'd missed him enough to come by with Tom.

God, he was acting like the fifteen-year-old he'd been, but this was the first time he'd toyed with the idea of a relationship. To prevent complications or real intimacy, he'd avoided women who might become attached to him and flirted with those who were attracted to looks alone. Which was how he had ended up in a cage that godawful night.

He wasn't going there.

Toweling off, he weighed his options. He could not rebuff Jamie again. It was too late to protect her feelings. She cared. No one had rung his doorbell for two years, unless they wanted money.

He would see her. It might be wrong and he might regret it, but either way regret was going to play itself out. He didn't want to see the bruised look in Jamie's eyes. It had threatened to reappear when they'd parted and he hadn't agreed to come to Andreas's game.

He pulled on jeans and a shirt, grabbed his jacket and keys, and headed for the garage.

The drive to Cedar Lane Park was not unfamiliar to Seth. His schedule wasn't crammed with social obligations so he'd attended a few of his students' soccer games over the past two years. He suspected some people thought it pitiful that he missed the kids enough to go looking for them on weekends. But the waiting for Veronica, while fearing the worst, had to be filled with some kind of activity.

He pulled into the parking lot, slammed the car door shut and walked up the slope to the field, wondering if Jamie would be surprised by his presence.

Friends. He crested the hill. The soccer field was full of red and blue children chasing the ball. While he might *feel* like Jamie was his mate, he was no longer a boy, and as wrong as his father had been about most things, he wasn't wrong about this—she could never be his mate. If nothing else, he wasn't prepared to explain his oddities of behavior, something a lover would demand. *I'm disappearing for the entire night, sweetheart. Again.* One of his few ex-lovers to last more than a month had decided he was cheating on her.

Though Tom might already have an explanation for Seth's strange actions. Ten years ago Veronica—out of control as usual—had shifted after a skinny dip, under the full moon. She'd been drunk enough not to be subtle and Tom hadn't been drunk at all, just fascinated, though whether by the shift or the nudity, Seth didn't know. To distract Tom, Seth had punched him. He never knew whether or not Tom actually observed Veronica's shift and his parents didn't wait to find out. Two days after the incident, Seth's family left town.

To Veronica's fury. She'd hated the moves and the secrecy. Unlike Seth, she had courted popularity with great success in Cedartown. Teenage boys had been enamored by the sixteen-year-old's sexual antics. Including Gordon's son, Brian. After the Carver family moved to Atlanta, Veronica had looked him up and a five-year on-and-off-again relationship ensued, part of Veronica's never-ending need for attention and drama. She'd gotten drama all right, the kind that ended all dramas.

Seth had never vied for the spotlight like his sister, but he was weary of the shadow life he was living.

As Seth approached, Jamie's face lit with pleasure and dark thoughts of Brian fled. She was pleased Seth had come. Something in his chest shifted free of the vise that held him still these last two years.

She brushed windswept hair off her face. Her eyes were bright from the cool fall weather.

"I didn't think you'd come," she said.

"I like to do the unexpected," he drawled.

"I'll say." The words had an edge, but she didn't elaborate. She turned to the woman on her right. "Seth, this is Tom's wife, Cynthia."

Blonde, shoulder-length hair and sharp, blue eyes. Cynthia extended her hand and he met it with his own. "Hi, Seth." Her gaze bored into his before it flicked up and down. Interested, but cool.

"Hello," returned Seth. Her slight, knowing smile made him wary.

"Andreas is playing defense." Jamie gestured to the far side of the field. "He'll be pleased you're here. Especially since you're an old friend of his mother and uncle." She grinned. "For some reason, that pleases him."

"Tom didn't come?"

"He's manning the sideline." She pointed and Seth saw Tom's tall, stooped figure across the field. "Waving the flag."

"Ah. Good for him."

"He's an involved uncle. Which Andreas needs, given his father's lack of interest." Jamie eyed him. "What's your opinion of absentee fathers, Seth?"

Taken aback, he didn't respond immediately. Jamie looked away, as if regretting the question. It must be difficult for her to be a full-time parent.

"Well, not high," he said.

"Tom enjoys his uncle time," Cynthia put in proudly. She turned to Jamie. "I'm going to keep Tom company, okay?"

"Sure," agreed Jamie.

Cynthia glanced at Seth, assessing. "Nice to meet you."

"Same here." As soon as Cynthia was out of earshot, he asked, "Does your sister-in-law have something against me?"

"Why?"

"She looks at me as if she knows something."

Jamie shrugged, but wouldn't meet his gaze. "Maybe you're nice to look at."

It was odd, being goaded by compliments, but he found himself amused this time. "You're nice to look at, too."

"What a charmer. You have a unique way of showing it." She slapped a hand over her mouth. "I didn't say that. I promised myself I wouldn't refer to the night you told me to get lost."

He was glad they were standing apart from the crowd and no one could overhear them. "It was not *get lost*, Jamie. You stormed out, for one thing."

She waved her hands between them, as if batting away the argument. "My fault. Sorry. I open my mouth and these words fall out. No worries though. I'm completely recovered and all I feel about that night is equanimity."

"I can tell."

"You seemed happy to see me at the door until you remembered not to be."

"I was happy. Tom's presence surprised me." He bent to look at her. "I'd like for us to be friends." His face heated up because he sounded ridiculously formal.

She hesitated, as they stared at each other. Her large brown eyes pooled with emotion.

"Good." Her expression was unreadable as the whistle blew. She turned to watch Andreas run in from the field.

Jamie walked over to make sure Andreas drank his water at halftime. He was sometimes too excited to pick up the bottle. As he finished gulping a good amount, Jamie said, "Look, honey, Mr. Kolski came to watch your game."

Andreas waved to Seth, spilling water in his enthusiasm. Jamie rescued the bottle and recapped it.

Seth came up to them. "Hi, Andreas. You got some good kicks in there."

Andreas glowed.

Seth also chatted with two other children from Eastdale. One was a striking child with dark liquid eyes. He was beautiful, but thin, his cheekbones too prominent. His soft-faced mother was urging him to eat a granola bar during the break. Andreas's sturdy build made Jamie grateful she wasn't concerned about his weight. She had enough worries.

Andreas observed his mother's interest in the boy. "Sanjay's in my class, Mom."

"Hi, Sanjay," said Jamie.

Sanjay, his mouth full of raisin and roasted oatmeal, smiled.

"I'm Jamie Buchner." She extended a hand towards Sanjay's mother.

The woman's limp hand shook Jamie's with little enthusiasm. Smiling nervously, she withdrew, wrapping her coat more tightly around her. Jamie tried not to feel rebuffed. Puzzled, she sought Seth's gaze but he was watching the coach call the team over to talk strategy—this mostly involved paying attention.

From a short distance, Cynthia studied Seth, and Jamie almost regretted telling her sister-in-law she was pregnant with his child. Then Cynthia and Tom came over, and Tom greeted Seth.

"So, you left Cedartown about ten years ago?" Cynthia asked Seth.

"Seth's family moved around," offered Jamie.

"Did they?" The speculative tone of Cynthia's voice seemed odd but she added, "Many families do, don't they?" She turned towards the field. "Ah, off for the second half of the game." Children ran onto the grass, some of them confused as to where they should go. Into the milling chaos, coaches shouted out redirections.

"T-ball is a fun game to watch at this age, too." Seth smiled and Jamie felt weak at the knees because Seth enjoyed watching children play sports. "None of the kids keep their position on the diamond so the entire team of players, herd-like, goes after a ball when it's hit."

"Maybe Andreas will try T-ball next spring," said Jamie.

"Hey, I'm neglecting my duty. Off I go." Tom jogged across the field, flag in hand, and Cynthia followed him.

Seth watched as if he didn't know what to make of them.

"Cynthia takes some getting used to." Jamie wanted to put Seth at ease. Cynthia might not blab but her behavior wasn't totally discreet. "She's a bit cold but means well. And, she can keep a secret."

Seth's eyes, pale blue, matched the autumn sky. "Secrets." His slightly sneering tone made Jamie fear he knew hers. "I dislike people who are too interested in secrets."

Jamie blinked. "I just don't like keeping them." She had a terrible desire to tell him about the baby. Except that a confrontation here and now made no sense.

She watched the children though she knew Seth was looking at her after that cryptic statement. His fingertips brushed her cheek. "Do you want to tell me something?" he asked, puzzled.

She shook her head with what she hoped was a vague expression and was relieved when the second half began. They could concentrate on watching the game. Conversation dwindled but she enjoyed listening to Seth cheer on the kids.

When it was all over and families headed to their cars, Cynthia pulled out her camera and insisted they get a group photo.

"I'll take it," offered Seth. "You can have a family shot."

"No." Cynthia pointed at Seth. "You stand with the rest of them. I don't want to be in the picture."

Seth looked annoyed.

"Mr. Kolski, come for the picture. Please," begged Andreas when Seth didn't budge. His shoulders slumped forward at this difficult-to-refuse request, although he still didn't move.

While Cynthia clung to her camera for dear life, Seth eyed her with some suspicion. Jamie felt like laughing at what was becoming a farce.

Tom turned to Seth, looking weary. "Get over here so we don't camp out on the soccer field overnight. You don't know Cynthia and cameras."

Seth stood to the side, waiting for Cynthia to hand over the camera.

"The truth is," Tom pitched his voice low, "Cynthia dislikes her own pictures. Humor her, will you?" Cynthia pretended to not hear her husband's aside.

When Andreas placed a hand in Seth's, he gave way, allowing Andreas to lead him over to the group. Cynthia got her picture and they split into three cars, heading to their respective homes.

That night, after Andreas was fed, cleaned and tucked into bed, Jamie sat on the couch sipping apple juice. She pressed a hand to her belly. Hard to believe that life lay beneath her palm.

Seth had come to the soccer game. He wanted to be friends. He'd parted with, *See you later.*

Tom thought Seth was smitten.

Never mind that. What counted was the baby. She intended to forge a relationship with the baby's father.

CB

Every Sunday at ten a.m., Derek called and Andreas picked up the phone. Her heart hurt to see her son's eagerness. He played by the phone from nine-thirty on, in case his father rang early. But Derek was always prompt.

On the hour, Andreas picked up the receiver and chatted with a ruthless enthusiasm that dismayed Jamie. Andreas was desperate to keep his father on the line as long as possible.

Andreas's first hopes of entertaining his father were pinned on yesterday's soccer game. And Seth Kolski. Jamie squirmed. She doubted Derek had forgotten her teenaged admirer. Andreas repeated the name Kolski three times, confirming Jamie's doubts.

The conversation between father and son ran shorter than usual and uncharacteristically, Andreas walked glumly towards her, as if to hand over the phone.

"Okay," said Andreas quietly, as he always did when Derek ended the conversation. "Okay." Andreas never said goodbye. "Mom, Dad wants to talk to you."

Jamie took the phone. "Hello?"

"Hi, Jamie. How's Andreas?"

"He's good. Had a good first week of school."

"Great." Derek cleared his throat. "Is Seth Kolski his gym teacher?"

"Yes."

"The same Kolski we knew in high school?"

"Yes."

"Andreas should stay away from him."

How typical of Derek to give such a ridiculous command. Jamie pinched her nose. "He's his gym teacher, Derek."

"He came to Andreas's soccer game. Why?"

"I invited him, along with Tom and Cynthia."

"Who's Cynthia?"

Jamie rolled her eyes. Derek couldn't remember the name of his son's aunt. "Tom's wife."

"Right. Well, Tom and Cynthia make sense, but don't invite Seth. He's a weird one, Jamie. Best to stay away."

"That sure is *your* motto."

"I wasn't talking about me."

"Of course not."

"I'm serious, Jamie." His lecturing tone made her want to scream. "Kolski's sister disappeared around the time Brian Carver was killed."

"What do you mean, *disappeared*?"

"Disappeared," he repeated, as if one word was sufficient for such a complicated event. "No one saw her again. Police searched for her. They think she might have been involved in Brian's death."

Jamie hunched over, one arm wrapping around her stomach, as if to protect the baby from this disturbing news about its aunt. She walked away from Andreas and whispered into the phone. "Why would they think that? A wild animal attacked Brian."

"She might have been an eyewitness. They wanted to question her. But she vanished."

"I hope she's okay."

"Jamie." His exaggerated patience grated on her nerves. "You're getting off track. The point is, keep away from Seth. That family has weird baggage."

"You sound like the gossipmongers who fed on the Kolskis' disappearance from Cedartown ten years ago. It's not like Veronica could rip open Brian's throat."

"You're missing the point. Seth comes from a troubled family."

"Yeah, so, is disappearing genetic or something?" Her voice was rising.

"Calm down now."

"You know squat about Seth. He's financially responsible, owns a house and contributes to society by teaching. Which is more than I can say about most people. Yet you utter dire warnings about him. Either say something substantial or say nothing at all."

"Okay, I'll find out more about him."

"That's not what I mean." She didn't want Derek to have anything to do with Seth.

"I've got to go. I'll call next Sunday."

She slammed down the phone, then realized an anxious Andreas was watching her. *Damn.*

"Why are you yelling at Dad?" asked Andreas.

Jamie knelt in front of her son. "I'm sorry you overheard our argument, Andreas."

He chewed his lip. "Will Dad still call me next week?"

"Yes, he said he would. Our argument doesn't affect his chats with you."

Andreas's face cleared. "Daddy wishes *he* could come to my soccer games."

Liar. She forced a smile that fell as soon as her son looked away.

◌ঽ

Watercress, mushroom and potato soup looked better in the cookbook's picture. Attractiveness aside, Seth would have been satisfied with a tastier soup. It was bland. Perhaps if he'd prepared it three days ahead as the instructions suggested, but Seth thought that lead time excessive. Not that he really knew. He hadn't cooked for anyone since well before Veronica's disappearance.

After a full week of good sleep, he felt more human. Thursday night he'd acted upon a wild whim and invited Jamie, Andreas, Tom and Cynthia for supper on Saturday after Andreas's soccer game. Seth had planned to spend the morning with meal preparation, the afternoon at the game and the evening socializing.

Radical, but that's what happened when you decided to be friends with someone. You made plans.

His schedule was off. The housecleaning had taken longer than expected, as had the shopping, given that the first supermarket didn't carry watercress or fresh mint. He'd called

Jamie to let her know he couldn't get to the game and continued on with domestic chores.

Now the guests were almost due and, while the soup was puréed, he'd put in too much watercress. Or something.

When the bell rang, the raisin pumpernickel rolls were still, in theory, rising.

He pulled open the door to find Andreas on the welcome mat, bouncing. "Is this your house?"

"Apparently," he said, smiling.

Andreas jumped inside. "We won!"

"Great."

"I kicked the ball four times."

"Did you play defense or forward?"

"Both!"

"Cool."

"Hi, Seth." Jamie was amused by Andreas's excitement, or perhaps Seth himself since she was staring at his shirt. His flour-covered shirt, he realized, looking down. "Have you been baking?"

With a hand, he swept clean his T-shirt. "Trying to bake."

"Run into problems?"

"Uh, no. Everything's fine. I'm a little behind schedule. I hope that's okay."

"Sure."

Tom marched up the front steps with a determinedly pleasant expression. "Seth." He held out his hand and Seth grasped it. "It's good of you to cook vegetarian for Cynthia. Thank you."

"You're welcome."

"Hi, Seth." Cynthia made her way in, glancing about with great interest. There was enthusiasm, though for what, Seth couldn't fathom. Maybe she didn't get asked out much.

A sizzling splash from the kitchen had Seth rushing to the back of the house to rescue his soup before it became irretrievably burnt. He transferred the soup to a clean pot.

Jamie followed him in.

"Sorry." He indicated the mess.

She waved off the apology.

"I don't think it's burnt. Yet," he added.

"Can I help?"

"Oh, no. I just have to whip up a salad." As if he made salad for five every day. "Would you like a drink?"

"I brought some wine," Jamie told him. "Why don't I handle drinks while you do what you need to do."

He passed her a corkscrew and she dealt with the wine. After placing a glass on the counter for him, she went in search of her brother and sister-in-law who were chasing Andreas down to bring him back to the kitchen.

"Hey, buddy," said Seth at Andreas's reappearance. "The TV's that way." Seth pointed his knife and soon only Jamie was left in the kitchen with him. He liked having her nearby, helping out, interested in what he was doing, even if it was only cutting vegetables.

He smiled at her and she tilted her head in question.

"Sorry I'm running late," he apologized.

She shrugged off his concern. "Is that cauliflower salad?"

"You don't like cauliflower?"

"I love cauliflower," she declared. Seth suspected she would have said the same about whatever he was making. "It looks complicated though."

"Not really." In fact, five spices in one salad was new to him. He wasn't feeling grateful to the cookbook at the moment.

"You've made it before?"

"No. But the cookbook made it sound straightforward."

"They always do," she said darkly.

He opened the oven door and closed it again, feeling harried by the glacial expansion of his pumpernickel rolls. "They're not rising."

"Did you put in yeast?"

"Of course I did," he said with some indignation.

A dimple showed in her cheek but she didn't smile. "Just bake them. I'm sure they'll rise." She walked over, pulled the rolls out of the oven and turned up the heat. "It's so sweet of you to cook. How many dishes are there?"

"Four." He'd only worked on three. "Damn. I forgot to marinate the beets."

"Cook them then. I'll dice. Where's the knife?"

They worked in companionable silence. Jamie's presence gave Seth relief from his solitude. She warmed him. He glanced over, admiring the way her rich brown hair fell forward as she cut beets. It took him a moment to realize Jamie was worrying her lip.

"Is something wrong?" he asked.

She took a breath. "Do you cook often?"

He was puzzled by the intensity of the question. "That bad, eh?"

She shook her head and laughed, then sobered. "Actually, that's not what I want to ask."

Her troubled tone stopped his salad-making and he turned his gaze on her. "What is it?" He wished he could say, *Ask me anything.*

"I was wondering about your sister. Veronica."

Damn. The cozy moment vanished. His throat clogged up. He found himself staring at the vegetables.

"Oh, Seth..." Her voice trailed off in worry and confusion. "Is she not all right?"

It was a question he couldn't answer, a question he pushed away when he could. Because, despite his months-long search as man and wolf, he'd lost Veronica's trail within days of her disappearance. No amount of running as wolf had found her scent again. Nor had his two private investigators discovered a clue to Veronica's whereabouts. He didn't like to think too carefully on the subject because the conclusion was too awful to contemplate. He needed hope.

He swallowed hard and looked at a point beyond Jamie, feeling helpless and blindsided, wishing the subject could have stayed buried. And yet, Jamie's concern made him feel less isolated. Someone else worried about his sister. Before now, it had only been him.

He needed to give Jamie an answer of sorts. He closed his eyes before he spoke. "She, uh..." He grimaced. "I don't know where Veronica is."

"With your parents?" Jamie suggested.

He shook his head sharply. "She's missing. I think something bad happened but I can't talk about it."

"I'm so sorry." Jamie's voice trembled. That Veronica's fate hurt Jamie, that someone cared, eased Seth's pain a little.

"You're a nice person, Jamie." He leaned down and kissed her cheek. Contact helped, even if he couldn't speak about Veronica. "How are those buns doing? Hey, they're rising. There will be one success this meal."

Quiet-faced, Jamie didn't respond.

Cynthia wandered out of the den.

"You're not enjoying Yu-Gi-Oh?" Jamie asked a restless Cynthia.

"I couldn't quite follow the storyline."

"There is no storyline," explained Jamie. "They duel."

As the two women set the table, Cynthia whispered to Jamie, "Did you tell him?"

Jamie shook her head and Cynthia let it drop.

Tell him what? Excellent hearing was not always advantageous. He didn't want to hear Cynthia's questions. Not tonight. Discussing Veronica had been more than enough heart-to-heart for him. He wanted company, not intimate conversation. He couldn't be intimate, on any level.

For that matter, it appeared he couldn't cook either because by the time they sat at the table, Seth had given up on the meal. Nothing looked as it should. The rolls had risen but were as hard as rock. The soup remained bland despite excessive salt. The beets were plain. Only the cauliflower had any panache.

"Yum, beets," exclaimed Tom. "And at exactly the right time of year."

"I don't like that," Andreas whispered urgently to his mother who answered in a low voice.

"He doesn't have to eat beets," said Seth, then wondered if he'd stepped on parental toes. He hated the thought of force-feeding his food to anyone.

"I like beets," declared Andreas.

"You don't have to eat cauliflower," allowed Jamie.

Seth handed out paper towels for napkins but no one minded. They all dug in, Tom and Cynthia eating heartily, while Jamie picked at her food with a game expression on her face.

Come to think of it, her face was thinner than five weeks ago and she looked weary.

She caught him watching her. "It's tasty, Seth," she assured him, chewing vigorously.

He went along with the charade and nodded. Obviously the meal wasn't her cup of tea. She ate the rolls with less distaste than anything else.

"So, how long will you two need a chaperon?" Tom spoke out of the blue, while downing his third glass of wine.

"Tom," remonstrated Cynthia to no effect.

"What's a chaperon?" asked Andreas.

"A companion for your mother and Seth," explained Tom.

"I'll be one!"

"Sure," smiled Seth.

"Not that the meal isn't worthy payment," continued Tom. "Why are you picking at your food, Jamie? Are you pretending to be a bird?"

"Tom," snapped Cynthia while Jamie's face reddened.

"That's okay," said Seth awkwardly.

Jamie glared at her brother. "I do like the food. *Tom.*"

"Good." Tom grinned.

"I liked the beets," piped up Andreas. "Can I watch TV again?"

"Wash your hands." Jamie sighed.

"If you want, Andreas, I'll play a game of Pokemon with you when I'm done." Seth wanted to ease the tension radiating from Jamie. Although Andreas's excited response held its own reward. Besides, playing cards with Andreas was simple, straightforward, involving no unexpected questions from Jamie or covert glances from Cynthia.

The boy beamed and raced off to the bathroom.

"Better you than me, right now. Pokemon is too complicated after this." Tom raised his wineglass. "I need to be alert to play."

"You need to be alert, period," muttered Cynthia.

Tom's eyes narrowed. "What'd I miss?"

"Absolutely nothing," said Cynthia to Seth's bemusement. Maybe Cynthia always acted as if people were out of the loop. Annoying, but not quite so worrisome if Seth wasn't the only person she treated this way.

However, Jamie sank further into her chair and Seth wondered what her reaction was about. But before he could think on it longer, Andreas was at his side with a handful of cards. "I have a new Sandblaster deck."

"Awesome," replied Seth.

Chapter Six

"That's a nice cake, Mom," said Andreas.

"Thanks, sweetie." Jamie added the finishing touches to the icing, pink on white.

"Does Oma like pink?"

"She does."

"Is Oma five-four?" He read the number on the cake.

"Fifty-four, yes."

"Will Uncle Tom and Aunt Cynthia be there?"

Jamie sighed. "I don't think so."

Andreas's face fell. But for this occasion, it was her mother's disappointment, not her son's, that most concerned Jamie.

"Did you pack your overnight bag?"

His face brightened at the thought of a sleepover at Oma and Opa's. "Yes."

"Go get your shoes on, then."

She picked up the cake to carry it to the car and the doorbell rang.

"I'll get it," shouted Andreas. As she placed the cake back down she heard him fumbling with the door. "Guess who it is, Mom?" His voice went high with excitement. "It's Mr. Kolski!"

Her heart stuttered, then picked up speed. Seth? Dropping in?

"Well, open the door." Trying to stay calm, she walked out of the kitchen.

"Hi, Mr. Kolski," blared Andreas.

"Hi, buddy. How's it going?" Seth flashed Jamie a smile before he attended to Andreas's answer.

"We're going to my Oma's birthday party."

"Great." Seth had hovered on the threshold, but now he took an abrupt step backwards. "My timing isn't good, then."

"Come in," said Andreas expansively, one arm stretched towards the living room, the other reaching for Seth.

"You're on your way out, but thank you for the offer." He glanced at Jamie again. She needed to kick start herself so she could speak. It was hard when Seth was so important to her. "I brought a kite along, Andreas, but we'll save it for another windy day, okay?"

Jamie's insides melted. "That was so thoughtful of you."

Seth looked embarrassed by her gushing. "No big deal."

Derek had never bought Andreas a kite in his life.

"Oma and Opa have a big backyard," Andreas told him.

Seth knocked him lightly on the head with his knuckles. "You get points for persistence, bud, but this is a family affair."

"You're welcome to come, Seth," said Jamie. He would distract her mother from her brother's absence.

"I don't want to impose."

"No imposition, believe me. The party could use an extra body because Tom and Cynthia can't make it."

Seth hesitated.

"But I understand if it's not something you want to do."

101

"It's not that…"

"What kind of kite, Mr. Kolski?" asked Andreas.

Jamie shrugged. "It's your choice, Seth. You remember my parents."

"It's a bird, Andreas." Seth looked over her son's head at Jamie. "If you're sure."

"I am." She smiled with pleasure and Seth's uncertainty eased. "Look, we're about to head out. Why don't you follow us in your car?"

◌ℨ

In the midst of greeting Jamie and Andreas, Mrs. Buchner broke off her exclamations to stare as Seth pulled into the driveway. Maybe coming along was a bad idea though he couldn't back out now. Anyway, Mrs. Buchner had been a sweet, if voluble, lady. It was Mr. Buchner who hadn't liked him much. Especially after a few drinks.

Jamie's mother bustled over as he rose from the car. "Seth Kolski. Imagine that." Her gaze swept from his feet to his head. "My, aren't you tall? Still too thin though, and you need a haircut."

"Mom." Jamie joined them as if to protect Seth from her mother.

Mrs. Buchner patted his arm. "He doesn't mind, do you, Seth?"

"No."

"It was kind of you to come." She smiled, making him feel welcome. "My own son couldn't be bothered."

"Mom." Jamie looked slightly harried.

"Well, he couldn't. He's not here, is he?"

Jamie tried to lead her mother back inside, away from Seth. "Cynthia had a business weekend booked in Washington ages ago, you know that."

"My birthday doesn't change from year to year, does it?"

"I'm sure she had no choice in the matter," Jamie said firmly.

"If it had been *her* mother's birthday, she would have had a choice."

"Mom, Cynthia is estranged from her mother."

"And I can see why."

Jamie fisted and unfisted her hands.

"Come in, come in." Mrs. Buchner smiled reassuringly at Seth. "I don't know where my husband is. It's just my birthday."

Jamie cast Seth a look of exasperation. He winked at her as they entered the house.

"He's probably reading a book in the basement," said Mrs. Buchner.

"Don't you like books, Oma?" asked Andreas.

"I like *your* books, honey." She patted her grandson's head while Andreas looked confused.

"Mrs. Buchner," began Seth.

"No need to remove your shoes, Seth. We don't stand on ceremony here, like some folks." He decided not to guess who did. "Sit down, sit down."

He didn't move. "I'm afraid I didn't know it was your birthday today."

"And why should you? You haven't seen me for years, unlike some people."

"Still," put in Seth, before Tom and Cynthia were mentioned again. "I did bring a kite. I had thought to fly it with Andreas."

"What a nice idea. So thoughtful." He expected a negative comparison but she turned to Andreas. "Honey, I'll watch you fly the kite from the window while I finish making the meal."

Beside Seth, Andreas vibrated with excitement.

"I'll meet you in the back after I get the kite," Seth told him. Andreas raced out the back door as Seth walked to his car.

Jamie followed. "You don't have to stay for supper, Seth. I'm sorry. I thought your presence would restrain my mother."

"Don't worry about me. I don't mind." At least Mrs. Buchner, unlike some mothers, enjoyed having her kids around. She even cooked for them.

"She's hurt by Tom. She and Cynthia don't get on well," Jamie explained.

He bent and kissed her lightly. He'd missed those lips.

"Why did you do that?" she demanded.

Not quite the response he'd expected. "Do what?"

"Kiss me."

He felt his mouth quirk. "You tempt me."

"*Friends*, remember?" The irony was strong in her voice. "You talked about us being friends at Andreas's soccer game."

"Did I?" He took a step closer. He was tired of living by his rules. They made him miserable and they hadn't saved him from nightmares. It was time to come to terms with Veronica's absence and Jamie's existence. He couldn't be alone all the time. "Well, friends can kiss each other."

Her eyes went flat and her mouth thinned. "You're playing games."

He stilled.

"I'm only going to say this once, Seth. I do want to be your friend and if that's it, then that's it. But I am not going through another episode of the *let's have sex and then get out of my space* routine."

"It wasn't just sex."

"That's right, though you wouldn't admit it at the time."

"Jamie—"

She held up a hand to stop his advance. "I'm not sleeping with you again. I'm a mother, I have a son to take care of and I can't allow you to play mind games with me."

He kept a lid on his temper. She didn't know what he was dealing with. And couldn't know. "Do you think upsetting you entertains me? Is that your low opinion of me?"

"I have a high opinion of you—"

"I can tell."

"But you have to understand my position as a mother."

"*Look*, I've never been seriously involved with someone before."

"*What?*"

Why'd he go and say that? *Jesus, shut up, Seth.* He raked a hand through his hair while Jamie searched his face for something. Truth, perhaps.

"Never?" She wasn't reassured by his statement and he didn't blame her. He was a freak. He could feel the heat radiating from his face. Great, he had Jamie's pity. Just what he wanted.

Andreas rounded the corner of the house, crunching gravel in his wake. "Where's the kite, Mr. Kolski?"

"Um," said Seth, distracted by his unexpected confession. "What?"

"The kite," repeated Andreas patiently. "There it is." He pointed into the trunk of the car Seth didn't remember opening. "It's blue! My favorite color."

"Good." Seth pulled out the brightly colored contraption and slammed the trunk down.

"Can it fly?" asked Andreas.

"I hope so." Seth glanced at Jamie whose face had softened at Andreas's arrival. He offered her the kite. "Would you like to fly it? I don't have to stay."

Andreas's lower lip thrust forward as he looked between Jamie and Seth. Jamie opened her mouth to speak.

"Not you, Mom," Andreas practically wailed. "I want Mr. Kolski to fly the kite."

Jamie ignored her son's protest. Her eyes didn't stray from Seth's face. "I'd like you to fly the kite and stay for supper." She placed a hand on his arm before she turned and walked to the house.

He didn't have time to think about their exchange because Andreas was beside him, demanding Seth's full attention, pulling on his hand, leading him to the backyard, chattering about the wind and the trees and the blue bird.

CS

"What a nice man," said her mother.

"Who's that?" Her father emerged from the basement. "Not your son, surely."

"Dad," put in Jamie. "I hope you don't mind but Seth dropped by my place this afternoon and I invited him to dinner."

Her father's expression was blank. "Seth who?"

"Seth Kolski, Andreas's gym teacher."

He frowned and walked to the window. Seth was kneeling beside a rapt Andreas, talking. Seth demonstrated how to let out the string before handing over the kite.

"Nice kite," her father observed and Jamie relaxed.

The phone rang. It was Tom. Jamie's earlier message, reminding her brother to call their mother, had borne fruit. She shouldn't have to play his secretary when it came to family occasions, but she couldn't face her mother's unhappiness when Tom didn't phone. Especially these days, when she felt so on edge. So *pregnant*. Her hand crept to her stomach.

"Feeling sick?" her father asked.

Her hand dropped away. Her father could be uncomfortably observant when she didn't expect it. "Oh, I'm quite fine, thanks."

His expression suggested he thought otherwise, but he didn't push the issue. They sat and watched the afternoon basketball game while her mother chatted happily to Tom. In time, the table was set and Jamie called in Seth and Andreas.

"Aw, Mom," whined Andreas while Seth began to reel in the plastic bird.

"I'm starving, buddy, so don't complain," said Seth.

Jamie came to understand he wasn't exaggerating. During the meal he ate with a speed just short of rude while her mother served him seconds and thirds of chicken, mashed potato and carrots until Seth became self-conscious.

"A man needs to eat," her mother declared with delight. "Tom never eats this much."

"Tom has a desk job." Her father thought this explained everything but Jamie figured either Seth had a high metabolic rate or he hadn't eaten for days. He should look after himself, given his soon-to-be responsibility.

She felt a twinge of guilt. Time was running out, as was his potential goodwill if she hid the pregnancy for too long. But God, she didn't want to tell him. She feared the end of their friendship. Even if it was a friendship based on somewhat false pretenses because, if not for the baby, she would have avoided him.

"What kind of desk work?" Seth asked after a long silence.

"He's a programmer." Her father lifted his chin with pride.

"Yes?" said Seth encouragingly.

"Tom isn't more specific." Another oft-voiced peeve of her mother's. "Since he met Cynthia, he's become secretive about his job."

Jamie rolled her eyes. "Mom, that's not true. It's just that you don't understand Haskell or C programming languages."

"Well, Cynthia is secretive about *her* job."

"She's not allowed to talk about her job."

"Oh, yes." Her mother's tone of voice suggested just the opposite. "She works for the *government*."

Jamie sighed. "Mom, let's not discuss Cynthia right now."

"Honey." Her mother was all concern and Jamie regretted that she'd allowed weariness to creep into her voice. "You're not eating much."

"Sure I am."

"Mom doesn't like to eat," Andreas piped up helpfully.

"You're not developing an eating disorder, are you?" asked her mother.

"Mom, please!"

"Edna," reproved her father.

"Well, I worry about you."

"I know that full well," Jamie muttered.

Seth stepped in. "Most eating disorders begin much earlier. It's commonly a teenaged problem."

Her mother was relieved. "I remember your sister as a teenager, Seth. Always too skinny, I guess it runs in the family. But she was a pretty thing. How is she now? Is she married?"

Looking as if something tasted wrong, Seth slowly chewed his mouthful of food. By the time he swallowed, Jamie realized he wasn't going to be able to speak of Veronica at the table.

"Mom. I'm afraid Veronica went missing about two years ago. Seth hasn't heard from her since..." Jamie gestured uselessly. "It's quite sad and rather difficult to talk about."

Her mother's eyes widened in horror as she sat back in her chair. "I'm so sorry, Seth."

Her father cleared his throat. "Sorry to hear that."

"Thank you." Seth applied himself to his potatoes rather mechanically.

Andreas watched Seth. Then he got off his chair and walked around to give Seth a big, serious hug. Tears started in Jamie's eyes.

Seth smiled at him. "Thanks, Andreas."

In the silence that followed, Jamie almost wished for her mother's chattering complaints. Until they started up again. "I wonder if Tom and Cynthia think about starting a family. I'd like another grandchild."

Jamie forced the now-cold potato to slide down her throat.

"Goodness knows, she's not getting any younger. I didn't think my son would marry an older woman but it's the new fashion."

Jamie cast Seth a look of despair and he winked. She was too old to be soothed by his winks, but she felt better all the same.

"If Cynthia quit her job, they could have a child," her mother continued. "Unemployment is so high these days because too many women work when they should be at home raising their children. Like you, dear." Her mother patted Jamie's hand.

"Oh, yeah, Mom. I'm in such a great position."

"Derek sends his checks on time."

"Daddy's going to phone tomorrow," Andreas said brightly.

"That's nice, dear."

"He phones every Sunday and we talk for fifteen minutes. Then he has to go to work." That Andreas was unaware of how pathetic his father's effort was, made the statement all the more painful to hear.

Her father cleared his throat again. "Maybe you could show me some of your new Pacman cards after supper, Andreas."

Her son's face lit up. "Po-kee-mon, Opa."

"That, too," said her father wryly.

"The sooner you eat your meal, the sooner you can show Opa your cards," Jamie told him.

Andreas concentrated on his vegetables. Then they cleared the table for cake and gift giving, sang "Happy Birthday" to her mother's great pleasure and, while her mother relaxed, Jamie cleaned up the kitchen.

By then the card game was over, or her father had been overwhelmed and Seth had taken his place. It wasn't late but Jamie felt tired and thought about heading home. A coward, she'd hoped Seth would leave before she did, but he wasn't bolting out the door at the first opportunity. On one level this pleased her to no end. Derek had hated hanging out with family. Unfortunately she could not use family as a shield if she and Seth left together. Andreas was staying overnight at her parents.

If she and Seth had the opportunity to be alone, she would feel obliged to tell him about the baby. While she liked to justify the dragging of her feet as a bid to avoid rejection of herself and her child, damage would be done if she kept the secret too long.

Watching Seth with Andreas and her parents, she could pretend Seth already knew about the pregnancy and was happy to be a part of her life. There was a silence and tension to him, yet Seth fit in well and Andreas adored him. Her son's openness and eagerness to be loved scared and hurt Jamie at times.

Though Seth looked oddly vulnerable here tonight, too. Growing up, he hadn't had a good home life. Maybe he was looking for that. Or maybe that was wishful thinking.

"Well," said her mother. "You two might as well take off for the evening."

Seth looked up from the game and Jamie felt her face flush.

"I'd better push off myself." He quieted Andreas's protests by promising a rematch.

"Do you and Jamie have plans?" her mother asked Seth.

"Plans?" Confused, he turned to Jamie for guidance.

"No," Jamie told her mother firmly.

"But you don't often get an evening off." Her mother spoke to Seth. "We like to take Andreas Saturday nights."

"Ah." Looking at Jamie, his eyes darkened with interest. Which was gratifying despite her desire to escape. "Are you heading out now?" he asked.

"Of course she is," said her mother.

"I'm here, Mom. I can speak for myself."

"Well, you're not saying much."

"I can't get a word in edgewise, that's why."

Her mother grumped and turned away, leaving Seth and Jamie in the kitchen.

"Sorry," she apologized. "You needn't feel cornered into making plans with me."

"I don't." His words were clipped. "I dropped in on you this afternoon, remember?"

Be brave and do what's right. "Okay, let's leave. Actually, I would like the chance to talk to you." *Liar.* The idea filled her with dread.

Jamie called Andreas for hugs and kisses. Seth received them, too. As she reached for her coat, her mother assured her, sotto voce, that there was no reason to be nervous because Seth was a gentleman.

You have no idea, Jamie replied wordlessly with a hug.

Seth and Jamie walked out to the driveway, gravel loud under their shoes, small echoes in the quiet night. She supposed, with a sinking stomach, the time had come to lay her cards on the table. The worst result—to find she'd chosen yet another man who backed away from fatherhood. What kind of mother was she, to always make babies with such men?

And, too, she felt wistful about the potential destruction of her budding friendship with Seth. She would miss him.

Did she have to predict the worst possible outcome? Maybe she'd be pleasantly surprised.

"Would you like to come to my place?" she managed, despite her creeping melancholy.

He cocked his head. "Are you that tired, or that unenthusiastic?"

Both. "I am tired." She swiped at a loose strand of hair.

He regarded her with concern, catching the errant hair and tucking it behind her ear. "You're tired and you're not eating well. Is everything okay?"

His sweetness hurt and she found herself ducking her head.

"You were happy to see me this afternoon, but you look pretty glum right now." He was puzzled. "Did I offend your parents, or something? I'm afraid I don't get to a lot of family gatherings."

"Oh, Seth, no," she burst out. "You were wonderful."

"Could have fooled me," he said softly.

"I need to tell you something."

"Sure." But his expression was now guarded and her hope evaporated. He didn't want close, just companionable. Maybe it was hormones, but she hadn't felt this fragile for a long time, even during her divorce. She couldn't tell Seth she was pregnant here. At her house, he might be less inclined to take off in his car right away. Jamie looked back to see her mother in the kitchen window.

"Mom's watching, Seth. Come back to my place and we can talk, okay?"

He nodded. "You sound so serious."

"I know." She gave a weak smile that no doubt did little to hide the feeling that the rest of her life depended on the outcome of this evening.

Would Seth take responsibility for their child?

Chapter Seven

Seth stood in Jamie's kitchen. Obviously troubled, she busied herself with mugs and coffee while forgetting to plug in the kettle. He was torn, wanting to pull her into his arms, to give comfort, not to get sex. But he was also aware that one might lead to the other despite Jamie's *don't touch me* vibes. Vibes he could overcome.

No. He wasn't going to do that. Not when she had something to tell him.

He didn't like her to be so pale.

"I only have instant coffee," she told him.

"I remember."

"What else do you remember?" She circled around her cupboards rather blindly.

He leaned against the doorway, waiting for her to come back to him. "Never mind the coffee."

She stopped moving, as if caught in the middle of the kitchen, and faced him. "Friends offer each other coffee. Then again, so do lovers."

He walked over and caressed her cheek with his knuckles. She flinched.

"What is going on, Jamie?"

"I'm confused." She crossed her arms but he could see her chest moving too quickly, as if she were panicked. Yet he could have sworn she wasn't frightened of him. "I have the wrong feelings for you, see? We're supposed to be friends."

He couldn't help himself. His mouth curved. "Let's explore those feelings."

"I'm not going through that humiliation again." Her harsh voice made clear that teasing would not solve the problem. Her pale cheeks, stained by two red patches, alarmed him. He feared she would faint.

He grasped her arm and, overcoming her slight resistance, led her to the couch. Without relinquishing her, he sat them both down so they faced each other.

"You're cold," he said.

She shrugged.

He pulled in a long breath. "I handled our night together badly. I'm sorry. I'd like to see you but I don't want you to expect too much."

She looked away. "I won't." The weariness in those two words asked for some kind of explanation.

"There's something you don't know about me." He sounded hoarse.

She stared at him and his chest became tight, as if his rib cage could contain his desire to tell her everything.

Her voice was controlled. "Of course there's something I don't know about you, Seth, because I barely know you. In fact, there may be something *you* don't know about *me*. Or perhaps you think I'm an open book because all you need to know is that after having sex with you I want a relationship."

"No." He would have released her hand but now she grasped him, as if she wanted him to understand something.

115

"You worry about my eating habits, you fly a kite with my son and you charm my parents. But we"—she pointed between the two of them with her free hand—"we're just about sex. I think, and don't take this the wrong way because despite everything I am interested, but I think you should grow up. You're twenty-five and I wouldn't mind some clear signals here."

"I'm not some callow, immature youth who wants his freedom. I am single for a reason, Jamie."

"Which is?"

He paused, unable to speak of it.

She withdrew, shrinking away. "I know. You can't tell me. Still, Seth, I'm sure it's profound."

"You have no idea," he said tightly.

"You're right. I don't." Her voice dropped. "You didn't tell me Veronica had disappeared. I had to ask you."

"I can't talk about her." But the hairs on the back of his neck rose. This time the pain of Veronica's name was accompanied by a shadow. As Jamie's words sank in, he stood and stared at her, wondering *why* she'd thought to ask about Veronica in the first place.

"What?" asked Jamie.

"Did you know that something had happened to Veronica? I assumed your question came out of the blue." A stupid assumption. Careless. "Because you're interested in family."

She frowned. "I *am* interested in family. But Derek told me Veronica was missing."

He blinked, surprised at Derek's interest. "Why would Derek talk about Veronica?"

"Why not? He knew her from high school. She dated the boss's son."

He ran a hand over his face, trying to gain some perspective on this new information. None of this meant they could tie him to the night Brian had died.

Jamie stood and faced him. "What is going on?"

"Why did you tell Derek I'm here?"

"I didn't. Andreas did."

"Why does Derek care that I'm here?"

She hesitated.

"*What did Derek say?*"

"To stay away from you," she said colorlessly.

"He knows we slept together?"

"Of course not! I don't share my private life with that man. Andreas told him you attended his soccer game."

"So you think I'm dangerous."

"Why would I think that?" she asked, mystified.

Seth didn't answer. There was no point when he could say nothing.

"You're not making sense." She pulled in a long raggedy breath. "Talk to me, Seth."

He began to pace. "Maybe I should leave town." His parents had moved around for a reason—so people couldn't pin them down. He'd hated that nomadic life. Besides, he had Sanjay's welfare to consider.

"You can't leave," said Jamie.

He shook his head. She was right, but she didn't know about Sanjay.

"You *can't*," she repeated. "My first child has been abandoned by his father. My second child doesn't deserve the same fate, despite my poor taste in men."

He tried to decipher Jamie's words. "You have one child. Andreas."

"That's right. But I will have another. I'm pregnant, Seth. The child is yours." Though her voice was precise, her eyes pleaded with him. "This isn't how I meant to tell you. The conversation got away from me. But you need to know."

He stared. The words made some kind of sense but not the content. He couldn't be a father. He'd made that decision long ago.

"Seth, say something." Her voice cracked on the last word and the entire conversation became less unreal. She was here and needed something from him. He focused.

"Are you sure?" he asked. Not the best question, but there had to be some sort of mistake and he could help her sort it out. He just didn't know which mistake it was. She *couldn't* be pregnant.

"Am I sure that I'm pregnant or that it's yours?"

"Jamie." He ran a hand over his face. "That you're pregnant. You can't be pregnant. I used a condom."

"I know. I was there. It doesn't change the fact that I'm pregnant."

He wanted to swear, but Jamie was too brittle to withstand harsh words. Not that he understood his own reaction. Confusion reigned, yes, and dread was strong, but strangely enough exhilaration and hope attached themselves to this terrible news.

"I'm going to be a father." He realized he sounded puzzled more than anything else. He tried to feel the weight of this new burden. His mind circled through a few memories—violent ones of his father, good ones of Sanjay. He didn't know where this news fit in to the pattern of good and bad fathers. He just knew this development was dangerous.

She gripped her elbows, waiting for his reaction, and now he understood her tiredness and loss of appetite. He searched for his own strength. He was going to need it.

"I can't believe it," he managed. Insufficient, but a start. "I never meant to have children." As the expression on her face began to close, Seth bumbled on. "My parents, especially my father, were *terrible* role models."

"You're not your father, Seth."

"If anyone were to have my child, I would have chosen you."

Her smile was tentative. "It wasn't a choice, but an accident. I think we rested together too long after we made love." She lifted a shoulder, trying to cover her sadness. "That's the only thing I can think of."

"Come here."

She frowned as he held open his arms. Perhaps it was wrong to give her real hope for the future, but she should know he cared. "This isn't seduction. This is a hug. I need it and you look like you do, too."

She came into his arms, then, and clung. A slight tremor ran through her body and he murmured soothing noises. Resting his chin upon her head, he smelled Jamie and flowers. So sweet. Special. He rocked her until she seemed calm. The moment passed and he stepped back.

Wiping a tear from her eye, she looked straight at him. "Will you be an active part of this child's life?"

He turned over the answers in his mind. *I don't know*, was truthful and misleading. *I want to*, sounded craven and weak. *Maybe*, worse.

She was steeling herself for his answer. He could see it in the set of her jaw and the flatness of her eyes.

"We need to talk this through," he said in his most reasonable tone of voice. "Let's sit down again." He reached for her elbow.

She jerked away from him. "Talk about what?"

He paused, unsure how to proceed.

"Don't you dare suggest abortion."

He stood there, stunned. That option had not crossed his mind. His smile was crooked, he knew. "I don't want to." While the child should never have been conceived, he couldn't act against it. He could only protect it.

At that admission, Jamie closed her eyes in apparent relief. "Thank God. I really can't face that discussion."

"You don't have to." He led her to the couch. "Do you need something?"

"I'm thirsty," she admitted.

He used the moment to escape to the kitchen for drinks, taking a couple of minutes to regroup.

"Do you want some milk?" he called, surveying the refrigerator. She needed to drink a lot, that much he knew about pregnancy.

"Okay."

When he returned to the living room, she remained seated, back ramrod straight. He gulped water. His throat was dry thinking of what to say next. It was important the information came across in such a way that Jamie would protect her child, a child who might carry wolf genes.

"Obviously, you have a certain suggestion in mind," she said.

He hesitated.

"Spill, Seth."

"It would be best if I am not known to be the father of this child."

She gazed at him. "Are you serious?"

He nodded.

She slammed her glass down on the side table. "What the hell kind of response is that?"

He pushed on. "You have to protect this child."

"Of course I do. I'm its mother."

He needed time to explain everything but her sharp reaction made his words come out slowly and painfully. "Listen—"

"I will not put father unknown on the birth certificate."

He winced.

"You couldn't refuse to take responsibility. Oh, no. It has to be more mysterious than that." Her anger was not misplaced.

He loathed himself for getting her into this mess. He hadn't wanted to leave her body that night. He'd resisted pulling away and this was the result. "Derek was right. You should have stayed away from me."

Her eyes widened. Evidently she hadn't believed her ex-husband. Nor did she believe Seth at the moment either. He paced, trying to figure out how to convince her not to tie the child to him. Though werewolves were rare and being found out rarer still, it was a possibility. He didn't want the child burdened with a public heritage.

"Sit down and tell me what is going on, Seth. Now. Like it or not, we have something that binds us together." She was pleading with him, despite the words that followed. "Your name *will* be on the birth certificate."

"Not once you know me better, it won't."

She glared at him. "Get out."

"Look—"

"Stop messing around. I want straight talking, or I want you to leave."

"Jamie, the last thing you want is the truth."

Furious, she marched towards the door.

"You're not ready for this," he warned.

She stopped and turned, crossing her arms. "Let me decide that." Her big, brown eyes threatened to swallow him up. He wanted to give everything to her and yet his biggest secret was a burden, not a gift.

"Brace yourself, okay?" he said.

Something in his expression must have gotten through because her impatience gave way to wariness.

"Okay," she agreed carefully.

"I'm a werewolf."

She blinked, confused. Certainly not frightened. Her brow began to furrow with...irritation. A wild hope erupted in him. Maybe she thought this small detail was somehow manageable and she was about to say, *Is that all?* annoyed that he'd made a big deal of it.

But it wasn't a small detail, except in an ideal world where people wouldn't fear and despise him.

She searched his face and apparently decided it had truth written all over it. Her brow cleared. "You're serious."

He nodded.

"Oh, Seth." A hand rose and clutched her forehead. "Oh, dear." She swallowed, dismay writ large. Despite her distress, he was relieved she didn't regard him with total horror.

She removed her hand from her head and spoke forcefully. "You need help. Professional help."

"There isn't a werewolves anonymous, if that's what you mean."

"I said *professional* help."

"I don't need help. I just am. A professional would be frightened or disgusted or excited in disgusting ways. But I don't do any of that to you."

She shivered, as if to correct his misapprehension. But her face was still open, clear, no longer wary. Though he hoped this *help* mode would pass. Did she think meditation or positive thinking would stop him from shifting?

"Seth, there are good people in the mental health field now. Good drugs, too. Doctors *can* help you."

His mouth dropped open.

"What?" she asked.

He started to laugh which simply deepened the concern with which she regarded him.

"Of course," he said. "You don't believe me. What was I thinking? It's such a reality to me. I hide what I am and think the least hint will make me obvious to all. Instead, a bald statement means I'm not believed. I should have come at this sideways."

She regarded him with forbearance. "Okay. Well, turn into a wolf, then."

Despite himself and the situation, he felt his lips curve. "I need a full moon." Not strictly true, but he didn't have the energy to force the shift now and he didn't want to frighten her.

"Ah, the full moon." She paused and the wariness returned. "You're not playing games with me, are you? Because I will never, ever forgive you, if you are. It was difficult for me to tell you I'm pregnant."

His humor fled. "I'm not playing games. Think on what I've told you and see if it makes sense, okay?"

She went pale again, and he wondered if she remembered his wolf visits. But enough for one night. He wasn't going to push the truth at her now, if she was resisting. Give her time.

"Let's make coffee," he suggested.

"I don't want coffee. I'm exhausted. I'm not sleeping well and you're not helping."

"I love you, Jamie." Shit, he hadn't meant to say that. He reached for her and she hit his arm away.

"You should leave." Bad timing for a declaration of love.

"Can I come back?"

"After you've made an appointment with your doctor."

"I don't have a doctor."

"Get one."

"And if I don't?"

"We won't see each other," she said grimly.

"I think you'll come around to my point of view."

She rubbed her head. "Oh, Seth, stop."

"All right."

She pointed to the door. "Leave. You need help. I need sleep. Then I'll figure out how I'm going to cope with a father who wants to be involved but has mental health issues."

"I'm sane, Jamie."

"God, I hope so, Seth."

"It would be better I weren't." He was unable to hide his bitterness.

They stared and Seth couldn't bring himself to look away. He didn't want to leave. The chasm between them would simply grow.

"Go," she whispered, eyes dark in her pale, tired face. He raised a knuckle to her cheek and she accepted it. Then, despite the fact he feared this evening was the end of whatever they'd ever had, he did as she asked. He left.

⚃

She slept deeply that night and woke refreshed. Perhaps because she no longer bore the guilt of withholding information from Seth. Not that the situation between them wasn't worse. Werewolf, good grief! What was she supposed to do with that kind of explanation, watch *Buffy*? Or was that a vampire show?

She sighed. Sarcasm was not going to help Seth, or herself. No wonder the man hadn't had a serious relationship, despite being gorgeous and twenty-five.

In the living room, Andreas roared as his T-Rex jumped off the fireplace ledge and onto another plastic dinosaur. Her parents had delivered him half an hour ago. Since then he'd waited for Derek to call and his impatience began to show.

"Mom, can we have a fire now?"

"Uh, no. We don't have fires on warm Sunday mornings."

"I'll put away my dinosaurs," he offered as incentive.

She shook her head.

"I want marshmallows," he persisted. "Opa knows how to cook them just right."

"That's nice. You can make fires and marshmallows with Opa, then."

Andreas gave up and returned to his play. She heard the sound effects of another dinosaur flying through the air.

As she retreated to the kitchen the phone rang.

"I'll get it, Mom," called Andreas. He leapt up from the floor, almost crashing into the end table in his haste to get his hand on the receiver. He started talking a mile a minute. "Dad! Guess what? I slept over at Oma and Opa's last night and ate marshmallows and watched hockey. There was lots of fighting and some blood. Oma didn't like that but Opa didn't mind. He says it's all part of the game. And it was Oma's birthday yesterday and Mom made a pink cake and Mr. Kolski showed me how to fly a kite."

Jamie winced. Seth's name again. She *really* didn't want to discuss Seth with Derek this morning. Listening to Andreas chatter with half an ear, she unloaded the dishwasher.

Fifteen minutes later—Derek was nothing if not predictable—Andreas was saying, "Okay, okay," and walking over to the kitchen.

"Dad wants to talk to you, Mom."

She took the proffered phone and encouraged Andreas to return to his dinosaurs by the fireplace.

"Hello, Derek." She headed to her bedroom, in no mood for Andreas to overhear her conversation this morning.

"I thought I warned you away from Seth," Derek said without preamble.

"You did."

"It would be easier if you listened to me."

"What are you talking about?"

"I spoke to Gordon, to find out specifics, as you asked."

"I asked nothing of the sort."

Derek ignored her. "My boss went ballistic at the mention of Kolski." Derek's voice was tense, stressed, as he got when work was at its worst. "I don't know why you had to invite that man to attend my son's soccer game."

"Well, for starters, you didn't attend."

He swore.

"Listen, Derek, it was your choice to bring Seth's name to Gordon's attention, not mine."

"I'm concerned about my son."

"You have a rather distant way of showing that."

"Jamie, we're not talking about me, we're talking about the entire Kolski family, who are on the run from the law."

"Really? Teaching here in Cedartown is an odd occupation for an outlaw."

"Don't be smart, Jamie."

"God, no, I wouldn't want to be smart. Only Derek can be smart."

"Don't start." He pulled in a breath. "Seth Kolski won't be Andreas's gym teacher for much longer if he is implicated in the murder of Gordon's son."

Jamie felt her body shiver, though she was warmly dressed. "So, instead of Veronica, you think Seth ripped out Brian's throat?" She tried to scoff but her voice sounded reedy and thin. Seth couldn't actually *be* a werewolf. It was a delusion of his.

"Jamie—"

"Look, was it an animal who killed Brian, or not?"

"An animal, yes."

"Without doubt?"

"Yes, yes," he said impatiently.

Jamie's frantic heartbeat calmed. No matter that Seth thought he was a werewolf, he was human, and a human had not killed Brian Carver.

"Someone could have arranged that death, Jamie." Derek's tone suggested she should see the obvious. "Gordon wants this possibility explored."

"Gordon is an asshole."

"That doesn't mean he didn't care about his son. Brian's death almost destroyed Gordon and he wants revenge."

"Has it occurred to you that Gordon isn't too objective here? He wants to blame someone. That doesn't mean Seth is to blame." But Seth's words came back to her. *It would be best if I am not known to be the father of this child.* Surely his misguided belief in his own ability to shapeshift had nothing to do with the Carvers. The phone shook in her hand.

"I'm giving you a real warning here."

"I've heard your warning, Derek, and now I have to go. Andreas is calling me. Bye."

She hung up and stood in her bedroom, hands gripping elbows, lightheaded with panic. Derek's phone call had scared her. She was even willing to consider the possibility that what Seth claimed was real, though the images that followed were disturbing. Werewolf. Torn throat. Brian's death.

No. She refused to believe in werewolves.

She had to talk to Seth.

Cʒ

Most days Andreas caught the bus, but this morning it passed by the house while he was putting on his jacket.

"Mondays," said Jamie. "Okay, Andreas, out to the car and I'll drive you to school."

"Will you pick me up?"

"Nope."

"Aw, Mom."

"You like the bus, Andreas."

"I like you more."

She laughed. "I'll remember you like me better than a bus the next time I'm feeling down." Which was now. She hadn't been able to reach Seth by phone yesterday. And he didn't have an answering machine.

She wasn't just down, she was worried sick, and Andreas had picked up on her distress because he'd gone into burble mode. On the way over, he chattered about Mrs. Sanders and Seth and art and gym, in no particular order.

It was good Andreas had missed the bus. Now Jamie had an excuse to see Seth. He usually greeted the kids at the door as they disembarked from the buses, making sure everyone made it into the school safely.

"Mom, I get to see Mr. Kolski in gym today!"

"That's great, Andreas." It was no accident, she reflected, that Andreas was so focused on Seth. He knew Seth was important to his mother. "Maybe we'll see him in front of the school, too." *Please.*

"That's not the same as gym, Mom."

"No."

But Seth wasn't at the door. The principal was—a nice enough woman despite the orange tint to her hair and excessive hair spray.

Really, Jamie, be nice.

She hugged Andreas who squirmed at this public display of affection. He disappeared into the throng of children entering the school.

"Hello, Mrs. Crawley," Jamie said as casually as possible, hoping any redness to her cheeks could be attributed to the brisk autumn wind. "Where's Mr. Kolski this morning?"

"Our teachers get sick sometimes, Mrs..."

"I'm Jamie Buchner. Andreas Debison's mother."

"Of course." Mrs. Crawley watched the latest bus disgorge its small passengers, obviously expecting Jamie to disappear.

"He has the flu, does he?" Jamie's voice was inappropriately cheerful but she couldn't help it.

Mrs. Crawley frowned. "Goodness, people are interested in Mr. Kolski this morning. We already received a phone call inquiring about his health."

"Oh." Jamie's ability to stave off her fears was dwindling.

"My dear." The older woman, surprised by Jamie's concern, tilted her head. She patted Jamie's arm to reassure her. "He'll be fine, I'm sure. Back tomorrow. Mr. Kolski is never ill, you see. Never misses a day of school." Her smile widened. "Before now."

Seth wasn't ill now, either. Between her morning sickness and her fear, Jamie thought she might vomit. So she merely attempted to smile and that was enough for Mrs. Crawley to move away from her, over to a rowdy group of older boys who had congregated by the birdhouse.

Jamie stumbled to the car.

CB

Tom opened the door, still in his pajamas, hair sticking on end, disgruntled by the interruption. "Jamie?"

She nodded.

"Is this important?"

She nodded again. He worked best in the morning, at home, and he was probably in the middle of some Very Important Project, but she had to talk to someone. Tom was the obvious choice.

"Okay, come on in."

She followed him to the kitchen. "How was Washington?" He'd arrived back late last night.

"Fine. Cynthia stayed on to visit her father."

"Oh. I'm glad he deigns to see her these days."

Tom shrugged. "He's a bigwig."

"Yeah?" She couldn't think about Cynthia's father right now.

Tom looked at her and frowned. "Are you all right? You seem out of it."

How to explain everything? It would be easier if Cynthia had told Tom about the pregnancy.

"Do you want some coffee?" He indicated the full coffeepot.

"I hate coffee," she said with vehemence.

He raised his eyebrows. "That's a new development."

"You can say that again."

His gaze swept to the side and back at her, as if she wasn't making sense. So, Cynthia had been the paragon of discretion and Tom didn't know. She'd have to start from the beginning. Her own fault for swearing Cynthia to secrecy.

He tightened the tie of his bathrobe, as if to prepare himself. "Uh, Jamie, is something wrong?"

"Yes." She burst into tears.

She wasn't a tidy crier. Standing in the middle of Tom's kitchen, she whooped and snuffled, despite trying to get control because Tom looked appalled. She managed to grab a chair and sit down. When she reached for the tissue box across the table, Tom retrieved it for her. He patted her awkwardly on the shoulder.

"Cynthia won't be back for a few days," he said with obvious regret.

"I don't want to talk to Cynthia." She blew her nose, though she was still sobbing and gulping. "I want to talk to you."

"Oh. Well. Okay." His forehead creased with deep thought. "Did you have a fight with Derek?"

"Derek can't make me cry."

"Mom?"

She shook her head, still sniffling, but the worst was over. "Mom annoys me. She doesn't make me cry."

"I thought she might have started in on you meeting someone new and you found that painful." He had some hope for this scenario. "Jamie, the best thing you can do with Mom is ignore her. Don't let her get to you. She means well."

"Mom's not the problem, Tom."

He slouched towards the coffee machine. "More serious?" he said with trepidation.

She nodded.

He poured himself a cup of coffee and folded his lanky body into a chair opposite her. "All right, who do I beat up?"

She smiled, despite herself. "Since when do you fight?"

He held out his long arm, bent it at the elbow and made a fist. "I'm a clever guy. I can figure it out."

"I'm worried about Seth."

Tom released his fingers from the fist and laid his hand on the table. "Seth?"

She leaned forward, trying to rein in her intensity, because she didn't want to cry again. It was tiring. "He thinks he's a werewolf, Tom."

Tom stared, expressionless.

"It's not a joke. Or, I'm pretty certain it's not a joke. I wish it were, though then I'd have to kill him. I read up on the internet and some people think they're werewolves. The condition is called lycanthropy. It's very rare."

"You can't believe everything you read on the internet, Jamie."

She gaped at him. Here, she'd revealed something astoundingly bizarre and he was mouthing platitudes about the internet. "Is that the most important point you can make, Tom?"

"What do you mean?"

"I feel better now that I know I'm naive about the internet. That solves everything."

Tom rolled his eyes. "Look, I'm willing to listen here, but don't critique my support-group skills."

"*Seth thinks he's a werewolf, Tom!*"

Tom held up his hands in surrender. "Okay, okay. When did he tell you this?"

"Saturday night."

"He must trust you a lot."

"*Tom!* Are we having the same conversation? You latch onto the oddest aspects of what I say. Internet, trust." She jabbed her finger at the table, as if physical gestures would get through to Tom better than loud words. "I'm worried Seth is schizophrenic or something, and needs to take medication."

"Possibly," Tom allowed.

"Seth wasn't at school this morning. Nor could I reach him by phone yesterday. Why would he disappear right after he told me he's a werewolf?"

"Do you think he's in danger?" asked Tom.

"Why would he be in danger?"

"I don't know. Because he thinks he's a werewolf?"

She shoved two hands into her hair in frustration. "Can you say something helpful?"

But Tom looked like he had trouble taking it all in. He grasped onto a previous part of the conversation. "You phoned Seth's house."

"Repeatedly."

"Try one more time." He reached for the cordless and handed it to her. "Dial."

She let it ring eight times.

Tom jumped up. "Okay, I'll get dressed and we'll drive over. See if he's in. Maybe Seth turned off his ringer because he's been out all night prowling."

"It's not the full moon."

"I doubt that matters to a real werewolf, Jamie."

She groaned. Her brother was a pain, and he didn't take her concern seriously, maybe because he didn't know she was pregnant with Seth's child. Or maybe because he didn't know about the wolf who had visited her with Seth's eyes.

"After all"—Tom came back down the stairs—"what is the worst thing about believing you're a werewolf? In itself, it's harmless enough."

"I don't think it's healthy, Tom. One needs a sense of reality."

Tom shrugged. "He has that. He can make conversation, hold down a job, prepare a meal of sorts. That's more than I can manage."

"If you were at all inclined, you could cook."

"That's what wives are for."

"Why doesn't Cynthia whack you on the head when you say these things?"

"We accept each other for what we are." Tom's tone was surprisingly serious. He jerked his head towards the front door. "C'mon. Let's go."

On the way over to Seth's, they lapsed into silence while Jamie, since she didn't want to think werewolves could be real, tried to consider Tom's point of view. Maybe she was overreacting to a werewolf identity crisis. But she had a hard time thinking lycanthropy wasn't a serious problem.

"The trouble is," she said finally, "Seth thinks there's something wrong with him. He hasn't even had a serious relationship."

"Jamie, that's not so unusual at his age."

"He's a year older than you, Tom."

"Yeah, but I met Cynthia."

"You know, talking to you sometimes has as much logic as talking to Mom."

Tom wasn't offended. "I inherited her brains. We think outside the box." He flashed her a smile.

"You're impossible."

"Look, do you feel better after coming to see me, or not?"

"I suppose." After all, he was driving her to Seth's. Good thing, as she didn't feel up to paying attention to the roads.

But when they arrived, the house was deserted. Tom debated the wisdom of breaking in, but wasn't serious. As they retreated from the front door, Tom said, "Seth likes you. He'll call again." He put his hand on the car door. "Unless you'd rather he didn't. Then I'll talk to him."

She stifled hysterical laughter. "I want him to call again."

Tom looked thoughtful, assessing, as if he wanted to tell her something. Which was unusual. Tom wasn't into confidences. Even so, she should tell him she was pregnant. But she waited for him to speak since he obviously wasn't going to open the door he stood beside.

"I saw a wolf once," Tom told her.

"Yeah?" *So have I.*

"At a party years ago, when I was a teen. Remember Seth's sister?"

Jamie nodded unhappily.

"Well, one minute there was Veronica, then she vanished and there was a wolf. It was weird. Before I could make sense of it, Seth punched me and called me names, acting all freaked." Tom shrugged. "I put it down to fifteen-year-old hormones and screwy parents. The Kolskis left a couple of days later."

"Why were Seth's parents screwy?"

"His dad used to hit him a fair amount," Tom said with distaste. Jamie remembered some of the bruises though when she'd asked back then, Seth had attributed them to schoolyard fights. "And his mom thought Seth deserved it."

"Oh."

"Yeah." He hunched forward, voice lower. "Cynthia thinks her dad is a werewolf. That's why he keeps his distance from her. Not because he's too busy doing important things."

"Huh?" Jamie squinted at her brother as if better eyesight would make his conversation easier to follow.

"Don't tell Mom and Dad," he added. "They already dislike Cynthia enough as it is."

"Have you tried to reason with her?" She refused to believe this werewolf myth. *Refused.* Though her hand crept to her stomach.

"Why? It doesn't do much harm. Whether he's werewolf or not, she still wants to see her dad."

"He should be more eager to see his own daughter."

"Cynthia's mother never told him she was pregnant, so Cynthia and her father have a relationship to build."

She brought the conversation back around to her more immediate concern. "It's not normal, Tom, to have these beliefs about werewolves."

"I don't care. I only care if it causes a problem."

"If Seth stays away from his job, that's a problem."

"Perhaps."

She chewed her lip. "That's bizarre, Tom. Seth thinks he's a werewolf and Cynthia thinks her father's a werewolf. What a strange coincidence."

"Well, Seth isn't your husband."

"That's hardly the point," she ground out.

"It's not a total coincidence, actually. Cynthia and I both researched werewolves, she because of her father, and me because of Veronica. That's how we met."

"What do you mean, because of Veronica?" Jamie didn't hide her frustration. Tom couldn't believe in werewolves too, thinking outside the box, or no.

"I wondered if Veronica was a werewolf," said Tom, as if he were saying, I wondered if she was musical. "Remember Veronica had those golden eyes? Unusual, like Seth's eyes are unusual. The wolf I saw had eyes that were exactly the same golden color as Veronica's, almost glowing."

Wolf's eyes. Pale, glowing blue, like Seth's. She'd been trying not to think of them and now she had to confront eyes she could not forget. The blood drained from her head. Her world turned gray and Tom's voice said, *hey*, from afar as she slipped into darkness.

She came awake from a vivid, if incoherent dream, disoriented, and Jamie realized she wasn't in bed. In fact, Tom was lightly patting her cheeks and her head was cradled in his lap. She felt peaceful, if strange. Till the word *werewolf* echoed in her head and everything came crashing back in a tense jumble of worries.

Tom carried on as if there'd been no lapse in consciousness. "I think you're the one who's sick, Jamie. You haven't looked all that well for a while."

"I'm pregnant." After all this talk of werewolves, that statement seemed almost mundane. "And I've seen Seth's eyes before, in that of a wolf."

Tom sat her up and slowly let go, making sure she could sit on her own. "Stay here." He held her arms, as if she might run off. "I have a water bottle in my car."

He sprinted three steps, retrieved the bottle and came back to her. She gulped down a mouthful.

"Do you believe in werewolves, Tom?"

"Actually—and don't take this the wrong way and faint on me again—yes, I do."

138

Chapter Eight

In the week that followed, Andreas watched for the return of Mr. Kolski at school. Jamie appreciated her son's unceasing vigilance although it was to no avail. Seth had truly disappeared.

"He's still away, Mom," Andreas announced every day. "Do you think you should take him chicken soup in case he's sick?"

"He doesn't seem to be at home, honey," Jamie would respond, trying not to sound fretful and apprehensive when she was both. Andreas looked at her with big eyes.

On Friday, long after his daily report, Andreas was sadder than usual. Listlessly, he played with his dinosaurs. Declaring them to be sick, he laid them out on the fireplace ledge to sleep.

After dinner, he said, "He's not coming back, is he?"

"Who?" she asked, to give herself time.

"Seth. Mr. Kolski. He's gone gone, isn't he?"

"I don't know, Andreas."

She arranged for Andreas to sleep at her parents' Saturday night so she could stop pretending everything was fine when she felt awful. Not just because Seth was the father of her child, but because something might have happened to him.

Tom came over and Cynthia phoned from Washington almost every day, worried about Jamie and Seth. Cynthia, backed by the authority of her father, whoever he was, insisted Jamie could not go to the police because their involvement would worsen Seth's situation, whatever that situation was. Jamie wished she knew what was going on. Cynthia's assurances that her father would find out seemed useless, given that he was in Washington. Nevertheless, Jamie did understand the take-home message—no missing-person report, no police. Because if they found and jailed Seth—without killing him first—he'd go crazy in prison. Werewolves had to avoid prison at all costs.

Jamie didn't quite know what to make of Cynthia's statements. Did the existence of her father make Cynthia a werewolf expert? Her sister-in-law thought so. Jamie, well, she still couldn't wrap her mind around the werewolf business. But in the moments when she didn't believe, she remembered Seth's eyes.

Saturday passed in a blur although Jamie did focus enough to play a game of Pokemon.

"Good job," Andreas praised her, as if she needed reassurance. "You almost won that time."

"Thanks, sweetie." She ruffled his tousled towhead. Fair, like his father. Large like his father. Yet Andreas had her eyes and her smile. "I love you."

"Aw, Mom, does that mean you won't play another game?"

"I can't, Andreas." One game of Pokemon was her limit. "Let's play Uno."

"All right."

At her parents', Jamie's mother fussed about her appetite and Jamie was thankful her mother could not imagine Jamie pregnant outside of wedlock. Not that she'd be quite so grateful once she broke the news to her parents. But that conference was a few weeks off. She wasn't yet showing.

"And why do you insist on wearing baggy clothes?" asked her mother. "No wonder Seth isn't taking you out tonight. You need to make yourself up. Dress nicely. Especially since he's younger than you."

"Mother."

"You have a lovely figure and you should show it off."

"Seth is out of town," Jamie snapped before her mother moved on to the topic of why push-up bras were better than the more comfortable athletic bras. An inappropriate conversation that her mother would have no problem revisiting.

"I don't know why Seth is away," she added as her mother opened her mouth to say more. "And I'm quite tired. I'm heading home for an early night."

"Stay for tea."

"No."

"Leave her alone, Edna," said her father.

"But she shouldn't spend the evening all alone," her mother protested.

"I'm going to read a book."

"Books are not company."

Her father raised his eyebrows at Jamie. Her mother had never been a reader and couldn't understand the love both she and her father had for books.

"Go on, Jamie. We can handle Andreas, can't we, Edna?"

"Well, of course we can. That's not the point."

"Come here for a hug, Andreas," called Jamie. He was setting up his Pokemon game, an activity her father regarded with something of a long-suffering look.

Hugs and kisses were exchanged and Jamie retreated to the quiet of her car. As she drove home, the full moon rose in the east and she found herself longing to hear her wolf again. That night, despite her exhaustion, she lay awake waiting for the familiar howl. But the sky was silent.

CS

The next morning she stumbled into the kitchen. Her dreams had been frenetic and vague, but Jamie was physically rested. As she searched for juice, she heard a rap at the back window. Slamming the fridge door shut, she looked out the dining-room window and screamed.

Seth winced. Wet, bare-chested Seth. He must be freezing this cool September morning.

He retreated and, fearing he'd disappear as quickly as he'd materialized, she rushed to the back door, almost tripping over her feet. She flung the door open and stared. He was naked, as if he'd been running around the forest without clothes on. She gazed at him and he must have seen a welcome in her expression, because he smiled. Crookedly, but a smile.

"Are you going to let me in, or am I too crazy?" He crossed his arms. The stance seemed to be more of a bracing for bad news than a bid for warmth. He didn't shiver, either. "I haven't seen a doctor, I'm afraid."

Gaping was only going to accomplish so much. She closed her mouth and motioned him inside, not sure what to say. "Don't leave," she blurted.

He tilted his head in acquiescence before entering. "Andreas isn't up yet? He might find my sudden and spartan appearance unsettling."

"He's at my parents for another hour or so."

"Good."

"Seth?" Her voice sounded high and shaky and she didn't know what she wanted to ask him. *Are you okay? Are you cold? Are you a werewolf?*

"Yes?"

"I, I..." She was shaking and looked down, only to see he was responding to her presence in a way that she would not necessarily have noticed if he'd been dressed.

Her glance flicked away and up. His expression was wry.

"I don't suppose you have any clothes around that would fit me?"

Her face reddened. Here she was, flustered by his arousal, when she hadn't known where he was all week, or why he'd gone missing.

"I've been worried sick about you," she said with a force that surprised them both. And burst into tears. Again. She'd already gone through this routine with Tom.

But Seth wasn't Tom.

"Hey." He gently pulled her towards him.

She raised both fists to knock against his chest with no real strength. Then she covered her red, wet face as she snorted and snuffled unattractively against his breastbone. He stroked her hair with his large, warm hands and made shushing noises, without speaking any words of real reassurance. Presumably he had none to give.

"You smell nice," she told him once she could speak without sobbing. "Like forest and damp grass."

"That's where I've been." He placed both hands on her shoulders and eased her away so he could examine her face and wipe away the last of her tears.

She nodded acceptance of his statement. "You didn't need me to make you more wet."

"The drizzle doesn't bother me."

She snorted laughter. "I'm the drizzle?"

"I was referring to outside." The morning was gray and misty, despite the efforts of the newly risen sun.

"You're warm." She stroked his side. "I'd freeze out there without clothes."

"I'm always warm after I shift."

She cocked her head.

"Shift from wolf to human," he added, a challenge in his eyes, a challenge to believe. "The change creates a lot of heat."

"Oh," she marveled as her cold fingers absorbed warmth from his skin. She became self-conscious then of his erection and stepped back. "Um. I have something of Tom's here. He stayed one night when Andreas begged for a sleepover."

"If you insist," Seth drawled.

Her chest tightened with lust but the rest of her just wasn't there. "For someone without a serious relationship in his past, you do quite well."

"I didn't say I was a monk. I like sex." He stepped forward. "As do you, if I recall. At least with me."

She backed up quickly and he stopped. His teasing expression vanished.

"Seth, we need to talk."

He nodded but his guarded expression upset her and she flung her arms around him again, both to make sure he was really with her and to get rid of the shadow.

"I missed you."

His chest rumbled. "I think you're sending me mixed signals now."

"I am mixed. There is so much to say and I don't know where to start."

"Okay, okay." He set her apart from him. "Truth is, I'm starving. Feed me and we'll talk. Then I'll get out of here before you collect Andreas."

Her heart sank. "I don't want you to go."

His blue gaze darkened. "I'm sorry. This is why, you know, I asked for a casual relationship. You can't count on me."

She swallowed. "What do you want to eat?"

"Bacon?"

She shook her head.

"Sausages?"

"None."

"Eggs?"

"A dozen. I have cold cuts in the fridge."

"I'll start on them."

"I'll get Tom's clothes first."

She excavated sweats and a T-shirt from her closet and threw them at Seth, then went to the kitchen to crack eggs and toss bread in the toaster. Seth vacuumed up the contents of a package of ham and salami.

"Is this why you're hungry all the time? Because you..." She couldn't say he was a werewolf, yet, though he waited her out. "Because you spend the nights outside?"

"Yes," he said between swallows. "Do you believe I'm a werewolf now?"

"Well, on a continuum of not believing and believing, I'm closer to the latter." She flipped the eggs. "I still can't quite comprehend it, but obviously something is going on." She buttered toast and was surprised how good it felt to do

145

something for Seth as simple as feeding him. Other problems seemed insoluble. *How does one make a life with a werewolf?*

From the stove, she glanced over and his blue eyes caught her in their strange, almost fantastic light. Intensified by emotion.

"Why didn't you call me?" she asked.

"I thought you would despise me."

"Oh, Seth," she said. "I can't do that." She placed a hand on her stomach. "We're bound by this baby and, besides, I have a crush on you."

He burst out laughing. "You have a crush on me!"

She turned away, grinning at the eggs. "You don't mind?"

"I can handle it." His expression sobered. "I'd ask for more, if I could give you more."

"It's more than a crush, given that I've been frantic this past week."

"I'm sorry. I had to work myself up to this visit. I wasn't sure you wanted to hear from me. I'm amazed that you were eager to see me. And grateful."

She plopped a plate of eggs and toast in front of him. "I wanted to hear from you. That said, I'm not sure I'm ready to see you change into a wolf. Even if you and my wolf have the same color of eyes."

"*Your* wolf?"

She smiled. What a ping-pong kind of state she was in, bouncing from anxiety, to laughter, to giddiness, to sorrow. All mixed up and pregnancy hormones didn't help keep the emotions straight. "I always thought of him, of *you*, as my wolf after that first chat in Atlanta."

He grabbed her hand and kissed her knuckles, his new short beard a soft caress. "You were right."

A tear leaked out of her right eye and she wiped it away.

"I'm so sorry, Jamie, to get you involved."

"Don't be sorry," she said furiously. "I'm not sorry. I want to find out what is going on and what I can do."

"If anyone asks after me, don't tell them I was here."

"I can keep quiet." She waited for more from him, but he plowed into his eggs and toast, and she remained silent, letting him eat what he needed.

Once he finished, he pushed away the plate and peeled an orange. "Sunday afternoon, they came to my house."

"Who?"

"Police. Detectives. Plain clothed, but Jamie, no one comes to my door like that. I escaped out the back window." His lips twisted. "Turned wolf."

She frowned. "During the day?"

"I can force the shift when the need arrives."

"You didn't think to stay and defend yourself?"

He shook his head. "I can't risk incarceration. Cages make me nuts."

"You've been in prison."

"I've been in a small space." He placed both hands on the table. "My parents didn't teach me much, but they did hammer into me the importance of not getting caught and identified as werewolf. If people get their hands on me, they'll have the right to do anything they like because I'm not human." She recognized suppressed rage when she saw it. Tension washed off his muscles.

"You are human."

His smile was sharp and completely lacking in humor. "How do you know?"

"You are," she declared. "And so is this baby I'm carrying." Not that she knew how she was going to handle its wolf nature.

"The baby won't be wolf, Jamie."

"It won't?" Relief grabbed hold of her throat.

Seth watched her carefully. "Not unless you carry the werewolf gene yourself, which is unlikely. We're extremely rare."

"I'd love this baby no matter what, Seth, but I can't cope with a werewolf baby without your help."

His face softened. "The gene is sex-linked and recessive. If the baby is a boy, no werewolf gene, because you're the X gene donor. I hope like hell it's a boy."

"If it's a girl?"

"She'll have my X chromosome with its recessive gene. But if she passes that gene on to her son, she'll have a werewolf baby boy. Like her father. Kind of like baldness, but with more consequences."

Jamie stood, hand on her stomach, trying to breathe, as if all this information made the air thin. Seth rose and picked up that hand, led her to a chair and gently pushed her down. He knelt beside her, earnest. "You'll have to tell her, Jamie. You'll have to tell her not to have babies at some point. It's dangerous to have a werewolf child with no one to run with. I know. They put themselves in jeopardy."

Jamie found herself glaring at Seth. "You'll be here. *You* can help your daughter."

He felt like her gaze would bore a hole through him and he would carry that hole around forever, missing her and the child, boy or girl.

Then he panicked. He still held out hope for a boy, but Jamie had said daughter. "You know it's a girl." Not a question, but a fact.

"No," she replied and was up again, fetching him a cup of her awful instant coffee and slamming it on the table.

He grabbed her wrist. "I'm sorry."

"*Don't* apologize to me for being what you are. Just don't."

"You must hate me for bringing all this into your life."

"Hate is not the word."

"What word is?"

She paused, her eyes going liquid, and his chest ached. "You said you loved me last week."

He didn't move but she wouldn't continue.

"I still do," he managed.

"I don't know if I love you. I hardly know you. But I want you to be all right and I want you to be with me. And Andreas." She paused. "I know you wouldn't bite Andreas."

He almost laughed. "Uh no, I wouldn't bite Andreas. Though you might like to know werewolf bites don't infect the bitten. That's fiction. The only means of transmission is genetic." He touched her stomach lightly. "Like how we made this baby."

"Good."

"Are you relieved I'm not dangerous?"

"Seth, you've never been dangerous."

"Your faith is touching. Though God knows where it comes from."

"You, you idiot."

"Well, for what it's worth, I don't eat people. I eat animals sometimes, but human blood tastes terrible." He could feel his mouth curling with distaste.

"You know that human blood tastes terrible." Her voice was flat, without emotion, and he didn't want to continue.

He had to. He had promised himself he would hand everything over to her. "There's something you should know, Jamie."

"Okay." She crossed her arms, took a breath.

"Ready? This isn't something you want to hear." His throat was clogging up with emotion, as it did every time he thought of that awful night.

"Okay, Seth." The slight impatience in her voice made it easier to say the words.

"I killed Brian Carver." Four words, but they were difficult ones. He couldn't quite bring himself to look at Jamie. His heart banged in its cage of ribs. He'd never laid himself on the line like this. It had always been secrets and hiding and evasion except, sometimes, with Veronica. But Jamie was the mother of his child. She had a right to learn this about him. A right to decide whether or not she wanted him in her life.

"I think I knew," she said quietly.

He laughed, short and harsh. As he made eye contact he saw she wasn't looking at him with revulsion. "How?"

"I put two and two together." She caught his hand, felt its tremor, and laid it against her cheek. "I know you had a good reason."

He stood, feeling wild again. He would kill Brian a second time if he had to relive that night but Jamie's utter faith in him was alien. "He was going to expose Veronica or kill her. He couldn't quite decide. It depended on which threat he thought would enrage me most. He said no one would be upset to see a wolf's carcass. Such an easy way to get away with murder." Seth took a deep breath. "I had to protect my sister."

She nodded, not releasing his gaze. "What happened to Veronica?"

His energy deflated as suddenly as it had filled him and he sat again, exhausted. "I thought I'd saved her. Because Brian talked the entire time as if Veronica was alive. If she was dead, I figured, he would have gleefully told me." He ran a hand over his face. "But now, I don't know. She disappeared that night and I've never seen her since. Though I looked hard. I picked up her trail, only to lose it, it was so faint. Still, that trail is what gives me hope. It wasn't a bloody trail, you see. She wasn't dying. She was alive after Brian's death."

He looked at her, as if Jamie could validate his hope, and she nodded.

"But I don't know any more. Maybe Brian was playing games. Maybe he thought it fun to act as if I could save Veronica when I couldn't."

Her eyes filled with tears and he rose to kiss them. "Don't cry, Jamie. All I give you is sorrow when you give me such joy."

At which she started sobbing. "I hate Brian."

"That's no longer necessary. He's dead."

Anger sat like a sheen of liquid in her eyes. "Did he hurt you too, or just Veronica?"

He tried to say the words. He wanted to tell her. It was such a relief to trust Jamie.

"Seth?"

"He caged me."

"*Caged* you?"

"The wolf me. It makes sense to cage a wolf, no?"

"I think I'm going to throw up." She stood still for a moment, taking it all in. Then she picked up his hand and stroked it. Looked up at him. "I don't like it when your hand shakes."

"I can't talk about it any more," he admitted. He felt wrung out. The week of running wolf had taken a lot out of him. These confessions drained him, too. He stared at her.

She hadn't turned against him. Rather, she caressed his unshaved face and he wanted to explain how much these touches meant to him.

"I need to go," he said, instead. His mind told him avoiding her was her best protection, but the rest of him didn't believe it.

"Stay. Please."

"Andreas is coming home."

"I'll phone my parents. He can stay with them today while we talk this out."

"Talking won't make everything go away."

"I'm a woman, Seth. I believe talking helps." She tried to smile at her joke.

"I need to sleep first. I'm wiped."

"And where were you going to sleep?"

"There are places." He'd planned to turn wolf again, though he was weary of the form and feared staying wolf too long. It made human interaction difficult and awkward, as if his body and mind forgot the proper human motions to go through.

"Sleep in my bed."

Despite everything, he smiled. He wanted her badly, quickly, without finesse. That desire hadn't abated since he'd entered the house. But she deserved more than that. The shift from wolf charged him sexually, but he'd never been able to use it to his benefit, or anyone else's. Women didn't wait all night for him to return from his run. He'd always come back to an empty house. For a brief, blinding moment the promise of having a home and family shimmered, like a mirage. He blinked it away.

"Seth." She was touching him again though she removed her hand when the tremor passed through his body. He didn't want to explain the lust that in no way excluded the love he felt for her. "You look beat. Sleep."

♋

"Hi, Mom," said Jamie.

"Hi, honey. Are you coming over for a visit this morning?"

"Actually, I was wondering if you could watch Andreas today."

"Oh?" Her mother waited a beat. "Well, why don't you join us? We'll all spend the day together. You're alone too much and I don't like it."

Jamie squirmed. "I didn't sleep well last night and I thought—"

"Jamie, what has gotten into you? Why aren't you sleeping?"

"Mom, will you and Dad take Andreas for the day? Without me?" She hated begging someone to be with her son. She never wanted Andreas to feel unwanted and under normal circumstances she'd never ask. But she absolutely needed to deal with Seth.

"Why don't we come over there, if you want to stay at home?"

"Mom, please!" She ground her teeth, trying to think of a way to convince her mother she needed time alone without pushing all her mother's worry buttons.

"Of course we will," she heard in the background and her father took the phone. "What's going on?" he asked.

"I'm pregnant and exhausted." Jamie surprised herself and, she was sure, her father. He questioned her so little, she liked to answer when she could.

Another silence. She'd made a mistake, no doubt, and she couldn't even reveal the child's paternity. She steeled herself for questions.

"Andreas can stay here with us." His voice was matter-of-fact. "I'll bring him home at what time?"

"For supper. Thanks, Dad. You're the best."

"You get some sleep," he said, with gruff concern.

"Okay. Thanks, Dad," she repeated, feeling the tears on her cheek. God, she cried so easily these days.

"And eat more," he ordered.

She smiled. "Okay."

Placing the phone on its cradle, she closed her eyes in gratitude. She had a few hours with Seth.

She crept into the bedroom and watched Seth, who was already asleep. He sprawled under her blankets, covered from the waist down, Tom's clothes removed. Her gaze fell on the back of his right shoulder where a mass of white, raised marks stood out against his dark skin. That he'd been hurt, troubled her. She hated whoever had hurt him.

Brian.

She'd ask Seth but not right away. There were other things to ask, like what he was going to do. His expression was tense. His worries could not be banished by sleep.

Now they were her worries, too.

Chapter Nine

He was bleeding again, which amused Brian. As did the shaking.

Seth panted, striving for control, trying to gather enough air in his lungs, to match the rapid thrum of blood. But the blood was angry, pulsing and couldn't contain his rage. The wildness was not entirely of his own making, but induced by drugs he could not escape.

Brian slid his hand between the silver bars and Seth tried to evade the needle that sought him. The sharp point did not enter him. Instead, a hand stroked his forehead.

"Seth."

He couldn't speak. His voice, like the rest of him, was trapped and he refused to trust the smooth stroke of fingers.

"Seth, wake up."

The hand cupped his cheek, as if he was human. He must have shifted from wolf again. How humiliating.

He couldn't save Veronica if he was incapable of controlling his reactions. He became frantic, because Veronica was going to die.

"Seth." The voice was urgent now, and familiar. "You're dreaming."

He ducked under and away, and woke seated on the bed, facing Jamie. His skin was damp. His face no doubt showed shock, as he read concern on hers. He shut his eyes, to compose himself, and a tear escaped.

Impressive. He cried in his sleep and woke in a sweat. He felt like an idiot. Apparently, he was determined to reveal to Jamie what a mess he was. He scrubbed his face, as if that motion could erase the last few moments, and waited for her to leave the room. No doubt, she was as embarrassed as he was.

She slipped into the bed beside him, not quite touching. He opened his eyes in surprise.

"Hey," she said. "That dream didn't look like much fun."

He cleared his throat, though his voice came out rough. "I'd better get going." After this performance, he didn't want to be asked to leave. It would be easier to pull his tattered pride together if he wasn't catching his breath.

"Stay a while. Andreas is at my parents' until dinnertime."

"It's better if I go."

"Why? Because you have bad dreams?"

"No." He tensed his body so he wouldn't betray the tremor his cooling sweat induced. "I don't want them to know your baby is mine."

"Them?"

He gestured vaguely. "Authorities. Look, Jamie, once Brian knew Veronica was a werewolf, he guessed I was. I don't know who he might have told. It's better if you're not linked to me."

She didn't look impressed. "If Brian told someone, they'd have looked for you before now, no?"

"Not necessarily." He soldiered on with the idea he felt bound to present to her. "Best would be if you could marry someone else." God, that stuck in his craw, but he plunged forward with the idea. *Make the child safe from his taint.* "Pass the baby off as his."

"Uh-huh." She faked deep thought. "How the hell am I supposed to do that when I'm nine weeks pregnant?"

He stared at a point past her shoulder. "You haven't seen anyone else?"

She looked pissed. "You know I haven't."

"I don't, really." He played with the twisted sheet because, in his gut, he did.

"Are you trying to push me away or make me angry?"

"Your feelings might be different since our last chat, given I declared I was a werewolf."

"I haven't become engaged since last week, Seth."

"I'm not making sense, but what I'm trying to convey is that the child will be most safe if you created a family with someone else."

"It takes time to create a family." She leaned forward. "I know we left the bar together that night, went to your place and had sex." He lifted a hand to her face. He'd never forget. "But I don't sleep with strangers, especially when pregnant."

He couldn't help himself. He traced the line of her jaw. "So beautiful, inside and out."

"Does that mean you'll stop this ridiculous conversation?"

"I'm trying to be practical."

"And failed abysmally. I don't meet men I want to marry all that easily. It'll probably take me another three years to sleep with another guy and by that time it will be too late to pass this baby off as his."

He gave up the fight. "I never planned to be a father, but I'm grateful you'll be the mother of my child."

She rose on her knees and touched her lips to his, then retreated.

It wasn't enough, now that it was clear his mate was not choosing someone else. He followed her retreat and she stopped moving so he could reach her. Her lips were soft and pliant, though she didn't open her mouth. So he explored the hollow of her cheek, the softness of her neck, and she shivered.

She pulled back, warning in her eyes.

He was rock hard and while sex wouldn't solve any of their problems, it would sure feel good. For both of them.

"I love your lips." He traced them with his thumb and opened her mouth from one corner, preparing her for another kiss.

She stood up and away from him, and he didn't follow her. Maybe his cooled sweat was unappealing. He hoped she'd forgotten his tears.

"I can't do this sex and separation routine. Not now. It tears me up." The quaver in her voice hurt him.

"Would it help to know I'm devoted to you?"

She smiled. "Yes." Then her smile fell. "I want to get you a lawyer. They can't chase you away from me, from us." Her hand stroked her belly.

"They won't help me, Jamie. I know."

"How do you know?"

"We moved around a lot when I was a child. For good reason. People never helped us. Never. We're not like you."

"Your parents drank too much."

"An effect, Jamie, not a cause."

"And your dad beating you up, what was that? Cause or effect?"

He looked away, wishing he could hold up something clean and honest and worthy from his past. But his life seemed littered with shame and secrets and humiliation.

"You're like me," she declared, throwing him off balance. "You are. You love kids. You want a family. Even better than me, you have a job."

"I'm a werewolf, Jamie, and I need to hide it."

"Don't run away."

He swore. "I'm not taking off on a personal whim because I'm incapable of committing." He grabbed her hand, as if contact would make her believe. "Before I met up with you I hadn't slept with anyone for two years."

"Two years?" She was struck by the confession. "Why? I thought you had casual sex frequently."

He laughed. "I did. Before Veronica disappeared. That kind of messed me up. Didn't..." How not to sound like an anxiety-ridden asshole? "The night we met, I didn't plan to hit on anyone. I just needed the anonymous camaraderie of a bar. You might not believe it, but we werewolves are social creatures." She gripped his hand more tightly. "When I recognized you in the bar, I was happy to see an old friend. Someone I could trust a little."

"Little being the operative word. You didn't want to see me again." Her voice became fervent. "You can trust me, Seth."

"I just can't sleep with you." He should feel like a jerk, focusing on sex, but it was difficult not to, given they were both in her bedroom. And he yearned to connect with her again, make her understand how important she was. Words had only ever accomplished so much for him.

Her nails bit into his hand, though she didn't realize it. He felt bad, as if he should be above sex. But there might not be any future for them apart from something like this brief encounter. He could visit, but he was a fugitive.

Perhaps that wasn't something Jamie could accept. Or she couldn't accept he was wolf.

"I haven't made love to someone who knows what I am." A lover who *knew* appealed to him enormously. He blew out a breath, as if he could exhale the eagerness and desperation creeping into his voice. "Not that my peculiarities are much of an attraction for you. You may feel leery."

"That is not what is going on, Seth." She retrieved her hand and crossed her arms, pissed off again, which was strangely reassuring. "I'm too attracted to you to feel leery. Besides, I like you."

"Too attracted?" he murmured.

"Seth! I'm worried about our future and the baby, and most especially at the moment, you. Don't guilt me into sex, for God's sakes."

He nodded acquiescence. "What about a back rub?"

She frowned.

"That's a bribe, not guilt," he pointed out.

As he trapped her hand again, tugging her gently towards him, she let out a long, labored sigh. "You're very manipulative."

"Only for a good cause." He circled his thumb on her palm. "You're too cold. Let me show you my other methods of persuasion. You've convinced me that guilt is a lousy motivator." He pulled her into his arms and nuzzled the back of her neck. Some of her stiffness receded. "I have fantastic memories of our night together."

"So do I," she said in a low voice.

"Then what are you worried about?"

"Not birth control, that's for sure."

He placed his palm on her rounded stomach. "It's in there?"

"Yes. Still quite tiny."

"By the way, in case you're worried, I've always practiced safe sex because, well, I didn't want to scatter little wolfling genes around the country. Besides, werewolves throw off human diseases when they shift."

"Well, that's certainly convenient." Her hand came up to touch his face. "I'm not worried about the sex per se, Seth. I don't have good memories of how we ended."

"We'll end well this time, promise. You know what I am now."

She leaned into him, as if his chest would protect her from his wandering hands. He traced a line around her ear and down the back of her neck with his thumb. "I've missed you," she choked out.

"Jamie," he said wonderingly. "I missed you, too. This is the first time I've had someone welcome me into their house for a long time."

She clutched him tighter. "I want you to stay."

"I know." He nibbled the tendon between her neck and shoulder and she buried her face in his shoulder.

Stroking her neck with both thumbs, easing her face away, he rained kisses on her forehead and eyes.

"I'm in my first trimester, Seth," she breathed.

"I can be gentle." His hard cock strained against her soft bottom and the desire to force his way in now was strong. But delay, and its exquisite torture, would have its own rewards.

"That's not what I mean. My skin is funny when I'm pregnant. Weirdly sensitive."

His hand crept under her shirt and up her side, skimming the swell of her breast. "Your skin feels wonderful." At the alarm on her face, he added, "We'll take it slow. Promise."

"I don't know how I'll react when you leave later."

His hand stopped moving. "I'm leaving no matter what we do. But if you think you're safer emotionally if we don't make love, I'll cope. And keep coming back." He eased his grip on her and prepared himself for her withdrawal. Instead, she burrowed into him and he closed his eyes as his arms came around her again.

"I don't feel great," she warned, though relieved laughter was now in her voice. He planted soft kisses on her head. Perhaps she feared he would take her too fast and hard. "My nausea isn't quite so bad now that I know you're okay."

He smiled against her ear, a low chuckle escaping. "I hadn't thought an admission of decreased nausea could be a turn-on, but it works."

"Does this work better?" Her fingers came around his painfully hard erection.

He moved to claim that hand. "Don't do that."

She looked up, surprised.

"I'm, uh, kind of primed after being wolf." He waited for some hint of revulsion to show and be quickly extinguished by Jamie's goodwill.

Instead, she looked curious. "What do you mean?"

He could feel his face heat up and to distract her, his hand covered her soft, heavy, beautiful breast and she gasped. He palmed the nipple lightly. "I'm always aroused the morning after I'm wolf."

She tilted her head, as if studying an interesting idea. "Huh."

"It's not that I can't hold on, but I'll need some cooperation."

"Every morning after?" she asked impishly.

He had to smile, though the smile faded as he gazed at her, trying to remember everything about her, so he could take the memory out and let it comfort him when they were apart. "I've never met someone the morning after. It's always been during my off-wolf time. I needed the distance."

"You're trying to make me feel special."

"You are special, there's no trying to it."

"You mean you've given up on keeping your distance from me?"

And this, Seth realized, was what Jamie needed. Some assurance she was important. Which was funny given she was all-important. He captured her face, soft cheeks against his hard-used palms, and he watched her breath speed up simply at his touch. "I love you, Jamie."

Her eyes widened but before she could come up with what she deemed an appropriate response, he laved her lips with his tongue. She opened for him.

She could hardly think, what with the soft stroke of his hands as he undressed her, and his mouth claiming hers. Seth might not have done long-term relationships, but he sure knew how to kiss, playing with her lips, then her tongue, coaxing her to join him. Which she did, settling into his embrace, relaxing at his touch, instead of preparing herself for it.

As if he knew how easily she could be jolted out of their lovemaking.

His hand traveled south, exploring her bellybutton and her stretch marks. She couldn't help but stiffen.

He pulled back. "What's wrong?" Gently, he palmed her thatch of hair.

"Nothing's wrong."

"You tensed up."

She didn't want to make any reference to Derek, but Seth could read her body. "During my last pregnancy, sex wasn't always successful."

"Can I ask why?"

"It's me. I'm very sensitive—"

"In a good way."

Soft laughter bubbled up her chest. "That's because you make me feel good."

"Yeah, it's all me."

His skillful fingers brushed lower still, barely touching her cleft. Her chest tightened in anticipation.

He laid her out on the bed. "Lie back and relax."

She pushed up on her elbows. "I want to be involved here, too, Seth."

"Oh, you are."

She should explain she wouldn't come now, that she was too dry in early pregnancy, but he distracted her by lowering his mouth to her breast. At first, his mouth was so light he breathed on her nipple but gradually his hold intensified as her chest rose and fell.

His fingers entered her and it didn't hurt. She gave way to the sensation of liquid pulls deep in her belly and let him work his magic. Time passed. At some point this soft, gentle, careful approach was no longer enough, despite that she had feared anything else till now.

"Seth," she demanded.

He grunted, his mouth busy.

Her hand reached between his legs and found his hard cock, its head slick. She ran her hand up and down his length once and he pulled away.

"Jamie," he warned.

"*Now.*"

As he opened his mouth to question her wisdom, she rose up and kissed him, winding fingers through his beautiful hair. He groaned as she straddled him.

He broke the kiss. "Jamie?"

"Let's talk afterwards." But as she went to kiss him, he held her away.

"This won't hurt the baby, right?" His voice was troubled and labored.

She laughed, shaking her head. "It's a little late to ask now."

She lowered herself, tight but damp, stretching to accommodate him, never relenting in her kisses, because she loved his tongue dancing with hers. The last time they'd made love, the focus had been on intercourse. She wanted, right now, to be connected to him everywhere.

His arms came around her and he thrust, once, twice, a third time and, banked with pleasure, she came. Through the haze she heard him voice his release, a noise deep and satisfying.

She sagged against him and his hand came up to hold her jaw in place as he tamped down their kiss before their mouths parted. Nestled against his chest, his chin over her head, she felt the last of him pulse into her.

"I haven't made love to a pregnant woman before."

"So many firsts," she murmured against his skin.

"I didn't hurt you? I haven't made love without a condom before so I kind of lost it once I was inside of you. You're so amazing."

She felt like her smile would crack her face open, she was so blindingly happy. "You sure know how to say the right things, Seth. But I got carried away, too. Maybe it was a mutual thing. You know, we were both involved."

"Cute." His hand grasped the left side of her butt and squeezed. "You were great. I'm sorry you were worried at the beginning."

"I just..." She glanced back as his hand slid down her butt cheek to her soft inner thigh.

He turned her chin towards him and kissed her. "Never mind that. You just what?"

She tried to focus on what she wanted to say and not Seth's deft fingers. "I worried our lovemaking wouldn't be what you expected, given I'm pregnant." The hand edged inwards, stroking the fold between her thigh and her sex. "What are you doing?"

"Talking to you." He stirred beneath her, hardening against her stomach.

"You have a funny way of talking, Mr. Kolski," and she moaned when his fingers entered her.

He eased her upwards and, with his tongue and lips, he explored her throat. A throat that vibrated with pleasure as his fingers stroked her sex.

"There are so many ways of talking. I like what you're saying now."

She made another inarticulate noise. He flipped her on her back and gazed at her as if awestruck.

"What?" she asked.

"I'm so lucky." His fingertips skimmed the silver stretch marks that scarred her proudly.

"There will be more of those."

His gaze darkened.

"We're going to figure out a way for you to see each and every stretch mark this baby makes, Seth." Like hell anyone was going to keep away her lover, and the father of her child.

He didn't argue. Wordlessly, he placed hands on each side of her face and studied her as if she were the most important thing in the world. She lifted her pelvis and he entered her. Still staring, he moved silently until she cried out, "Kiss me," and he did.

03

He woke to find Jamie burrowed against his side, as if she thought he might sneak out while she slept. Her bare shoulder was cold and he reached across to pull the duvet over her. Her eyes opened.

"You better not be going anywhere, Seth."

"Not yet." They had a couple of hours left. "But I don't want Andreas to know I'm here. It's not fair to confuse him with my presence here and absence at school. Frankly, it's better if no one knows about me."

She regarded him steadily. "It's too late for that."

Peace deserted him in an instant. That old, constant companion, wariness, returned. "What do you mean?"

She kissed him. "It's okay. But I'm afraid I told Cynthia about this pregnancy and your role in it well before I told you."

Cynthia. Jamie's sister-in-law who eyed him with suspicion. Crap. The baby might be a carrier. He hadn't wanted anyone to tie him to his child.

Jamie wrapped her body around him, clinging, and some of his distrust abated.

He could think this through. "Can you tell Cynthia you were mistaken? You thought I was the father, but it was that other guy." He braced himself for her reaction.

Jamie's face showed no anger. "Cynthia thinks her father is a werewolf."

Seth half-rose. "What?"

"That's why she won't have children. That's how she and Tom met."

"Tom believes Cynthia's father is a werewolf?"

"He saw Veronica change, Seth."

He turned away, trying to take it in. "Tom and Cynthia came to my home knowing I was a werewolf?"

"Knowing Veronica was a werewolf," Jamie corrected him. She slid her hand down the length of his spine and up his side to his scarred shoulder. Her finger traced the web of scars. He wished she'd ignore them.

"Who did this to you?" Her voice was hard.

He didn't want to talk about it. He never did, but after lovemaking, the topic was a downer. Besides, he loathed pity. He eyed the clock. "I had better go."

"You had better eat." But her hand and her focus didn't leave his shoulder. Her feather-light brushes, an acknowledgment of the pain, soothed him. "I never wanted to kill anyone before," she said in a faraway voice.

Seth shifted his gaze back at her and saw fury, not pity, on her face.

"This happened in the cage, right?"

His breath shuddered out. "You can cage a werewolf, Jamie, but they go crazy."

Chapter Ten

"Cage?" Jamie prompted, nuzzling his shoulder, wanting to ask more, but wanting to ask it right.

He lay down on his stomach, profile tilted away from her, silent. She pressed the length of her body against his side, and his arm came out and encircled her waist. He turned.

"How'd Brian get you in the cage?"

"He drugged me. Or, one of his women drugged me."

She played with his hair, softly brushing his ear.

"She picked me up at a bar," he explained.

Jamie burrowed deeper. "Was this woman your lover, too?"

"No."

A breath she didn't realize she was holding bailed out. "I'm glad you weren't betrayed by a lover."

His smile, though, was thin. A shoulder lifted and fell. "I might have been. I went home with her for that purpose. To fuck. It had been a while and she was colder than I liked, although cold usually made parting easy, despite less satisfactory sex."

Her fingers danced over his face and he kissed her palm.

"She gave me a drink. I passed out. Woke up naked in a cage. That was fun. More fun was turning wolf in front of Brian.

The woman was gone by then so I suppose I can be grateful that she didn't see me shift. Small mercies and all that."

His gaze had been diffuse, not quite on her. Then he focused on her face. "Shapeshifting is a private moment. We don't like others to see."

"You can't control it?"

"Normally, I can. But not when I'm drugged, not when the light of the full moon is shining down upon me. I'm not going to shift on you here, if that's what you're worried about."

"I am worried about many things, Seth, but not your shifting."

"You wouldn't want to see me change."

"Not if you don't want me to." She ran a hand over the rough skin of his scar again, then sat up to examine it.

"Razor wire," he said. "Brian put it around the door of the cage—it was quite a big cage, he wasn't totally without thought for my comfort—and, as drugged wolf, I rammed against it a few times, tearing up my shoulder."

"That's terrible." Her words felt inadequate.

"It wasn't the worst thing about it, Jamie. Brian kept telling me he was going to hurt Veronica." Seth looked away. "I couldn't let him do that."

"How did you get out?"

"I faked unconsciousness. It wasn't difficult given my exhaustion—I'd been crazy for hours in that small space. And Brian's judgment was impaired by whatever drug he'd taken himself. He felt all-powerful. Wanted to touch a werewolf. He got contact, all right." He snorted. "Good thing he was stupid or I'd be dead or worse."

Jamie's throat was constricted but she forced herself to ask more. "Was this before or after I saw you at Gordon's?"

"Before. I was a bit of a mess afterwards." He looked slightly embarrassed. "I wondered what you made of all my trembling."

"I thought you were shy."

He smiled at that. "Despite all that was going on, I was happy to see you. It had been years." He kissed her forehead. "I came to Gordon's after I killed Brian, hoping to find Veronica, but I didn't smell her. She sometimes slept with Gordon, you see."

Jamie winced.

"Yeah." Seth let out a long, painful breath. "She always said she used guys but I think she ended up being used. That's why I bought a house for us. I thought if I could drag her away from Atlanta and help her set up a new life in Ohio, she might stop all the self-destructive sex." He rubbed his face hard. "People deal with loneliness in different ways, but still."

Seth sat up. "I don't want to talk about this any more. Maybe it's good you know, maybe we can talk later, but I have to deal with now."

"Okay." She climbed into his lap, grateful that this confidence did not make him push her away. Instead, he welcomed each and every touch and caress.

"Does your shoulder hurt?" she asked.

"It aches sometimes but we werewolves heal well." He grabbed her shoulders. "Now you understand it's dangerous for others to know about werewolves. I wish you hadn't told Cynthia. I assume Tom knows, too."

"They're safe, Seth."

"They can't tell anyone."

"No." She cradled his balls in her palm.

His hand fastened on her arm. "You're trying to distract me."

"They won't tell, Seth. Remember my mother complaining that Cynthia is too secretive? And Tom didn't tell me about Veronica turning wolf till last week. They don't reveal secrets."

His expression relaxed. She reached up and locked lips with him, before trailing kisses down his chest, his stomach and to his cock, which she took in her mouth.

He lifted her head up.

"Why are you doing that?"

"I like to," she answered seriously. She knelt, circling the head of his cock with her tongue, tasting his salty come.

"Jamie!"

She managed an inarticulate, questioning noise.

"You don't have to prove something to me."

She took a short break. "Like what?"

"You don't have to prove I don't disgust you, say."

Again she lifted her head. "I want to remember everything about you until I see you next. Now shut up for a few minutes. Or talk, but let me do what I want."

He rested his hands on her back. "I'm not used to this."

After a certain interlude, she disengaged long enough to ask, "Used to what?"

"This."

She had to laugh because he wouldn't name it. Then she kissed him deeply. "I would imagine you're not used to me going down on you, because I haven't before now."

She went back to work and fun, enjoying the length of him, his thickness, his smooth head.

"I, uh, I used to concentrate on the woman having fun. Made me feel like less of a louse, you know." He groaned and a moment later she was flat on her back.

"Hey, I wasn't done."

"Yeah, you were." He nudged her legs apart, thumb on her clit, while the head of his shaft worked her open. "You're good at that."

"I know," she said smugly. It had felt wonderful to decide to take him in her mouth on her own, without being urged. Seth's surprise had delighted her.

He filled her to the hilt and she cried out. He stopped and she assured him, "You didn't hurt me."

"You sure?"

"*Yes.*"

He hesitated.

"Seth. Do. Not. Stop."

He moved, long, hard, strokes that did not stop, even when she came. Time was suspended until, as another wave approached, he demanded, "Jamie, look at me."

She kept her eyes wide open, watching his face, intense, concentrated fully on her. Everything began and ended with him, between them time stayed still.

Then he stiffened, right before shuddering in her arms as he pumped into her. She clung, unwilling to let go of this moment, she didn't want him to withdraw. Time, if life were at all fair, would stop again and she could catch up on her emotions and the events surrounding them.

"Seth," she said, temporarily exhausted, as they lay tangled together, catching their breaths. "We have got to think up a better game plan than spending the afternoon in bed."

"Yeah."

She wondered if they'd sleep again, but just when she felt she might drop off, he rose and pulled on his pants. Reality asserted itself. Their time together was ending. She pushed herself off the bed. "You need to eat before you go."

He was all muscle and no fat. She didn't want him to lose strength. His frame could too easily become gaunt. "We have an hour before Andreas is due back."

"Okay."

She wrapped a robe around herself. The thought of Andreas filled her with warmth while the thought of losing Seth horrified her. She wanted them both together, now.

He munched on an apple while she dragged stuff out of the fridge. "From now on, I'm going to be better prepared to feed you. Leftover pizza?"

"That's great."

"It's not great, Seth. Nothing is great." Her euphoria over the strength of their feelings for one another was overwhelmed by sadness. He had to leave. He would not stay for fear the police would come for him. Cages of any sort were impossible.

"You are great. We're great. I'll come back. But I want an all-clear sign."

Her heart sank.

"Jamie, we can't ignore what is going on."

"I know."

"If you take in the two deck chairs, if the deck is empty, I'll know to be careful. Okay?"

She slammed the microwave door shut.

"Don't be miserable, Jamie. This is more than I deserve."

"Bull. You deserve a family. You deserve me."

"This is more than I've ever had." His voice was soft. "Don't ruin it right now. Let's part with some hope, some joy."

She walked into his arms. "Come back tomorrow?" she asked.

"If I can."

She had to make do with that.

ೞ

Andreas ran into the house and launched himself into Jamie's arms. "Mom! Are you better now?" he asked, as if she'd been in mortal danger.

"I'm fine, honey." Above Andreas's head, she frowned at her father who shrugged. She hoped her mother hadn't scared Andreas with an ominous description of Jamie's health.

He wrapped pudgy arms around her neck. "I don't like you sick."

"I'm not sick. I was resting." She held him tight. "Did you have fun at Oma and Opa's?"

"Yes." He pulled back, his face brightening. "Oma's learning Pokemon now."

Jamie laughed. "Well, what do you know." She stood, keeping a hand on Andreas's shoulder.

"Do you want something to drink, Dad?"

"No, no. I'd better be going." Worn out by his full day of childcare, her father still smiled indulgently as Andreas rushed back to hug one of his long legs.

"Bye, Opa. Thanks for the ice cream."

Her father patted Andreas on the head.

"Ice cream?" asked Jamie.

"Opa took me to Dairy Queen."

"Nice, though I would have thought it too cold for ice cream."

"No!" exclaimed Andreas. "It's never too cold."

Her father shook his finger at Andreas. "You have to eat your supper, remember? And be good to your mother."

"Okay," said Andreas automatically.

"Thanks, Dad." Jamie kissed him goodbye.

After her father shut the door, Andreas asked, "Mom, I'm always good to you, so why does Opa keep telling me that?"

"Well, you know, Opa is *my* father and fathers worry about their children, even when they're adults."

"Like Dad worries about me?"

"Yeah," said Jamie with less enthusiasm and truth than she liked.

"Dad didn't forget me today, Mom." As if Andreas knew how low her opinion of Derek was. It made her heart clench to see her boy rise to defend his father. "He called me at Oma and Opa's."

She kept her voice light and even. "Yes, honey, I know. Because he phoned here first, wanting to talk to you." While Seth had lain sleeping in her bed, she'd redirected Derek to her parents' house. Though she'd wanted to accuse him of working for slime like Gordon who slept with his son's girlfriends. "Did you have a nice chat?"

"Uh-huh. He's sad about missing my soccer games."

Jamie nodded attentively. "I guess he would be. I know he was anxious to get off the phone with me and talk to you." Derek hadn't wanted to chat, which was out of character, especially these last few weeks when he'd been obsessed with Seth. Jamie had expected Derek to tell her, again, to avoid her werewolf. Well, not in those words. Derek would probably say, *Stay away from Seth Kolski.* Jamie smiled, thinking how ridiculous that notion was. Yet nothing about the situation was funny. It was as serious as a heart attack and she was tempted to giggle. Bad sign.

"Mom?" Andreas tugged on her hand.

Lordy, she had to be careful not to let all her worries completely distract her. She smiled down at Andreas's sunny face. It was lit up with news, she realized. He had more to tell her. She knelt down so they were face-to-face and looked directly at Andreas.

"Yes, honey?"

"Daddy is so sad about missing the games that he's coming here tomorrow." His brow furrowed. "But my game isn't until next Saturday."

She blinked. "What do you mean?"

"Daddy is coming here," Andreas repeated. "Tomorrow. Though my game isn't until Saturday. Right?"

"Right," Jamie echoed. "But, sweetie, your father lives in Atlanta." *And he better stay there.* This week, life was too complicated for visits. "He can't pop over for an evening."

"Well, he can take the plane, Mom," said Andreas, as if she were slow.

"Are you sure you understood what he was saying? I think he *wants* to be at the game but can't make it. Your father said nothing to me about a visit."

Andreas's lower lip stuck out, face defiant. "Don't you want him to come and see me?" he asked, suspicion plain on his face.

No.

"He should consult me first, Andreas."

"He wants to see me." Andreas jabbed a thumb at his chest and glared, daring her to refute his statement. Which she never would.

"I know, Andreas. And I'm always glad when you spend time with your father. Okay?"

Andreas looked guardedly mollified.

"Let me call your father so I can know his plans, okay?"

Andreas ran around her and picked the phone off its cradle. "Here." He handed it to her and she tried not to be irritated as her son watched her with great anticipation. Why was absentee dad now a celebrity? Okay, the answer to that was obvious.

Derek's machine picked up after two rings. "Not home," she told her son and proceeded to dial Derek's cell. She got a message there, too, but this time left instructions to phone her immediately.

"He's coming, Mom."

Surely not. "When did he say he might fly here?"

"Tonight?" Andreas said hopefully.

With a heavy heart Jamie ushered her son through his supper and evening routine. Between clearing the dishes and making sure Andreas brushed his teeth, she reluctantly pulled in the lawn chairs from the deck. She'd been counting on seeing Seth tonight.

No matter how small the chance Derek would come by, she couldn't risk her ex-husband catching sight of Seth. And so Seth was warned.

CS

Despite that Sanjay was a pup at this moment, not a child, he reminded Seth of Andreas. Both boys clung to him when he was around. Both boys missed having a father in their life.

Seth didn't want to bring another boy—or girl—into a fatherless world. One who would latch onto men because he couldn't be there for them. He wanted to be a father, not lurk in the forest making the occasional stealth visit. The joy Jamie had brought him earlier today was dissipating in the face of reality. What would she make of him now? He was wolf.

Sanjay rolled on the ground, tummy exposed, as if the act of submission would make up for the fact he wasn't returning home as Seth had demanded. It was late, Sanjay was exhausted. Sanjay's days at school had taken a lot out of him. No wonder werewolves, especially children, were so thin. They led double lives. The shifting and running drained them, sometimes dangerously so.

Sanjay whined, *I'll miss you.*

The boy wanted Seth to visit during the off-wolf times. At least once a month, Sanjay begged for more of Seth and it broke Seth's heart that he couldn't give it.

Especially when Seth feared he might have to stay wolf in order to hide. He could shift at any time of the lunar month and at any time of day. But it was harder to force when the moon waned. Besides, when his kind stayed wolf too long, they went feral.

As his parents had. Abandoning Veronica and him in their late teens, sick of the human world as, his father assured them, they would become. Though Seth had always sworn to cope with more skill than they had.

Now look at him. He nudged Sanjay to his tired feet, using affection and size to lead the pup home. Rani would be waiting for him, worried. Seth promised to return again tomorrow and Sanjay dragged himself home to his mother.

Seth was too lonely to go feral. Though the physical life of a wolf held its own appeal, losing his mind did not. One didn't think the same way as a wolf and, over time, it showed. He didn't want to show such deterioration to Jamie and lose her.

That Jamie had fed him, loved him and cried on him was all rather amazing. Seth couldn't stay away from her. He would visit tomorrow morning after Andreas had gone to school. But they had to do more than descend into their dream world of love and laughter and physical sensation. They had to plan a future, such as it was, that included Sanjay, Andreas and the baby.

He also had to discover who had set the detectives on him.

As he reached the clearing of Jamie's yard, Seth looked to the moon, tempted to throw back his head and howl to let Jamie know he was watching over her. Not that he'd allow her to see him like this. Now that she was aware of who her wolf was, Seth wanted to shift to human before their rendezvous. As far as he was concerned she was his mate—though she didn't know it yet. Nevertheless, his time as wolf could only belong to him.

Before he released his song of longing, he was arrested by what was missing on the deck. He moved closer. The deck had been cleared of chairs.

Staying within the shadows, Seth crept towards the voices.

C

Jamie stood in her doorway, leaning on the doorknob under the yellow light of her porch, and stared at her ex-husband. Derek thought she should invite him in at two in the morning simply because he was weary and disheveled.

"No," she repeated, refusing him entry, and to her chagrin he looked hurt. "I was on the phone with you this morning."

"Yes," he said, sullen, unsure how to decipher her statement.

"Why didn't you tell me an unprecedented event was imminent? That you planned to see your son?"

He shook his head in disapproval which, even now, made her see red. Her ex should have less hold on her after two years apart.

"You use such big words when you're upset, Jamie. It doesn't actually make you clever, you know."

She breathed in hard, held that air in her lungs, and counted. Shouting was not an option. Andreas was asleep.

It didn't help that Derek was right. She sounded stupid, talking in that forced, artificial way. But she wanted Derek away from her and her house. Away from Seth who might come here.

Something of what she was going through might have shown on her face, because Derek looked ashamed. He slid a hand over his head. "I'm sorry, Jamie, that was uncalled for."

"Apology accepted." *Please leave.*

"I thought you might be more welcoming. It is the middle of the night."

"Exactly."

He stepped forward, as if the distance between them could be breached, but stopped when Jamie moved to shut the door on him. The one thing that prevented her from making such a move was the fact he was Andreas's father.

"Dammit, Jamie."

"Keep your voice down."

"I'm concerned," he hissed.

"If you're that concerned, you should choose a better time to arrive on my doorstep. Let's take a rain check on this, okay?"

"I didn't want to get into it on the phone." The weariness crept back into his voice and she didn't think it was to manipulate her. Derek had been many things, but not manipulative. He preferred to give orders.

He looked tired and under other circumstances she might have invited him in to sit down and have a hot drink. But she'd been sleeping and he had no right to invade her house, no matter that he was the father of her child.

Father of her child. Where was Seth?

She dragged her mind back to her more immediate problem—getting rid of Derek. "I'm tired. Go to a hotel and we'll talk in the morning."

"I'm sorry my plane was delayed," Derek said stiffly. He cleared his throat and with some dismay Jamie realized she was going to hear a confession. "I quit my job, Jamie. I'm moving back to Cedartown."

She stared, unsure what he wanted of her. She should be happy for Andreas but today was really crappy timing.

"I thought you'd be glad to hear I'd quit my job," he added.

"Derek, I wanted you to quit when you were my husband. It is no longer my concern."

"Not even if I make it a point to become more involved in Andreas's life?"

"Why?"

"Well, you've always hated my work and my boss."

"I mean, why quit your job?"

Derek's laughter was embarrassed. "Gordon was going to fire me."

"Ah. Okay, well something else to chat about tomorrow." She moved to shut the door.

"If only you'd never mentioned Seth Kolski to me."

"I didn't. Andreas did." She did not want Derek to know Seth was important to her.

"Yeah, well, apparently I've been remiss these past two years. I never told Gordon that Veronica Kolski had a brother."

That stopped Jamie. "Huh?"

"My reaction exactly." Derek looked baffled. "It didn't occur to me it was important. I keep Gordon's accounts, Jamie. I don't dig into his personal life. I certainly don't keep track of his son's girlfriend's families."

"But that's what Gordon liked about you. You'd do *anything* to further yourself in his company."

Derek shook his head. "Not anything, Jamie."

"No," she agreed to avert an old argument. Jamie hadn't meant to bring back the accusation that Derek had wanted her to sleep with Gordon. She'd never quite believed Derek had formulated the idea so bluntly in his mind and it was old territory they could get lost in for hours of ugly fighting.

"Did Gordon think you were hiding information from him? You wouldn't do that."

Derek looked at his feet. "I'm at a complete loss. All I can think is Brian's weird death unhinged Gordon. He hasn't been the same since."

"Derek, it's time for you to leave."

"I'm sorry, Jamie." He raised his gaze to meet hers. "About Gordon. He was more of an asshole than I realized."

Jamie shrugged off the apology. That Derek had to lose his job to admit Gordon's attention had been more than innocent flirtation, did not make her grateful. But this was as close as she would get to an apology.

"Jamie, I've come back to you," he added in a rush.

"What?" she said with little grace. "You don't think I'd take you back now, do you?"

He straightened, voice and face solemn. "I'm ready to turn over a new leaf, Jamie. I'll prioritize family and I'll be faithful." He smiled, painfully. "No more workaholic. Counseling if you still want it."

"Derek, I wanted counseling three years ago!"

"I'm going to find another job and balance my time," he soldiered on, as if he'd rehearsed this speech any number of times. She didn't know if that made her feel worse or better about his clumsy attempt at rapprochement. She tried to speak again and he overrode her.

"I know I don't always have a good sense of when to stop working. It's like work sucks me in. And I've denied it's a problem for years. But that's going to change."

Yeah, since you've lost your job. He looked at her with hope and she felt appalled.

"Derek. It's too late for us. Years too late." Two years ago, she would have tried again, despite the infidelity. Not now. "I can't go backwards."

"Think about it," he urged her. "I've sprung this on you."

"No, Derek. Absolutely not. I want to be as clear as possible here. We will *never* get back together. What we had died." She wanted to kill whatever hope he entertained. She had too many other concerns and worries to think about this.

As what she said sank in, he turned away and she steered the conversation towards the one person who did need Derek. "Andreas would benefit from your time and attention. He's desperate for a father. For you. Make him part of the new balance."

To her irritation, Derek looked lost. "I'm a better father when you're around."

"That's not true." She slumped against the doorframe. "I'm exhausted. Go to a hotel. Come back tomorrow, though call me first. I don't want you dropping in."

He didn't move.

"I'm not comfortable with you staying here, Derek. I'm sorry. Why don't you pick up Andreas from school tomorrow and spend time with him? He'll be ecstatic. It will be a new beginning for you both."

Derek lifted his suitcase as if it were the heaviest thing in the world, and Jamie felt a stab of annoyance that he wasn't more excited to see his son. Nevertheless, she would be as supportive as possible.

"You can get a new job, Derek." She knew his sense of self-worth was tightly linked to his job.

He nodded, obviously not convinced. "I'll be at the Holiday Inn."

"Good. Take Andreas to the pool there tomorrow. He loves to swim but you have to watch him all the time because he's more enthusiastic than proficient." Andreas was an excellent swimmer for his age, but Jamie wanted Derek to keep a close eye on him.

Slight panic played on Derek's face. "I don't have a bathing suit."

She waved him towards his car. "Buy one. You know where the Wal-Mart is. And phone me in the morning."

Shoulders bowed, he walked down the drive to his rental car. With relief she watched him throw his suitcase in the trunk and slip into the driver's seat. *Go, go.*

Letting the front door close, she waited until the crunch of tire against gravel convinced her Derek had driven away. She pressed a hand against her forehead. Everything was happening at once. Seth's entry into their lives had unleashed a series of events that involved not just the investigation of Brian's death, but the return of Derek. She hoped the latter was a good thing.

She pulled on her jacket and went out the back to sit on the deck. Where Seth had reappeared yesterday morning.

Huddling against the cool autumn night, she stared at the full moon that had such a hold on her lover. "Seth?" she whispered. Though he was likely far away.

He walked around the corner of the house and she jumped, letting out a bleat.

"Shhh. I was trying not to startle you." His long loose limbs moved gracefully towards her and thought left her. The only thing she felt was blessed that she knew him as she did.

She placed a hand on her heart and waited a beat, till she could talk without her voice trembling with cold and emotion. One breath. Another.

"I didn't know you were here," she managed.

His face was severe, distant, making her uncertain. She sat again, so she could gather herself in a ball for warmth. He settled beside her, not quite touching. "I saw Derek. I eavesdropped, I'm afraid."

"That's okay." She sounded inane and shut her eyes.

"Jamie, can you ask Derek more about Gordon and what he might be up to? Ask him about Brian's death, if possible. But don't let him know about us, okay?"

"Okay."

He rose before she had the courage to reach for him.

"Stay," she asked.

His smile twisted as he looked moonward. "I'm not comfortable in this skin right now. It's my time to be wolf," he said, almost sadly, and she wished she could go with him.

"Come visit me as a wolf." She already missed him.

He shook his head and she couldn't read his face as he retreated into shadow.

"Why not?"

"That was before you knew who I was."

"Even more reason—"

"No, less," he declared. "There are some things we can't share."

"Well I realize I can't run with you," she snapped, suddenly angry. "I was suggesting a visit, but never mind."

"You have to deal with Derek tomorrow," he said, a hint of apology in his voice. "And you should sleep."

It was true. She rose. "You can rest here tomorrow during the day. I'll leave the back door unlocked, okay?" She tried to keep the pleading note out of her voice, though this wasn't all just for her own reassurance. She worried about him wearing himself out.

"I can stay wolf."

"How long can you stay wolf?" He'd fled his house a week ago.

"Forever," he said tonelessly. He didn't want this discussion now. He was restless, impatient, anxious to leave. She found she was hugging herself, wondering how she had again chosen someone who was wrapped up in an enterprise greater than her love. Derek's work. Seth's wolf nature.

He strode towards her and gathered her in his arms, solid, firm, and for the moment, unyielding. Then he let her go.

It was funny. Seth was naked and she felt the more vulnerable.

"You are so important to me, Jamie," he said, even as he retreated.

She stopped herself from reaching out for him. "I'll hold onto that."

"Good."

She wondered if he would change in front of her, but he walked into shadow.

ↄ₰

The following morning, Jamie met up with Derek at the Holiday Inn restaurant. His demeanor was stiff, as if he'd embarrassed himself the night before with talk of reconciliation. She supposed he had, but she—and Derek—had more important things to consider.

Like their son.

"I'm glad Andreas is enjoying kindergarten," said Derek, after Jamie had described Mrs. Sanders in great detail.

She wished Derek was keen to meet Andreas at noon. Andreas had asked about his father in the morning before the school bus came and Jamie's reply had been vague, for fear

Derek would bail, leaving his son devastated at a no-show. She'd made noises about Derek's fatigue and late plane.

Thankfully, Derek was with her, and they were about to head over to the school. He lacked enthusiasm, but his grim determination, bolstered by three coffees, meant he would spend the afternoon with Andreas.

They drove separately to the school.

"What will I do with him?" he burst out when they exited their respective cars in the parking lot. He ran a hand over his balding pate.

No recriminations. "Eat." That coaxed a smile out of him. "Swim. Eat. Play Pokemon."

Derek looked alarmed again.

"Andreas will teach you the rules and have a grand time doing so." She shrugged. "Then it will be time to return Andreas to me." *Where he belongs.*

She didn't quite approve of her attitude towards Derek, especially with him gamely walking to the school. A part of her didn't want Derek back in her life, wanted to keep Andreas to herself.

But it was important to foster this relationship as much as possible. Derek's presence was better than his absence even if she feared he would treat Andreas with indifference. Because, too often, Andreas had asked, *What's wrong with me, Mom?* Too often, Andreas had taken Derek's absence as complete rejection, especially those Saturdays when Derek hadn't showed for his weekly appointment.

"Don't disappear like you did in Atlanta, Derek," Jamie warned. "You must establish a regular, dependable presence in Andreas's life so he can count on you and trust you to be there for him."

"You were the one who moved away," said Derek in a low voice, but he didn't meet her eyes.

She gritted her teeth and didn't retort, though she wanted to lash out. "I know I moved away."

He stopped outside the school doors and waited for her to say more. She didn't.

He deflated without a sparring partner. "You're right. I can be a better father. I will be. I've had to get past my anger at you."

She sighed. "Now is not the time for this discussion, Derek. This is about Andreas."

"You left me and all I had was my job."

She counted to ten, then spoke quietly. "You slept with other women, Derek." His last woman hadn't liked him to have a son on the weekends. But the guilty look on Derek's face kept Jamie from voicing that fact. "Please, for Andreas's sake, let's try to have a working relationship."

He nodded curtly.

Besides, she had to bring the conversation back around to Gordon. "I'm glad Gordon is no longer your boss."

Derek's look of appreciation touched her. "We can both agree on that. The trouble is"—Derek pushed open the school's front door—"I've only worked for Gordon's company and now he won't give me a recommendation. After my 'betrayal'. I'm not sure how I'll find new work."

"You're good at what you do. That will count in the end."

"I hope so."

"It's odd for Gordon to become enraged by the existence of a brother of Veronica Kolski," she observed as casually as possible.

Derek shook his head in aggravation. "Apparently, years ago, she told Gordon her brother had died. God knows why, but Gordon sees this as some kind of plot I may be involved in. Not that I understand any of it."

"Huh." She hoped her "huh" sounded like an *isn't that interesting but that information doesn't affect me* "huh". Not a *this is critical to me* "huh". "The police would have known Seth Kolski was alive."

"Sure, but they didn't tell Gordon—more of this plot, you know—and he didn't know to ask. Because of me." Derek groaned. "Believe me, I've heard it all from Gordon these last two weeks."

"Well, police aren't going to bug Seth now," she said airily.

"Cedartown police will. Don't forget, Gordon comes from here and still has clout. He'll be able to get someone in the police department to ask around now that he knows Kolski is alive."

"Oh." Jamie's voice was small and Derek gave her a penetrating look.

"Why?" he asked.

"Andreas is quite attached to Mr. Kolski."

Derek waved that fact away. "Well, obsessing about Brian is now Gordon's main purpose in life. I mean, it's good to be concerned about family." Derek looked a little shamefaced. "But, you know, Brian is dead."

And Brian deserved to be dead. But Jamie just bit her lip. Before Derek could say more, kindergartners began to troop out of their classroom.

"Dad!" bellowed Andreas from down the hall. Breaking away from his class, he pelted towards them. Startled, Mrs. Sanders opened her mouth to reprimand him. Once she realized who Andreas ran towards, her frown transformed itself into a big smile.

With some apprehension, Jamie looked at Derek and was surprised and pleased to see him moved by Andreas's joy. As Derek lifted their son into his arms, his expression became fierce with love and his eyes shone with unshed tears.

Jamie didn't know what to make of this unsteady love, real as it might be at the moment. She hoped it would translate into a stable presence in Andreas's life. It was the right thing to hope for. Maybe, without the overwhelming enchantment of his job, Derek could pay proper attention to Andreas.

Your son is giving you a second chance. Don't you dare let him down.

Chapter Eleven

The drive home from Andreas's school was short. It passed in a blur as she drove over the small hills that wound down to her street. Like the hills, Jamie's barely coherent thoughts rose and fell, alternating between Andreas and Seth, unable to settle on either. She needed to go sit in her living room and *think*.

Andreas was with his father and she wasn't entirely comfortable with the renewal of that bond. Her feelings about Seth's situation were more straightforward. She was frantic.

She shouldn't think about Seth while driving, so she moved back to Derek and the loss of his job. Job loss wasn't the greatest of motivators when it came to making time for your son but she wouldn't undermine Derek's attempt to connect with Andreas. She prayed his interest in playing dad would last. Fatherhood was not something to be donned and doffed, depending on the job market. Her heart feared for Andreas's vulnerability.

Seth was vulnerable, too. Her hands turned white, gripping the steering wheel too tightly. She loathed the Carvers, both father and son.

Wait, wait, she told herself. She wanted to get home before she whipped herself into a frenzy of anxiety.

It was only after she pulled into her driveway that she saw two strange cars parked next to her house. She braked hard and gravel flew while she tried to gather her scattered thoughts.

She almost shifted into reverse and backed out. But it was too late. She'd been seen and heard by whoever was waiting for her. This was no time to suspiciously run away from her own house. Strange behavior would draw attention—the wrong kind of attention.

Cautious behavior was not so strange, though. She left her engine running and rolled down her window an inch to speak to the man in her driveway.

"Good day, ma'am." He was an older man, dressed in a not terribly elegant suit. Heavy, but not tall, he had swaggered as he walked towards her.

"What can I do for you?" she asked with as much self-possession as she could muster. Despite herself she darted a glance at the second car in her driveway. The occupant had not emerged. A Mercedes. Gordon liked that make of car and its presence frayed her nerves.

"I'm Detective Mackay." He flashed his identification. "I have a few questions for you, if you don't mind."

"Okay." She tried to sound puzzled. "Let me park my car." The detective stepped away, and she pushed down on the accelerator and edged towards the house.

Please, Seth, don't be here. Had he done as she suggested and come inside to rest? Stupid idea. But Seth was cautious and clever. *Focus on the man with questions.*

She got out of the car and tried to school her face to look mildly perplexed, rather than completely panicked, by the unexpected company of a detective.

His face seemed kind enough. She clung to that observation.

196

Before he could say anything, the door of the Mercedes swung open. Her heart sank as Gordon unfolded from the driver's seat. In an expensive suit. While he hadn't changed much in two years, her reaction to him had. Her distaste had grown into revulsion.

At her obvious flinch, Mackay frowned.

"What questions do you have for me?" Dammit, her voice quavered. She should have stayed silent. Though she'd never been convinced silence meant strength. But, oh, she wanted to be strong. Strong for Seth, strong for the baby.

And yet, the quaver might not be a bad thing because Mackay's face softened at her distress. He cleared his throat. "I want to ask you about a missing person, Seth Kolski."

Her first impulse was to acknowledge Seth, claim his importance to her, her love for him. Let Detective Mackay understand she had a deep stake in Seth's well-being.

She could do nothing of the sort.

"Andreas's gym teacher?"

"That's right." Mackay nodded.

"Oh, very smooth, Jamie." Gordon's smile was thin and ugly.

Mackay's gaze flicked between the two of them before settling on Gordon, darkening as he did so. Jamie hoped that Gordon still had the knack of overestimating his power over people.

"Mr. Carver, we agreed, before I took on this case, that I would ask the questions," said Mackay.

Hands raised, Gordon backed off theatrically. "Absolutely. That was a comment."

"And I will make the comments. Or you will leave." The detective's no-nonsense tone reassured Jamie. She took a deep breath and realized that all her emotional reaction was focused on Gordon. To manage Mackay, she needed to get rid of that man.

"Why is Mr. Carver here?" she asked.

The detective adopted a stoic expression, giving Jamie hope.

"I'd like Mr. Carver to leave my property," she continued. "I dislike the man. He used to get drunk and hit on me when I attended my now ex-husband's office parties." Jamie feared she would gag, the stress-induced nausea was so strong. Let the detective, whose eyes closed at her revelation, think it was fear of Gordon, not fear for Seth.

"That's ridiculous." Gordon's forced laughter grated. "A little flirting you've blown *completely* out of proportion."

Mackay looked at Gordon with barely concealed dislike. "I'll let you know how the case is progressing, Mr. Carver."

Gordon stiffened. "This investigation is about my son, Mackay."

"The investigation will be more effective if you leave now and we talk later."

The two men glowered at each other.

Gordon shrugged, as if his presence here mattered little to him. "The ladies know how to wrap you around their finger, I can see." Gordon's smug expression increased the flare of the detective's temper.

"Sir," said Mackay with little respect. "You can leave and let me do my job. Bags of money do not make you a detective."

"This has nothing to do with money and everything to do with justice." Gordon slid his gaze over to Jamie who ignored him.

"Of course." Mackay stepped between Jamie and Gordon, as if to protect her. The detective glanced at her with concern and she supposed her lightheadedness was showing. Stress and pregnancy weren't a good mix.

"I think I'm going to faint," she announced.

Alarm animated Mackay's face and he steadied Jamie by cupping her elbow. She was going to milk this encounter for everything it was worth. Fumbling for the key, she let herself and Mackay into the house while Gordon's car door slammed shut.

She allowed herself some relief once Gordon's motor started up.

"I'm sorry." She began to sniffle. It sure wasn't difficult. In fact, the idea she was putting on an act to fool Mackay didn't quite hold water as her next, truthful words came out. "I'm pregnant and I haven't felt well for the past month."

This admission of hers heightened the detective's coloring. He was embarrassed and he didn't want to be here. That was good, wasn't it? Because she wanted him to leave as soon as she'd convinced him she had no link whatsoever to Seth.

"Would you like something to drink?" she offered.

"No, no. That's not necessary."

"I'll get myself something."

"Of course."

She blew her nose a few times, poured herself juice and returned to Detective Mackay who remained standing.

"Please." She indicated a chair in the living room.

"Thank you." He sat and made a show of pulling out his notepad. As if this gave him authority. Well, perhaps it did. "I have a few questions for you. About Seth Kolski."

She frowned, as if puzzled. "Is he okay? Andreas gets very attached to his new teachers. Especially his gym teacher. He is such an active boy. Always on the move." She put on the brakes before her babbling ran away on her.

"We don't know where Seth Kolski is, so I can't tell you whether or not he's okay. He went missing the very day I arrived to question him."

She tried to look appropriately concerned.

"His phone records indicate you called his house repeatedly last Sunday, the day he disappeared." He smiled. "I was wondering if you could tell me what those phone calls were about."

She drank her juice, taking her time to come up with the right response.

"I'm sorry. I didn't know Andreas phoned Mr. Kolski so often. I thought I put a stop to it after I caught Andreas dialing. But I also napped that afternoon." She leaned forward to emphasize her next point. "You see, my son's father hasn't been around much this past year and Andreas latched onto Mr. Kolski. I think because he attended Andreas's soccer game a few weeks ago. Which was kind of him. He loves kids." *Don't gush.* She forced a smile back at Mackay though neither of them was happy. "Ever since, it's been Mr. Kolski this and Mr. Kolski that."

"Ah." Detective Mackay looked skeptical. "It wasn't you making the calls."

"No," she lied.

He scratched his jaw and watched her drink. No doubt he wondered what she was doing pregnant. Well, she wondered herself sometimes, but it was her business, not his. She badly wanted him to go away and feared the desire shone out her eyes, or something, because he frowned.

"I was led to believe that you might be, ah, involved, with Seth Kolski."

"Why?" Her surprise was real enough.

"Ah'm." The man's color was rising again. Good. Let him be uncomfortable. "Mr. Carver suggested it."

Damn Derek. She shook her head though she hated denying her relationship with Seth. "Why would Mr. Carver think that?"

Mackay spent an inordinate amount of time clearing his throat. When he spoke, his voice was clear, but wooden. "Mr. Carver didn't say."

Mackay didn't like Gordon. And he didn't like the case. Good.

"I'm pregnant, Detective Mackay, and I am not dating."

He stood then, obviously uncomfortable. "You haven't seen Seth Kolski since Sunday?"

"No. I drove Andreas to school on Monday and the principal told me that Mr. Kolski was sick. Perhaps you should talk to her."

He eyed her with more intelligence than she liked, but before she began to fidget, he snapped his notebook shut. "Thank you for your time, ma'am."

"Detective Mackay?"

"Yes?"

"I want Gordon Carver to stay away from me and my house. His presence unnerves me. I'm scared he'll think it's his right, because of this investigation, to question me."

"I'll take care of that, ma'am," drawled Mackay. That he disliked Gordon was great. That he didn't seem to believe what she'd told him, wasn't.

"Thank you, sir."

He nodded his goodbye and left.

She stood in the hallway looking at the front door, waiting to hear the crunch of tire against gravel that signaled the detective's departure. Then she waited some more, to be sure Mackay was gone.

The encounter with Gordon had been a shock. While Mackay had been affected by lies and womanly distress, she didn't think he'd bought her story.

At the sound of bare feet padding down the hall, she turned to see Seth moving with quiet grace. They stared, as if wary of each other. Things were changing and Jamie feared their bond would unravel.

She would not allow that to happen, even if Seth looked ready to bolt.

"You did a great job with the detective. You kept your cool." His praise wasn't warm but it was sincere. Jamie felt a smile play on her lips. Seth's admiration allowed her to relax a little.

"I cried," she said.

"An added touch. Your phone-call explanation was quick thinking."

"I hope he doesn't question Andreas." She didn't tell Seth she wasn't sure the detective believed her. Seth was tense enough.

"Right." His expression became wry. "I didn't know you phoned me on Sunday."

"What can I say, Seth? You're important to me. I was worried. I still am."

The stiffness in Seth's shoulders lessened.

"Seth, Mackay doesn't like Gordon. I think that's a good thing."

Seth dismissed the notion. "He's in Gordon's pocket, or his department is. He'll do Gordon's bidding."

"I hate it." She went to him and slid her arms under his shirt.

He held back for a moment, before gathering her to him, breathing in her hair. His mouth descended, caressing her eyes and cheeks before kissing her deeply.

I need you, she thought, relaxing into the embrace.

She was released. Set apart.

"I have to go." But he didn't move.

"No." She tried not to make the one word sound like a wail of despair.

"Jamie—"

"Stay for a while. I bought us some time." She wouldn't release his gaze, despite the distance he placed between them, despite the way his body seemed ready to spring.

"I'm not..." He looked at the ceiling, as if he could find what he wanted to say there. "I don't think it's a good time for us to make love."

"The doors are locked. We'll hear any car that comes down my gravel drive. They don't know you're here." She took his hand and dragged him to the bedroom.

She stripped and his pupils dilated, reflecting her need back at her.

"We're going to be together now, briefly, and later, all the time," she said.

"I'm feeling wild here, Jamie. I don't know if I can take it slow."

"I don't care. I want you." She wanted, most of all, to show she loved him, certain these body memories would help him while he roamed the forest alone at night. They kept her company.

He hesitated and then they were together, hands on each other, kissing with a desperation that scared Jamie, though she couldn't let him know. He should know she loved him and he had to come back to her. Despite his warning, he was careful at the moment of entry, eyes questioning.

"Yes." Her hands caressed his face. "Seth, I love you."

He answered with an overpowering kiss. Her mind emptied as he moved and touched her, inundating her senses with urgency. For the longest time she couldn't think, just feel, and the release from thought was a gift she didn't want to relinquish.

But she did, after they exhausted each other.

In the aftermath, they didn't speak right away, just touched. Jamie traced lazy circles on Seth's back until his breathing slowed and their skin cooled.

But reality could no longer be set aside. He tensed. She'd been waiting for that moment. It was his silent way of saying, *I have to go.* He pulled away.

"Cynthia might be able to help us." Her sister-in-law hadn't said anything new on the phone this morning, but Cynthia had been confident her father was going to save the day. Exactly how, Jamie didn't know.

Seth looked suspicious. "How?"

"Her father has connections. He might be able to shut down Mackay's investigation here in Cedartown." Jamie wanted to offer something more substantial, instead of this distillation of the vague noises Cynthia had made all week on the phone.

Seth was up and pacing, their lovemaking forgotten. "Sure, get him to do just that. That'd be a great help." He stopped and shook his head.

"What?"

"I'll believe when it happens. No one helps us, Jamie."

"That's your father talking. Besides, Cynthia's father is a werewolf."

"So she says."

"I can see you feel very trusting right now."

"What is there to trust?" he snapped. "Cynthia and Tom know what I am and I have to live with that."

"They want to help."

"There is nothing they can do or they would have done it, no? As far as I'm concerned they're a threat and I just hope you're right and they keep quiet."

Jamie didn't say more.

Seth stilled. "Don't worry about me. I'll take care of myself."

She frowned. "Do you have a plan?"

"Yes."

"Are you going to share it with me?"

"No. You wouldn't like it."

She felt cold at the brush-off. "Try me."

He stood now in the threshold of the bedroom door. "Making love is like a dream, Jamie. But it has to end. Every time."

She stared mutely, refusing to agree.

"Do me a favor," he said, his voice softening.

"Anything." He might need to push her away but she wouldn't do the same.

"If Sanjay Smith ever needs your help. Ever. You help him. Please."

"Sanjay." Jamie remembered the dark-eyed boy in Andreas's class and on his soccer team. "Yes." Seth trusted her with this information. It was a gift of sorts. "Of course I will."

"Thank you."

"Don't thank me for something I would do anyway. But I'm glad you asked."

He was restless, ready to run, she could see it in the tension of his body. "I'll come back when I can."

He slipped away. She was losing him, as if they'd already been as close as they could be, as if each day to come would increase the distance between them.

Wiping her face, she glared at her mirror, daring herself to give up. She wouldn't. She would fight. They would make it right, even if she couldn't see the way through now.

CB

Tom's kitchen looked as lost and disordered as Jamie felt. Fortunately for Tom's kitchen, Cynthia would return and set everything right.

The same could not be said about Jamie's life, though Cynthia was trying to work on that, too.

"When did you last see Seth?" Tom asked, expression grave. That her brother was unable to see any humor whatsoever in the situation, made Jamie feel worse. She hadn't thought the day would come when she wished her brother would not take her seriously. But today was that day.

"Monday."

"Did he say when he'd contact you again?"

She shook her head. "He said he'd come back when he could. I thought he meant a day or two, but it's Thursday now."

"Maybe the detective and Gordon's visit convinced Seth he should avoid your house. It's not safe there."

"He could phone."

"I don't know. Seth's not out of line in thinking that is dangerous, too. Everything can be traced."

"Where can he be safe? That's what I'd like to know. I want him in a safe place."

"My house might work. No one has thought to ask me questions about Seth. Tell him that if you can." He rose and pointed to the coffeepot, incapable of remembering she did not drink caffeine right now.

"No. Thank you." She sipped her milk and returned to the conversation. "Seth didn't like me telling you about him. He doesn't know he can trust you."

Tom absorbed this, taking no offense. "But he knows Cynthia's father is one of his kind. His name is Trey Walters, by the way."

As if a name could save Seth. "I doubt he'll believe her father is a werewolf until he sees him shapeshift. Speaking of which, why doesn't this Trey Walters get here?"

"He's coming."

"You said that last week."

Tom sighed. "I'm picking up Cynthia and her dad from the airport tonight, okay?"

"What's he done? Besides instruct Cynthia to tell me to keep Seth out of jail. Something I might have thought a good idea without Cynthia's help."

A bad joke would have suited Jamie better than the solicitude on her brother's face. "Cynthia's father is not forthcoming, but I believe he's working on the case."

"How?" she demanded.

"I don't know." At Jamie's frustration, he added, "We'll ask when he gets here."

"If he gets here," she muttered.

"Don't start talking like Seth. He, at least, has reason. You know you can trust me."

"Yes." Jamie did know. Right now, it was keeping her sane. "I hate doing nothing."

"Let Andreas keep you busy."

Her smile was weak but real. "Oh, I do. Poor Andreas. He's my anchor and he doesn't know it."

"I wouldn't say poor Andreas because he's your anchor. You're a great mother."

Jamie winced. If Tom felt he had to compliment her, he must think the situation was dire.

"How's Andreas doing with Derek?" Tom asked.

Jamie ran a finger around the rim of her empty milk glass. "Okay. Derek's taking him for the weekend. So I'll be on my own come tomorrow night."

"We'll visit Friday, don't worry."

"Thanks, Tom. You're the best brother."

"News to me!" he said with forced cheerfulness.

Jamie tried to not show her utter dismay at his un-Tom-like behavior by muttering a weak, "Yeah, yeah."

She pushed herself away from the table and rose. "It's time to pick up Andreas. We're spending the afternoon with Mom and Dad. Since they became Pokemon converts, Andreas's grandparents are the new celebrities."

"It's not the worst game I've played," allowed Tom.

"I don't think they understand it, to tell you the truth, but Andreas has yet to tire of explaining the rules to them. He enjoys the audience."

Tom came around and hugged Jamie awkwardly, which should have made her feel better. The effort was appreciated but the motivation frightened her. Tom would only hug if he thought she was in bad shape.

Chapter Twelve

Thursday evening, the moon rose. No longer full, a sliver had darkened. The waning had begun and with it the desire to be wolf receded. It would be Sanjay's last run of the month. Tomorrow, and for days afterwards, the boy could remain human.

Seth wished he could say the same for himself. He'd been wolf for over a week and a half. Even if he'd shifted to human during the day when he slept, he still feared being dragged away from himself, turning feral as his parents and perhaps his sister had.

That permanent wolfhood was the best scenario he could imagine for his sister, made him sad. But that fate was better than death. Maybe, someday, she would find him again and he could lead her back to humanity.

If he could sort out his present situation.

The one solution which he had so far resisted might still play itself out. Especially if he stayed wolf and let the hate he felt for Gordon rise into his throat.

But not yet, not yet.

Sanjay snapped at his heels, angry at Seth's lack of attention. The pup was always wild by the end of the full moon, from lack of sleep, from knowing it would be weeks before he saw Seth again.

Nevertheless, Seth had a hard time paying Sanjay proper mind. His thoughts turned again and again towards what he must do—destroy the threat that Gordon posed. Yet to kill Gordon in cold blood was something Seth was not quite ready to face. But soon.

Sanjay nipped Seth's shoulder, whining, eager for a game of tag, chase, or a tussle. Boisterous play was difficult when Seth felt so angry and so sad. Grieving for a life he couldn't have with Jamie. He had stayed away these last few days, though it was already too late to save her from himself. By becoming her lover he'd complicated her life. He couldn't regret what they'd shared, but he could despise himself for his weakness. He'd do Jamie a favor if he cut and run. What use was a wolf to a pregnant woman?

But he couldn't abandon her.

Or Sanjay, whose future was precarious. If Seth fled Cedartown, the boy would be on his own, his one keepsake a letter Seth would send his mother. The concept of leaving the pack, even a pack of two, was difficult to get across in wolfspeak, especially to a five-year-old. Seth hated the idea of Rani explaining to Sanjay that he'd been abandoned by a father-figure. Again.

Sanjay started to yip, the equivalent of a temper tantrum, because Seth moved too quickly and didn't allow the pup to catch him. Seth's restlessness was huge, making it difficult to romp.

Still, Seth slowed and Sanjay leapt at his shoulder. He rolled to the left, allowing them both to tumble down the bank. Sanjay reverted to his normal, enthusiastic self.

Seth prayed his potential daughter would not bring a pup into the world on her own. The isolation of a singleton was dangerous, not just to himself but to the few werewolves who did exist. Better if werewolves were continued to be thought a myth, not proved true by a vulnerable pup.

With that thought, he turned to Sanjay who deserved his attention. Sanjay, who had no one but Seth to guide him. They played hard and a couple of times Seth's intensity gave the pup pause enough for a querulous whine that Seth couldn't answer. What Seth could do was return Sanjay, worn-out and happy, home.

As they approached the large property, Seth was brought up short by the strong smell of exhaust and car. An unusual number of vehicles were parked in Rani's driveway late at night.

Sanjay whined in confusion. Seth rounded on him, forcing him down to the ground, ordering him to wait, to not move. He rarely growled but Sanjay needed to understand the seriousness of this situation. Seth crept forward to investigate.

It was fortunate most of Rani's property was woods. As Seth approached the edge of the lawn, he tensed, smelling men and one scent in particular, that of Gordon Carver. His expensive cologne mixed with a unique man scent was unmistakable. Seth trembled, felt his lips pull back in an angry snarl. He wanted to attack.

No. He had to think this through.

Why was Gordon here? With Mackay, who Seth also now identified. He teased out the smells of two other men, presumably police.

How could they have linked Sanjay to him? At school Seth had been meticulous about treating Sanjay like any other kid. He'd stopped some mild bullying, yes, but he always did. It would have looked strange not to, given the anti-bullying school policy.

Seth's throat rumbled in anger and he moved towards the men who threatened his pack. Blood pounded through his veins, violence was his companion.

Keep your head. Now was not the time to give over to bloodlust. If anyone suspected Sanjay's true nature, ripping out Gordon's throat in front of three witnesses could harm the boy irreparably. And who would protect him if Seth had to flee after the kill?

Sanjay trusted Seth to look after him. Right now, he lay crouching in the forest awaiting Seth's return. Seth had to take him to a safe place.

But first, drawn by Rani's voice, Seth crept towards her, wanting to protect her. Yet coming out of the shadows and entering their trap would not accomplish that. He did hope to overhear enough to understand what was going on before he took Sanjay to Jamie.

He could trust Jamie to help.

"We simply want to investigate the sighting of a wild animal in your backyard, Mrs. Smith." Detective Mackay spoke with some irritation.

"What sighting?" Rani's voice sounded shrill. "Who sighted what? Explain this to me, sir."

A large beam of light switched on. It swept Rani's backyard and Seth froze as it passed over him.

"Turn that off." Rani's now tearful voice gave her little authority.

"For God's sakes," muttered Mackay.

"Your ex-husband visited the other day, didn't he?" said Gordon.

"He saw nothing, nothing. He visited in midday when no animals were about. And he is not welcome here. None of you are welcome here. Please leave," she pleaded. "It is midnight."

"Finish your little charade and we can go," said Mackay wearily.

"My son," declared Gordon Carver, "was murdered by a savage animal. At midnight. This is no charade."

Seth backed up. As wolf, he would be everything Gordon sought and as Seth Kolski, he would be taken in by the police.

"Do you know anything about savage animals, Mrs. Smith?" asked Gordon.

"No." Rani's denial was soft, as if she'd gotten herself under control. "All I know is I want you to leave and I will be lodging a complaint in the morning."

"It's a straightforward matter of public safety, ma'am." A stranger, presumably a policeman.

Whoever was manning the light swept past Seth again, stopped and zeroed in on him. Before he could flee, he was caught in its glare. A shot rang out, missing him.

Mackay yelled, "What the hell are you doing, Carver?" and Seth was turning away, legs bunching as he leapt into a dead run.

A second shot grazed his shoulder.

He smelled blood but sped through the undergrowth towards Sanjay. He had to get the pup away. And quickly. Never mind that the pitch of Rani's voice was now high and unyielding.

When he reached Sanjay, the pup was alert, quivering, a whine of *Mommy* in his throat. Seth overrode Sanjay's plea with *Follow me, I'll look after you.* For one brief moment Seth feared the bonding had been insufficient, those innocent brown eyes would give way to distrust and defiance, and Sanjay would make a disastrous run towards his mother's distressed voice.

Sanjay's ears lay back on his head and he moved in the direction Seth wanted him to go, confused, frightened, but obedient, willing to trust that Seth knew what to do.

Which Seth did. First, he would leave Sanjay in Jamie's care. Then he would take on Gordon Carver who had shot him, who would shoot Sanjay. By tracking down Sanjay, Gordon had made a mistake tonight and he would pay for it.

They headed north, to Jamie's, following an old, well-trodden deer path. It led to the highway and they stopped, waiting for a break in traffic. The disturbing events and the abrupt change in routine made Sanjay nervous. He whimpered while Seth gave what reassurance he could. Sanjay had been ready to sleep, not hike across the county. Though the pup could understand they were going to Seth's friend, the why of it would have to be explained later. As would gunshots and his mother's cries.

They crossed the highway and Seth jerked to a stop, poleaxed by a new discovery when new discoveries were not welcome. The scent of a strange werewolf, pungent and fresh, filled his nostrils. His body tensed and quivered. His already weary heart hammered while Sanjay began to whimper, confused by Seth's reaction to the strange smell.

In other circumstances, a new wolf would have brought Seth an instinctive leap of joy. He was, after all, a pack animal. He longed for company. It was the biggest reason he'd taken Jamie home all those weeks ago—his inability to stay alone.

Sanjay leaned up against his leg, nuzzling his chest, asking for reassurance. Despite his worries, Seth rumbled soothing noises. Was this Cynthia's mythical father? There was no guarantee such an individual would help. It was almost too much to hope for. If he was anything like Seth's own father, for instance, he would be full of dangerous ideas, delusions of grandeur and his own agenda to boot.

Tonight, already fraught with danger, did not need this added complication.

Sanjay barked, impatient at the delay, not able to understand the scent's significance. Seth had to get the boy to safety, to Jamie, who could later return Sanjay to Rani, as a child.

Then Seth would look for the stranger.

⚃

The first howl entered Jamie's dreams and by the second she sat up, fully awake. Groggy, she pushed herself out of bed. After days of no contact, she hoped this was Seth.

The chance to see him again filled her with anticipation. Padding out of the bedroom in her pajamas, she grabbed her jacket off the hook. The night air was cool. She didn't want the visit cut short because he refused to come inside, while she became a shivering mess from the cold.

Quietly—she didn't want to wake Andreas—she let herself out to the dark deck. Unlike Wolf's last visit, she didn't switch on the porch light. Seth needed the safety of shadows.

"Wolf?" she called softly.

Two minutes passed and she feared she'd dreamed the howl. Just as she'd dreamed Gordon had disappeared so she and Seth could live together without this terrible fear of discovery.

Something moved at the back of the yard. In the darkness, she made out two figures. Her teeth began to chatter.

That was Seth's howl. Trust him.

A wolf and a small boy walked towards her. She shook her head at the sight and looked again.

They came closer. The boy was naked and reluctant, but not cold, given the way his arms hung loosely at his side. The wolf nudged him forward and Jamie realized Seth was limping. As her eyes became better adjusted to the night, Jamie saw that Seth's shoulder was matted with blood but when she looked into his eyes to speak of it, he turned his large head towards the boy.

Sanjay, whom Jamie recognized from Andreas's class. The boy glared at her while his clenched fist held tight to Wolf's ruff.

"Hi, Sanjay," she said gently.

Seth's blue eyes locked onto hers and she knew what to do.

She pulled off her coat and offered it to Sanjay who, with great dignity, wrapped it around his small body. Then grabbed onto Seth again.

"We'll get you some of Andreas's clothes, okay?" Her voice was reassuring, as if this were an everyday occurrence.

Sanjay nodded. Seth moved forward, leading him to Jamie. Sanjay made a noise of protest when Seth shook off his grasp.

"Do you know your mother's phone number, Sanjay?" Jamie wanted to phone and reassure his mother.

The boy shook his head, his eyes filling with tears.

"I'll drive you home."

Seth's bark was low and negative. She glanced at him and back to Sanjay.

"You'll stay here?" she asked.

"Yes." Sanjay's first, reluctant word.

"Andreas will be happy to have a sleepover."

Sanjay's wariness lessened. "Andreas is here?"

Jamie smiled. "Of course. I think it's time for bed, okay?"

"Can I eat first, please?" His young voice was stiff with politeness and fear.

"Absolutely." It took Jamie half an hour to settle Sanjay. His voracious appetite, followed by his uncertainty at sleeping in a strange place, prevented his evident exhaustion from taking over his slight frame.

She meant to put Sanjay in the guest room in order not to wake Andreas who would have too many questions Jamie did not want answered. But Sanjay wanted to see Andreas and begged to sleep in with him, not out of a sense of fun, but a sense of the familiar.

He deserved it, given his night. Jamie pulled out Andreas's trundle bed and made it up. As soon as Sanjay's head touched the pillow, he fell asleep. Such long eyelashes. What a beautiful boy.

A werewolf.

She slipped out onto the deck, with a flashlight this time because she wanted to look at Seth's shoulder. The entire time she'd been settling Sanjay, focusing on making him comfortable so he would sleep, there'd been a constant noise of fear in the back of her mind. Fear that Seth would walk away without saying a word.

To her great relief Seth was still here. His long, human frame lay stretched out on the grass.

"Seth?" Had he passed out? Was he hurt?

He roused himself and she wondered when he had shifted and how long the process had taken. She needed to learn these things about him.

"Is it difficult?" she asked. "To change form?"

He shrugged. A non-answer. Which scared her. He was pulling back, way back from her. She refused to go through this hell *and* sacrifice her feelings for him.

"Sanjay's asleep now," she offered. "Do you want to phone his mother?"

"You phone her in the morning. I think it's safer if I talk to her in person tonight. Once the police have left."

Her heart sank. "Police?"

One sharp, sudden nod.

"Why?"

He grimaced. "I don't know, Jamie."

She held out her hands but he shook his head. "I need to leave. But I wanted to give you parting instructions. When you phone Rani, that's Sanjay's mother, talk as if everyone knew he was sleeping over with Andreas. They're friends at school, etc. This was prearranged."

"I can do that."

He still refused to come to her. She dropped her hands and only then did he hold his open in supplication. "I'm sorry. I couldn't think of anywhere else to bring him, of anyone who would take him in and return him to Rani."

"I'm glad you brought him here."

Despite his refusal to take her hands, she switched on the small flashlight and went to examine his shoulder.

"It's nothing," he said roughly. "It's fine." But he allowed her to look at it.

"It's healing," she admitted. "Though you were limping earlier."

"I won't limp now."

"When did this happen?"

He eyed her, as if assessing her potential reaction. "Less than an hour ago. The shifting promotes healing. One of the benefits of being a werewolf. In case you thought there were none."

"I want to clean it."

"I told you, I'm fine." He turned away and something snapped inside her.

"Look, you've been away for three days, with no word. You've brought me Sanjay and I will happily look after him. But at least let me clean it."

He looked taken aback by her tone.

"Sit down." She pointed to the deck. "Now." She didn't usually give orders to anyone except Andreas, but she was fed up. Which was a relief, given that her emotions had been overrun by fear and uncertainty this past week.

"All right," he said with a hint of amusement. As she swung her small beam of light away from where Seth had lain, she saw a small puddle of blood.

"Seth, you've lost blood."

"Not a lot." He was impatient again. She shone the light on his face. He didn't look pale. She hoped that his lack of concern about his wound was justified.

She went inside to get disinfectant and antibacterial ointment. Maybe he was right and he had a great immune system, but treatment couldn't hurt.

As she came back out, she stood in the doorway. "Why don't you come into the living room?"

Once again, that weary half-smile played on his face. "I don't like being inside on nights like these." He pointed towards the moon. "Even when it has begun to wane. Besides, Sanjay shouldn't see who I am."

"What do you mean?"

"He doesn't know I'm Seth Kolski," he explained. "Nor does his mother, yet. They only know I'm a werewolf who looks after Sanjay."

"It sounds so lonely, not to share who you are."

"It's safer that way. I'm too big a secret for a five-year-old."

"How did you meet?"

"As wolves," he said tersely, as if anything to do with him being wolf wasn't of interest to her.

"How, as wolves?"

He glanced at her and her expression seemed to reassure him. "We can recognize that we're weres, not wolves. At first Rani was upset Sanjay spent time with a stranger but, after a while, she came to understand Sanjay was safer with someone who made him stay close to home. Sanjay used to wander far afield and was in danger of getting lost. Or hit by cars. If nothing else, I keep him away from busy highways." He tilted his head. "Is that what you wanted to know?"

"There's lots I want to know about you, Seth. I don't think you understand the extent of my curiosity."

This time his gaze steadied on hers. "We're not unthinking animals when we're wolves."

"I know. I've talked to you a couple of times, remember?"

He nodded.

She opened her first-aid kit.

"Don't bother with bandages. It'll come off in the shift."

"What caused this?" she asked.

He didn't answer as she cleaned him. "Seth?"

"A bullet."

"Shit."

"A nick."

"Yeah. And how do you know there won't be another?"

"I'll be more careful."

She sat back on her heels. "Was it Gordon?"

"I'm not talking to you about Gordon." Suppressed anger buoyed each of his words.

She took a deep breath. "I want to know what you're planning, Seth."

He sprang up. "You want to know that I plan to rip that bastard's throat out? Why?"

Hell, if she didn't watch it, she'd be crying and he didn't need that now. Self-pity was not something she, or Seth, could afford.

"Is there another way?" she asked.

"Don't worry. You don't have to be with me afterwards."

"Fuck, Seth. You don't like killing. That night wasn't just about Veronica's disappearance and the cage. It cost you something to kill."

Now Seth looked pale in the rising light of the moon. "There's no other way, Jamie." His voice was strangled. "Because things are happening that I don't understand. Sanjay's been linked to me. I don't know how, but I have to protect him. And you."

"Mackay?"

"He's looking for me, Jamie. I'm a missing person, and he showed up at Sanjay's. But how would he know I have a relationship with the boy when Sanjay and his mother don't even know it?"

Jamie gestured uselessly.

"And a strange werewolf is in the area. Male, not young. I crossed his trail on my way over here."

Hope leapt in Jamie's breast. "It's Trey Walters. Cynthia's father. Tom said he was coming tonight."

"It's a complication I don't want right now."

"Seth. Find him. Talk to him. See if he can help."

He looked away.

Tentatively, she placed a hand on his and he flipped it off, moving away. She couldn't keep the hurt from her face.

"I'm no good for you, Jamie."

"God, don't start that again."

His mouth was tight. "You only pursued me once you realized you were pregnant. Otherwise, you would have avoided the hell out of me, and rightly so."

"You pushed me away, Seth, as you're doing now."

"Keep your voice down. Can't you see we'll never make a go of this, even under ideal circumstances?"

"What do we know of ideal circumstances? Nothing has been ideal from the beginning."

His shrug was a jerk. "We're of different worlds. I'm about to go hunting in the forest. On all fours. Why would you want to saddle yourself with this baggage, Jamie? Explain that to me."

"You can't argue the wanting out of me." She smacked a fist against her chest, where her heart hurt. "It's there."

"I'm sorry I seduced you that night and dragged you into my life." His voice trailed off and she no longer cared if he pushed her away.

She went to him, placing both hands on his face. "I'm in love with you, you idiot, baby or no."

He shook his head at her before his body betrayed him, shuddering as he pulled her into his arms. The embrace was hard, swift and intense. And then he was striding away into shadow and she was crying.

Chapter Thirteen

Seth raced furiously, as if he could escape the turmoil of a love that could not change what he was. He focused instead on what he could do—talk to Rani, find the werewolf, kill Gordon.

In that order. He scouted out Rani's house and its environs. The interlopers still remained. He could smell them. Rani herself had retreated into her house. However, the police were leaving and dragging an enraged Gordon with them.

Gordon was not the only one angry. At one point, Mackay exploded with expletive after expletive that included threats of arrest for shooting at a dog in the city.

"It was a wolf," Gordon declared darkly. "I know what I saw."

With that, Seth's gut clenched. Gordon *knew*. He knew he had shot at a werewolf. If Seth had entertained any hope that his secret had died with Brian, it was now gone.

Gordon had tried to kill him. Seth would respond in kind.

"This is it," said Mackay, whatever that meant. But Gordon took it badly, railing against his son's death. He had to be forcibly removed from Rani's yard by the two policemen and frogmarched into the back of their car.

They left, but Gordon's Mercedes stayed behind, an expensive reminder of the threat Gordon posed to not only Seth, but Sanjay.

The windows turned dark as Rani roamed the house, turning off lights. She stepped out the back door and, as she did every evening when she waited for her son's return, sat on the dark veranda. Her figure looked more defeated than usual and she rocked slightly back and forth in silence.

Out of her sight, Seth shifted. He disliked becoming human under the full moon and this was the second time he'd turned tonight. His human skin felt wrong and uncomfortable. He had to push himself into it.

But he couldn't speak to Rani as a wolf. He needed to know what she'd learned from this evening's visitors and she deserved to be reassured about Sanjay's safety. Her posture suggested she was anxious, if not worried sick.

He rested after the change, itchy in his human skin, as if he was pretending to be something he wasn't. Not strictly true. He had his humanity, he just didn't want it tonight.

Once his breath stopped heaving, he pushed himself off the ground and walked softly up to the veranda. He stayed at the side of the house, in shadow. He'd still rather that Rani didn't recognize his human self. Besides, he was naked. But given the events of the evening, neither his hidden identity nor his nudity was of critical concern.

Protecting his pack was.

He sank down on his haunches, watching her bowed shoulders. As he was about to clear his throat, she lifted her head.

"Sanjay likes to play this game." Her voice was melodious and barely accented. He was pretty sure she'd been raised in Cedartown by parents who'd emigrated from India. "He sneaks up and tries to scare me. I've become quite aware of movement in the dark. Besides"—a smile hitched her voice—"I am part wolf, I suppose. My eyesight is keen." She turned to look directly at Seth. "Your movements are heavier than Sanjay's."

"He's safe."

She let out a long, trembling sigh. "They didn't shoot him."

"No. I kept him away."

"Thank you."

"He's at Jamie Buchner's, Andreas's mother. Andreas is in Sanjay's class." He didn't know if Rani remembered Jamie and Andreas. Rani kept to herself. "Jamie will phone you in the morning."

He sensed her dismay.

"I wish you'd brought him back, instead of exposing his secret to someone else."

"Jamie can be trusted." Of all things, Seth knew that.

"Perhaps." She clasped her hands together. "I don't like to trust people." It was almost a whisper. An admission, too, of how alone she was.

"Neither do I," Seth admitted. "But I didn't know how long the police would stay. I had to get Sanjay somewhere safe. If Sanjay's absence needs to be explained, you and Jamie can act like the sleepover was planned."

"They did ask about Sanjay, at the prompting of that man." *Gordon.* "I told them Sanjay was at my parents. They accepted that, or Detective Mackay did. That man sneered at me."

"Gordon likes to sneer."

She nodded.

"Why were the police here?" Seth asked.

She turned away from him. "I'm afraid I recognize you, Mr. Kolski. Even if your voice weren't familiar, I would wonder why a man like Gordon Carver would talk about you like you were the devil's spawn."

"He knows what I am."

"I wish he didn't." She did not blame him for what he'd brought on her family. She just sounded lost.

"How did he connect me to you?" Seth couldn't fathom what the missing link was.

She was silent for a long time and he realized she had something to tell him.

"Do you know?" he prompted her.

"I was married. Though not to a Smith."

He waited.

"To another Indian. An arranged marriage, with a man my parents deemed appropriate. That is, a man my parents thought they could control with money if my child was a werewolf. It runs in my mother's family, you see."

She looked down, as if she didn't want to go on.

"My ex-husband wasn't too happy I was already pregnant, but it was part of the agreement. However, when Sanjay was born, the baby looked too much like his biological father and too different from my then-husband. Who became ashamed. So, despite my parents' money, he divorced me."

She slid her head back and forth in a gesture that Seth didn't recognize.

"Well, the reasons for his leaving are complicated and not solely related to Sanjay. But that's not the point. The point is, he came back two years ago, looking for reconciliation, that is, more money. He saw the wolf pup out back. He saw Sanjay."

Seth listened to her breathing in dark, shallow, quick breaths that measured her distress.

"My parents paid him more money." She sighed. "He's an awful man."

"I'm sorry."

Her spine stiffened. "I don't need your pity."

"It's sympathy. I come from a family of werewolves. I know what it's like when a loved one is at risk."

She accepted that with a nod. "My ex-husband, like many people in this small town, once worked for Gordon Carver, before he moved south to Georgia. My ex recently communicated his little moneymaking scheme to his ex-boss." She smoothed loose hair back from her face. "I should never have married. It has been my biggest mistake."

"Does Detective Mackay know Gordon is looking for werewolves?"

"I don't know though at one point the detective did say this is a missing-persons investigation, not a horror film." She shivered. "It feels like one to me."

The last sentence was uttered in a small voice. Seth wanted to comfort Rani but when he stepped towards her, she tensed, and he remembered he was werewolf and naked, and she was neither.

"You mustn't let Sanjay run wolf until this is resolved," Seth told her. "For the next three weeks that shouldn't be difficult, given the moon is disappearing. By the next full moon this situation should have stabilized."

"Okay." The one word sounded beaten, almost hopeless. Seth wished he could tell Rani something hopeful. Instead, the silence lengthened between them.

When she spoke next, it sounded more like she was talking to herself than to him. "We may have to move, Sanjay and I. My parents may suggest it. In the hopes that my ex-husband and Gordon Carver can't find us."

"I would like to know where you are. So I can visit, perhaps."

She wiped her face briskly and Seth realized she was crying. "Sanjay will find it difficult without you. You're important to him."

"Sanjay is important to me."

She peered into the distance, where the darkness of night was ending. The gray of early morning had begun. "You should go, before that man returns here for his Mercedes."

"I should go," he agreed, but paused, looking for something reassuring to add. "Sanjay is safe now. And sleeping. Jamie fed him well."

"I will thank her for it. And I thank you. Goodbye, Mr. Kolski." Her formality made her sound more alone than before. She wasn't a werewolf, but she was isolated.

"Seth," he said.

He saw her mouth curve. "Goodbye, Seth."

"Rani."

He retreated to the woods to shift.

There would be no rest. A strange werewolf had crossed his path. Seth had to track him down.

⋄

The moan Jamie heard was her own. Above it, in discordant harmony, was an excited voice. Small hands pushed at her shoulder. "Mom. *Mom!* Guess who's in my room!"

She forced herself awake, head shaking in an attempt to clear muddled thoughts. These middle-of-the-night visits didn't do much to lessen her pregnancy fatigue. Next time she got pregnant, it was going to be planned.

Or she wouldn't have sex.

There, she felt better with that useless resolution. Never mind that it could do nothing to help her now. She focused on her little boy who bounced on her bed, talking a mile a minute.

Her brain sped up to process his words.

"My first friend to sleep over, Mom, and I didn't even know it. That's not fair. When did Sanjay come? Can I wake him up? I jumped on his bed twice already but he's still sleeping."

"Um." She held up a hand to stall further questions. "Sanjay's tired because he was up late last night."

As frustration overtook Andreas's excitement, she realized she'd made a tactical mistake.

"Why didn't *I* stay up late?" he demanded. "I miss everything. That's not fair, Mom."

She shoved her hands in her hair. "Andreas, please. Let me wake up."

He pushed out his lower lip. "Did you stay up late, too?"

"I'm an adult, sweetie."

"Sanjay isn't."

"No." She ruffled Andreas's hair and felt for Sanjay's mother who must be sick with worry. Andreas frowned at Jamie's sudden sadness.

She stumbled out of bed. Andreas trailed behind as she searched for and found the telephone book. There were a zillion Smiths. Jamie wished Rani had kept her maiden name.

Phew, Rani Smith was listed. Jamie dialed, hands shaking.

It rang once before someone picked it up. Male. Elderly. With an Indian accent.

"May I speak with Rani Smith?"

"Who's calling, please?"

Jamie paused. "I'm Andreas's mother, Jamie Buchner. Andreas and Sanjay are classmates."

"How is Sanjay?" The voice was unsteady with fear and hope.

"Good. He's still sleeping. I thought I'd talk to Rani about a pick-up time."

"One moment please."

In the background she heard a rapid-fire exchange in another language. Rani came to the phone. "How is Sanjay?" she asked anxiously.

"He's good, asleep but good. It took me a while to settle him last night."

"No problem, no problem." At Rani's choked voice, Jamie's eyes filled with tears. "I'll come over and get him now. Can I have your address, please?"

"Mom," shouted Andreas, tugging at her top. "Do I have to go to school today?"

Jamie covered the mouthpiece of the phone. "Yes."

"Does Sanjay?"

Jamie ignored Andreas and gave Rani her address. They were in this together, though Rani couldn't know they both had wolf genes in the family.

As she hung up, Andreas again asked to wake Sanjay and Jamie gave him leave.

Soon Andreas bounded back down the hall. "He won't wake up, Mom. I shook him."

Jamie rushed to Sanjay's bed, and was relieved to see the boy breathing. "He's exhausted," she explained to her son.

Andreas became sulky. "This isn't a very fun first sleepover, Mom."

"Well, honey, I'll try to do better next time." She'd plan it, for one thing. Planning, she was certain, would do much for her life. "Get dressed for school."

"Sanjay's not dressed." Andreas's face flushed and his eyes shone with unshed tears.

Jamie groaned at the incipient temper tantrum.

The phone rang and she jumped. As did Andreas. "I'll get it, Mom. Maybe Sanjay can stay."

"I don't think Sanjay is feeling all that well." Her words were lost on her boy who sped down the hall.

"Hi, Oma," said Andreas into the phone. He sounded disappointed.

Her mother was calling early this morning. She generally waited until Andreas was at school.

"Yeah!" Andreas rallied quickly. "Dad came to my school. He's never done *that* before. I'm going to see him today. He's looking for a house around here because he wants to live near me." His voice was rising. Between Derek's homecoming and Andreas's unexpected guest last night, Andreas was overwhelmed by life.

As was she.

"Guess what, Oma? Sanjay slept over last night."

Jamie winced. She hadn't wanted to talk to her mother about Sanjay. She could just hear her ever-curious mother asking Andreas, *Why?*

"Because he's my friend," Andreas answered, then paused. "I don't know. I only saw him in the morning. But now he won't wake up."

Jamie walked into the living room to take the phone from her son.

"No, Mom! *I'm* talking to Oma, not you." He clutched the phone to his small chest and walked out onto the deck.

Jamie rolled her eyes and went to pick up the other phone.

"...think I should talk to your mother now, dear. It's time you got ready for school."

As Jamie opened her mouth to second her mother's suggestion, Andreas exclaimed, "Hey, the grass looks funny. Like the time an animal died in our backyard and there was blood. Is that blood, Mom?" he called.

"Blood?" echoed her mother on the phone.

Jamie marched out to the deck, ready to scream at her son which was unfair. But she felt pushed to her limit. Deep breath, calm voice, if uttered through clenched teeth. "Andreas. Inside. Off the phone now. You eat breakfast and get ready for school."

"I don't want to go to school today."

"I'll phone back later, honey," said her mother. Andreas still held the phone but his arm hung by his side. "You shouldn't let him have sleepovers during the school week. It's too much. He's overexcited."

"Yes, Mom, thanks. Bye." Jamie clicked off the phone.

"Mommy, I am *not* going to school today," declared Andreas.

"Your father is picking you up after school and you're spending the weekend with him. What will he think if you're not there like we planned?"

Andreas reconsidered for two seconds. "Okay, I'll go."

"Good boy." She extracted the now dead phone from his clutches.

He eyed her, still unhappy with how this morning had unfolded. "I want to play with Sanjay."

"We'll have him over another time. Promise."

A worried line formed between his eyebrows. "That's not Sanjay's blood on the grass, is it?"

"No," declared Jamie. Her first task, once the house was empty, would be to spray the grass with water and get rid of that blood. Then she planned to sleep all day. The baby needed it.

∽

Jamie had managed to get Andreas on the bus, pass Sanjay over to a nervous Rani who would barely speak, and get rid of the blood on the grass. But before sleep came, the phone rang.

Her mother, uncharacteristically, began without preamble. "I'm coming over this morning, Jamie."

"No." *Keep your voice steady, girl.* If her mother suspected Jamie had serious problems, which she sure as hell did, she'd be over in a flash, no matter what Jamie said. "I didn't sleep well last night and I need a nap."

"Why aren't you sleeping?" her mother demanded.

"I don't know."

"Do you have insomnia?"

Eating disorder. Insomnia. Jamie wondered what her mother would diagnose next. Probably not pregnancy.

"I don't think so, Mom. I'm just adjusting to the new routine, with Andreas going to kindergarten now."

"He started weeks ago, Jamie. You've had plenty of time to get used to the new routine." The doubt in her mother's voice was strong and Jamie didn't know whether it was good or bad that her father hadn't told her mother she was pregnant.

"Well, you know me. It takes me a while to adjust to change." The words, nonsensical as they were, rolled off her tongue.

"That's news to me." Her mom sighed at Jamie's silence. "Why don't you and Andreas come here for lunch?"

"Derek is taking Andreas for the weekend."

"You're going to be on your own again, Jamie. It isn't healthy."

"Mom, I want to be alone. Everything's fine."

"You never want to leave your house." Suspicion again.

"I like my house." Jamie wondered where this was leading.

"You're not agoraphobic, are you?"

"Mom, please! I'll come visit soon, okay? But not today." Not when it would be evident Jamie was troubled.

"I worry about you, you know."

"I know." God, did she know. "You have no reason to worry." What a load of crap. But it got her mother off the phone and Jamie felt awful for lying. But how could she admit her real problems? *Seth's a werewolf* sounded unreal.

Except when she was around him. Then she knew.

Just as well Derek was taking Andreas for a couple of days. After spending a half-day with his son this week, Derek decided he could cope with a longer stretch. She was suspicious of his newfound enthusiasm for fatherhood, but Derek's job loss left him with much time and little to do. Perhaps father and son would bond deeply enough that Derek wouldn't leave Andreas hanging again.

But this was Derek's last chance. If he dropped out, she would block any further attempts he made to see Andreas.

Chapter Fourteen

Not only was Seth tracking the stranger, the stranger was tracking Seth. The wolf had been to Jamie's house, or its environs, and to Rani's, as Seth had the night before. His territorial, as well as protective, instincts were aroused. But he was relieved to see the stranger, presumably Trey, had been careful in his scouting expedition—for that's what it seemed to be—never approaching the houses too closely. Leaving little of himself, besides his scent, behind.

Trey was clever and quick-moving while Seth was exhausted by the night's events. This man had apparently flown in to help. Seth decided to give up the stalking game. Throwing back his head, he howled. He didn't keep the aggression out of his voice.

The response was not immediate and when it came, the stranger's howl, disgruntled and annoyed, was not a challenge. Seth loped through the woods, crossed the highway and plunged into woods again. Trey howled twice more during Seth's approach and it occurred to Seth that Trey might think he was incompetent, unable to locate him. If nothing else, Seth's parents had taught him how to use his wolf senses. After the first howl, he'd known where to find Trey. It was a game he and his sister had played as children. One day he hoped to train Sanjay, too.

He ran steadily, fast approaching Trey. By the time Seth came within meters of the new wolf, the fur on his back was raised. First meets could be dangerous, his father had warned, and some werewolves were psychopaths. Seth had met so few, he couldn't know if it was true. But all thoughts of danger fled when he realized the stranger was no longer wolf, but man.

Seth was surprised. His father had drilled into him the importance of meeting as wolf, not man. Wolves could tear men apart. Unless they had a gun. Yet Seth caught no whiff of gunpowder.

"I thought we might talk." The man's voice carried through the bush, low and matter-of-fact. Seth moved closer.

While the man lounged against a tree, Seth growled his greeting, suspicious, though he reined in his aggression. The man had, after all, given Seth the upper hand physically. Trey didn't think he was about to be attacked.

Trey stood, arms crossed, big in every way imaginable and extremely fit. Perhaps he thought he could take on wolf-Seth, like he'd thought earlier that Seth couldn't track him. But the stranger didn't meet Seth's gaze directly. Trey was not interested in provocation. He did not want a fight.

"I'd like to talk to you." At that point Trey met Seth's gaze. Seth jerked back with a jolt of recognition. The stranger had the same color eyes as Seth.

"Trey Walters." He smiled, a flash of teeth. Not much humor but some satisfaction. "You do have the look of me."

Shit. This was not the time to learn about his true parentage. He felt a growl gather in his throat. He'd never believed his father's accusations of his mother's infidelity. Still didn't.

"I'm your uncle," said Trey and that one word cleared away some of Seth's misapprehensions. He hadn't wanted to meet a new father. Trey gestured at Seth to move. "Go on and shift. I'll stay here. I want more than a one-way conversation and some wolf glyphs of emotion."

Seth turned and trotted out of sight. He knew shifting so close to a stranger could be dangerous. Werewolves were at their most vulnerable during the change. But although Trey was a virtual stranger, he was also family—no wonder his smell had been so familiar.

Besides, they needed to talk. So Seth let the world lose focus while he thought of Trey and Jamie and Sanjay. His family. As the pain intensified, Veronica's absence caught him by the throat. He wanted his sister to see her newborn nephew or niece, but she was gone. Gone. He passed out.

And came to lying on the ground, winded, trying to catch his breath. In human form and it felt right and good. If only he wasn't starving. He smelled Trey and remembered. He rose.

When Seth returned, Trey gave him the once-over. "You need to eat more."

Seth rolled his stiff shoulders. "It's been a rough week."

"So I've heard. Hungry?" Trey asked, as if Seth had to be. Seth wasn't used to someone who knew what it was like to shift and run and need to eat.

"Yes."

Trey eyed him, now that Seth was human. "You still have the look of me. Your mother Tessa was my sister." He reached out a hand to shake and Seth gripped it. "I'm also Cynthia's father."

"You're kidding." It hadn't seemed real when Jamie had told him.

"I don't kid." Trey handed Seth some jerky.

"What are you doing here?" Seth asked between swallows.

"Cleaning up. Some idiot is making too much noise for my liking about savage animals. I'm told a wolf killed his son." He cocked his head, assessing Seth. "You wouldn't happen to know anything about that, would you?"

His uncle's eyes were nonjudgmental, almost indifferent. Seth could match the tone Trey had set, even if what happened that night had sunk its claws deep within him.

"I killed Brian Carver," he admitted.

Trey nodded. "Why?"

"He was going after my sister. I had to protect her. He knew she was werewolf," he added when Trey didn't seem to think protecting Veronica was important.

"'Going after'. What does that mean?"

"Brian wanted to cage her, drug her, kill her."

"Did he?"

"I don't know." Seth bit out the words. "She disappeared that night. I never found her again. And I can't trust what Brian told me."

"What did Brian tell you?"

"That he was going to do these things to her. He hadn't yet. At the time I thought I killed him before he could hurt her."

Trey chewed on that. "He's better dead."

"Yeah," said Seth bitterly.

Trey's eyebrows rose a fraction. "I don't like kills, either. So we'll jail Gordon Carver." He passed Seth more jerky.

"How can you jail Gordon Carver? He's powerful."

Trey gave a ghost of a smile. "Not more powerful than I am."

Seth waited.

"I am going to jail him on money-laundering. Totally unrelated, but certainly not fabricated. Within his own company. He'll be too busy with his own problems to continue this werewolf investigation shit. He'll undermine his already shaky credibility if he talks about werewolves."

"Okay." Seth wanted to grab hold of this possibility of an end to the Carver nightmare, but until it happened it seemed unreal.

"You're a missing person till tomorrow," Trey went on. "Then you can say you went on a short sabbatical, family crisis, whatever, sorry for alarming everyone, but you're back now."

"The police—"

"The police won't bug you by tomorrow. You can go home then. They won't bug the pup, either." The flash of teeth again. "I've taken care of it."

"And how do you have such influence?"

"Special Agent Trey Walters."

Seth snorted in disbelief. "They let you into the FBI?"

"Yes. I'm good at what I do."

"I've heard about their training. How could you pass? It's impossible."

"No, it's not. I have exceptional control. It's something every werewolf should work on."

Goaded beyond good sense, Seth said, "Even when they're shot full of ketamine." He held Trey's gaze and refused to look away.

"You escaped." Trey dismissed Seth's shame. "You killed your captor."

"Right, I conquered."

"Sure."

Why reopen this raw wound with a stranger? He loathed talk of what had happened in the cage, even with a fellow werewolf. But Trey's unemotional reaction, no anger, no outrage, calmed Seth.

"So," Seth changed the subject. "I just go home."

"Without ripping out Gordon's throat, yes," said Trey, as if this condition were a huge complication. "I don't want to explain to my superiors that both father and son Carver were killed by savage animals. I will have a hard time hand-waving that coincidence away."

Seth stared at him steadily. "Gordon is a threat."

"I'll take care of him, I told you. I'm here until the arrest, which I expect to go down tomorrow."

"That's it."

"That's it." Trey was getting impatient, but Seth didn't care.

"It's too easy."

"It isn't easy at all. I've worked hard this past week. I'm sorry I couldn't get here earlier but I didn't believe Cynthia at first. I thought she was trying to get my attention." He paused and for the first time looked, well, human. "I'm not a good father. Runs in the family."

"Not necessarily." Seth could be a good father. He knew it.

Trey shrugged, losing interest in the conversation. "You're going to stay around here and look after the pup."

"That's been my plan for a while now."

Trey nodded. "Otherwise he'll cause problems for himself and potentially me if he doesn't have a wolf to guide him. Singletons are the worst. They come to bad ends or they become shits like your father. I don't know what Tessa saw in him."

"I'm staying here." Seth resisted the urge to say, *Mom didn't do so hot, either.*

"Your girl is pregnant."

"I'm aware of that."

"Good. I'll be glad to see a wolf who can parent effectively."

"You have no idea what kind of father I'll be."

"Cynthia is full of praise."

Seth frowned. He hadn't thought Cynthia liked him. "Yeah?"

"Yeah." Trey's tone was dismissive. He wanted Seth to leave.

"One more thing," said Seth. "Rani Smith—"

"The pup's mother."

Seth tried not to be taken aback that Trey knew everything. "Yes. Her ex-husband—not Sanjay's father—knows Sanjay is a pup."

"Hell." Trey looked away for a moment. Sighed. "I'll shut him up."

Seth didn't care how. "Thanks."

Trey pushed himself up. "So much for getting some sleep." He offered Seth the last of the jerky. They ate in silence, shook hands and parted with monosyllabic farewells. Trey strode off. It all seemed insufficient, for such a crucial exchange of information, but Seth supposed that information, and giving instructions, was all that interested Trey.

Besides, Seth didn't quite trust him. No matter how arrogant the wolf had been, arrogance did not guarantee competence, as his own father had so often demonstrated. Seth remained in the knoll, trying to take in the half-hour conversation. If Trey was correct it would be over soon. As Seth turned the thoughts over in his mind, his exhausted body gave way to sleep.

CB

Twice more that day, her mother phoned, and Jamie's nerves were shot. Somehow, staving off a visit from her mother was the last straw. Pretending all was well when it decidedly wasn't almost pushed Jamie over the edge.

Or maybe that last straw was not being able to read Andreas his bedtime book. At loose ends, she paced her living room, waiting to feel tired enough to go to bed, even though she'd slept the day away.

The ten-minute phone call from Derek's hotel room, with Andreas repeatedly telling her he was having fun, as if trying to convince himself, had upset her. Derek had assured her Andreas was fine. She reminded herself of Andreas's last words, *We'll see each other soon, Mom!*

She wanted to see Seth soon, too. No, she wanted to see him now. But mostly, she wanted to be part of one, big happy family with Andreas, baby and Seth. And have Derek in the area so that Andreas didn't feel rejected by his father.

Tears threatened again, which made her angry.

The doorbell rang. Damn. Her mother had made good on her threat to drive over and see what was going on. Despite her father's assertions that Jamie should be left alone. Despite Jamie demanding she be left alone.

She marched up to the front door, fed up with her mother crashing personal boundaries. Not that she would use such words, because her mother wouldn't know what she was talking about.

Jamie yanked the door open.

And froze.

Gordon smiled thinly. "Hello, Jamie."

Her mind shouted danger and her body waited a beat before catching up with the warning. She put all her strength into shutting the door on Gordon. But he was already stepping into the house, pushing the door against her and shouldering his way through the threshold.

She screamed and he slammed the door, locked it. The night had been cool enough to warrant closing all the windows. No neighbor would hear her scream in a shut-up house.

She spun around and ran for the back door.

A hand clamped down on her arm and jerked her to a stop. She turned to knee him in the groin and he sidestepped her clumsy move. Then smacked her hard across the face, shocking her with the force of his hand. She'd never been hit before.

"There's more where that came from, if you keep struggling," he warned, squeezing her arm to bruise.

The baby. He might hurt the baby. Her free hand came to rest on her tingling cheek while she smelled Gordon's expensive cologne and felt like she would hurl.

He manhandled her onto the couch. It didn't take much effort because somewhere between fear and shock, her fight and flight response had disengaged.

Instead, she shook and gulped breaths. Dammit.

"Let's have a chat, Jamie."

She didn't want to talk to him. Acid rose in her throat.

Gordon smiled. "A little pale now, are we?"

She vomited on his shoes.

He swore and slapped her again, less effectively this time because she was sitting. She retreated to the far corner of the couch.

"Don't vomit on me and I won't hit you again," Gordon assured her.

Where's Seth? echoed in her head. She needed him. Here. Now. More than ever.

"Though maybe I'll hit you if you don't give me the information I need." He leaned forward, loosening his tie, which unnerved her. "Tell me where Seth Kolski is."

"I don't know."

"You're involved with him." It wasn't a question.

She shook her head. "He's my son's gym teacher, that's all."

Gordon, with false patience, repeated his demand that she tell him where Seth was.

She began to cry. Maybe if she hadn't been pregnant, she could have been stoic, but she wasn't coping too well with the situation at the moment.

"Tears worked with that moron, Detective Mackay, but they won't work with me, Jamie. Besides"—his voice lowered—"you're prettier when you haven't been crying and I prefer my women to be pretty. I'll bet Seth finds you pretty."

"I've told you, I don't know Seth well."

"You barely know the man, eh?"

He seemed to be waiting for a response so she nodded.

"Yet you invited him to your mother's birthday dinner." Gordon shook his head. "If that's not a rite of passage, I don't know what is."

She stared at him. *Oh, Mom.*

"Yes, your mother was happy to talk to her ex-son-in-law's boss. She's a chatty woman. Touchingly concerned about Seth's disappearance, too."

Jamie blinked. Crying was humiliating. She was going to stop. "I can't help you. I don't know where Seth is."

"Women are so unreliable. They lie through their teeth. Veronica lied all the time. You remember Seth's sister Veronica, don't you, Jamie?"

She didn't answer but Gordon carried on anyway.

"Veronica fooled my son for many years, telling Brian Seth was dead."

Jamie frowned.

"Why would she do such a thing, you ask? Let me explain it to you—the lie allowed her to arrange for Seth to kill Brian. Quite clever, don't you think?"

Except it didn't make sense. And it wasn't true.

"At least that bitch—and isn't that an appropriate description for a she-wolf—was always good for a fuck."

"Shut up," said Jamie furiously, tears forgotten. "Just shut up."

"Couldn't get enough," rolled on Gordon, enjoying his audience. "Insatiable. I'll bet Seth is like that, too. Wolves, you know."

"Asshole," spat Jamie.

Gordon shoved his face in front of Jamie's. "Don't be rude. You're in no position to do anything but agree with me. Pleasantly."

His breath was sour, making her stomach heave, and she turned so she wouldn't smell him so strongly.

Gordon pulled back. "Your ex-husband called me a kook." He laughed. "*Kook*. Such an old-fashioned word and Derek used it to describe me. Before I fired him. Why, you ask? Because I'm obsessed with the violent death of my only son. Well, some men care about their family and I did. Derek, less so, don't you think?"

Jamie concentrated on keeping her gag reflex under control.

"Jamie, look at me."

She did. He was wrung out and furious, an unsettling combination. His normally well-groomed hair stuck up in odd directions and his face shone with sweat.

"Wouldn't you want to avenge the death of your son?"

She refused to speak of Andreas, to make him part of this godawful conversation.

"Don't you understand the importance of family?" he asked.

"Yes."

"Good, you understand why I'm doing this." Gordon pulled out a gun. "I'm going to hold you hostage until someone takes me seriously."

A moan bubbled up from her throat. The baby. *Be smart, Jamie. Don't fight him, it ups the ante.*

"They closed down the investigation into Brian's death today. As if God on high sent down a commandment. And for good measure they've created this trumped up charge of money-laundering against me. Who do these guys think they are? Do they think they're above the law?"

She closed her eyes, refraining to point out that Gordon thought exactly that about himself.

"Now Mackay won't look at the case again. Says it's not in his jurisdiction and he should never have been involved. Says his hands are tied." Despite the sneer in Gordon's voice, it trembled.

He expected something from her.

"Oh," she said, unwilling to venture anything else. Jamie was relieved Gordon calmed slightly. She'd feared he would begin to literally froth at the mouth.

"I have some influence, you know. I come from Cedartown. I just don't have enough influence to override orders from the FBI. Yet."

Cynthia had been confident of her father's ability to handle Seth's situation, as he apparently called it. At the moment, Jamie was in no position to judge Trey Walter's competence but, if nothing else, he had made some moves.

"You're going to help me," declared Gordon.

Her eyes widened. He came closer.

"You have dreadful taste in men. First Derek who couldn't keep his pants zipped unless he's adding up numbers. Then Seth, a freak who murders innocents."

Brian was no innocent. The thought rang in her head and she kept it there. No matter how badly she wanted to speak, she had to remember the baby she was safekeeping.

"How is holding me hostage going to help anyone find Seth?" she ventured.

"Who slept here last night?"

Jamie stiffened. He laughed, then knocked his head with his knuckles, twice. An odd action that made her uneasy. "I could have been a detective. I followed Rani here this morning. I can figure out who brought the little werewolf to you."

She retched but nothing came up. It was making her sick, this stress. Her hand clutched her stomach.

"You were prettier two years ago."

"I make a better impression when I'm not gagging. The gun doesn't improve my looks either."

Gordon grabbed her by the throat, a one-handed grip that pushed her head back against the couch. "Don't mess with me, lady."

"That hurts," she tried to say. His hand obstructed speech. She squirmed and the pressure on her throat increased. No one was here to help her. She felt desperately alone.

It became difficult to breathe. She began to thrash in earnest.

From far away, his words continued, endless, insane conversation that she somehow had to withstand.

"I'm in charge here," he was saying. "This is an investigation into my son's death. Into the animal that ripped out Brian's throat."

Her fingernails found Gordon's face and she gouged. *The baby*, she thought furiously. *He's going to hurt the baby.*

He let go and smacked her a third time, hard enough to make her head ring. Then he pointed the gun at her head as she heaved in big breaths, tears of pain streaming down her face.

"Tell me everything you know about Seth or we'll have another round of breathlessness."

"You hurt my throat," she whispered.

"Ah, well."

"Put the gun down," she croaked. "I can't think when it's pointing at me."

He smiled.

"Please," she begged, wringing her hands, desperate for a reprieve. Frantic, she tried to think up what to tell him. Safer to claim Seth had taken off, perhaps for Georgia.

Gordon liked the pleading. He stepped back and theatrically placed the gun down on the coffee table.

It was the movement she noticed first, an outside shadow, from the corner of her eye, before the room exploded into motion. Shattered glass flew everywhere as Wolf leapt through the window and into the living room, one bound before he reached Gordon. The growl came as Gordon fell, followed by the sickening thud of a man's head hitting hard against the cement corner of the fireplace ledge. Then Seth was on top, his large jaws ready to clamp down on Gordon's exposed throat, Seth's lips pulled back in a snarl.

That's when the scene seemed to freeze. Because Seth didn't move, and neither did Gordon. It took Jamie a moment to realize Gordon was unconscious—his face had whitened and blood was seeping into the carpet from the blow to his head.

Her vision faded but Jamie concentrated. She refused to pass out now.

Chapter Fifteen

The red haze of his vision flared but Seth held back, resisting the lure of destroying Gordon, the man who had attacked his mate. With brute force of will, Seth pulled back from sinking teeth into flesh. The mantra repeated itself over and over again in his head. *I can't rip this throat out.*

The difficulty of explaining similar father and son deaths would expose himself, his child and perhaps Sanjay.

With great care, Seth retreated from Gordon, putting distance between himself and the temptation to kill. As he did so, the pounding of blood in his head receded. He panted, trying to calm the bloodlust. He needed to think clearly.

And he needed to face Jamie. He turned.

Pale and wide-eyed, she sat on the couch. Despite the violent emotion within him, the desire to comfort and calm took hold, settling some of the roiling fury that wound through his veins. She was overwhelmed, she needed to be cared for. Not that a snarling wolf with fur full of glass shards was the best candidate, but he was all she had at the moment.

Unless he shifted to human.

"Seth," she whispered. Her hand moved towards him, then stopped, as if she didn't know what to do.

He stared at her, searching for revulsion, but her face was empty of everything but shock and pain.

"I needed you and you came." She was grateful. When he was late, too late. When he had brought this violence down on her.

Her eyes were shadowed and her face bruised and he didn't know what she saw when she looked at him. He wished desperately he was human right now.

"Don't leave me," she said.

And no, he could not leave her alone with Gordon's body. There was nothing for it, he would shift and look after her. He hoped she'd have the sense to close her eyes.

Going into himself, he worked at the feeling of human, of long limbs and a straight back, of organs that arranged themselves as Seth, not Wolf. After his weeks of running nights, his body welcomed the change to human. He was ready to return to humanity.

The fur receded and the skin smoothed. Pieces of glass slid off his body, the tiny shards hitting the glass-saturated carpet, clinking as they fell. It had been a big window and it lay all around him.

Heating up, he tried to watch Jamie, wishing he could apologize. But she had begged him not to leave and so he was here, shifting before her eyes.

Her dilated eyes told him nothing of her thoughts and he couldn't yet speak to ask. Her mouth fell slightly open, not gaping, more in the way of someone examining an interesting phenomenon.

And then he was overwhelmed by the fluid swirl of shifting bones and muscle, the pain shrieking through his blood as he lost touch with himself.

He came to, lying on his side on broken glass, his chest heaving. Jamie crouched beside him, repeating his name, concern in her voice.

"Yeah, I'm here," he groaned, embarrassed by his temporary indisposition. Another reason he liked to shift in private.

His hand wiped his sweating face and came away with blood. "Shit." What a bloody mess, literally.

Now that he was human, common sense began to prevail. As it soon would with Jamie. Once the shock wore off, she wouldn't want to be anywhere near him. The complications of loving a werewolf were deadly and dangerous. Because of Seth, Gordon had attacked Jamie. Imagine if Andreas had been home. She must be thinking the same thing.

"You've been cut." Her concern took him aback.

"Yeah, well, that's what happens when you jump through windows." He sat up. "I need to wash."

She reached for him and he brushed her hand away.

"Don't touch me." He wanted to be clean for her, not dirty; he wanted to be worthy and whole, not bloodied by violence and death.

"Okay," she said carefully.

He pushed himself off the ground and forced himself to examine Gordon who hadn't stirred, who wasn't likely to stir. There was the smell of death about him and Seth could not find a pulse.

"Is he dead?" Jamie asked flatly.

"I believe so." Seth's gaze went from Gordon's gray, slack face to the gun Gordon had pointed at Jamie.

"Don't touch it," warned Jamie. "I'll call the police. It will be evidence we acted in self-defense."

"Self-defense? How are you going to explain this?" Seth pointed to the broken window. "I haven't a clue how the police are going to interpret this scene."

"Well for starters, I pushed Gordon after he threatened me and he just happened to hit his head."

"Who jumped through the window?"

"I'm working on it."

Seth shook his head. "Let's just wait a moment before we phone the police, okay? We need some kind of coherent story." He didn't even want to think about the police and what they could do. If they took him into custody, he could hope for a release within three weeks.

Maybe.

Truth was, he wanted to run, get out before the police hauled him away. But he couldn't leave Jamie to face the consequences alone.

"We can wait," she agreed.

"Then let's leave this room. I need to clean up." Gingerly, he made his way through the shattered glass and out of the living room. In the bathroom, he ran the shower and stepped into it, welcoming the distraction of cleaning a multitude of minor cuts.

Jamie followed him and he ignored her, focusing on the cold water. Its punishing shock momentarily eased the horror. That bastard had almost killed Jamie. The gun pointed at her head had made Seth crazy with rage. He was still amazed Gordon's throat was intact. His control had been greater than he thought. He faced the stream of water, letting its coolness calm his body and his emotions, grateful he'd saved Jamie, regretful he hadn't been there sooner.

He pulled away from the shower to speak.

"Is the blood gone?" he asked Jamie.

"Yes." Her voice was brave, its tremor negligible, and he so wanted to comfort her.

He couldn't. The idea of police and handcuffs began to assert itself, throttling any ability to feel. The rest of the evening, if he could do the right thing and not leave Jamie here holding the bag, would be one horrible step after another, heading towards its bitter conclusion—custody.

He'd rather be a fugitive. Yet he couldn't make that choice when she needed him. Trey had enough control to be FBI. Surely Seth was strong enough for this.

She handed him a towel. "I'll get you clothes."

He nodded, then froze as wheels ground into the gravel of Jamie's drive. "You phoned the police? I asked you to wait."

"I didn't phone anyone."

They stared at each other.

"Go see who it is," said Seth. "Turn them away."

She walked to the front door while he vigorously dried himself and wrapped the towel around him.

"It's Tom's car," she called in relief.

He heard voices, three of them—Tom, Cynthia and Trey. Someone knocked.

"Jamie?" Cynthia's voice.

"Who's with you?" Jamie talked through the door.

"It's us. Tom and me and my dad."

"Are you okay?" asked Tom over Cynthia. "Mom has me all worried about blood in your yard."

There was a pause.

"Jamie, for God's sakes let us in." Tom sounded more and more worried. He banged on the door. "Jamie. Open up. Now."

Jamie looked at Seth questioningly and he nodded.

"Geez, Tom, hold on a sec." Her voice was casual, as if they'd dropped by to have coffee. She slid open the bolt.

The three stood in the doorway and Jamie didn't budge. Tom tried to see past her and found Seth. "Are we interrupting something?" he asked, observing the towel.

"Not what you think," replied Seth dryly.

Tom pushed his way in, since Cynthia and her father were too polite to do just that. Jamie stumbled aside.

"Be warned," said Jamie. "The living room..." But she couldn't articulate the state of the living room. Blood drained from her face and Seth reached for her. This stress couldn't be good for the baby.

Tom took one look at Jamie and said, "Hey, it's okay," with more hope than conviction, Seth thought, as he gathered Jamie in his arms. She was cold and shivering, shaking her head as if everything was crashing down on top of her.

"Tom's right," Seth murmured. "It will be okay."

"Who are you?" Jamie demanded. She stared at Trey with some suspicion.

"My father," began Cynthia.

"Yes, but *who* are you?" she repeated and Seth knew she had recognized his eyes in Trey's face.

"I'm Seth's uncle," said Trey.

As if it was the last straw, although this fact seemed minor compared to most others they had to deal with, Jamie went limp in Seth's arms.

ℭ

Jamie woke to three sets of eyes watching her while Seth stroked her forehead. At least he was no longer telling her not to touch him, she thought groggily. She hoped she didn't have to faint the next time she wanted Seth to hold her.

She closed her eyes. For a moment, upon waking, she'd been allowed to forget Gordon and his grisly death scene.

One pair of eyes showed more indifference than concern. Trey examined her and she was mesmerized by the pale blue magic that belonged to Seth.

Wolf's eyes.

"I'm Trey Walters," he said, as if their introduction had not been interrupted by her unconsciousness.

He extended a hand and Jamie sat up in bed to shake it.

Trey might be related to her lover, but Jamie understood some of Cynthia's coldness now. Her father's face was hard and lined. His words carried no warmth.

In fact, as his gaze turned to Seth's, he seemed annoyed. "I told you not to kill Gordon Carver. He was about to be nailed on money-laundering charges."

Seth didn't answer, though his body tensed in anger. Jamie snuggled more deeply into the arms that held her. If she could speed up her thought processes she would answer Trey's question herself because the man's attitude offended her.

"Actually." Seth's voice was clipped. "You told me not to rip out Gordon's throat, which I didn't. Though it was a near thing, given he pulled a gun on Jamie."

"Son of a bitch," said Trey, and that ended that discussion.

"You should drink." Cynthia proffered a glass of water, seemingly out of nowhere.

Jamie obliged, feeling self-conscious when all four of them watched her swallow. She tried not to wince as her throat was sore from Gordon's attack.

"Why did you all come over here tonight?" she asked.

"We came to rescue you," said Tom. "Cynthia suggested it."

Cynthia rolled her eyes. "What Tom means to say is Trey wanted to see Seth. He thought Seth might be here."

"And Cynthia and I wanted to welcome Seth to the family." Tom glanced out to the living room. "Not that I expected Gordon to crash the party before it started."

An uneasy silence fell.

Seth began to disengage from Jamie and she didn't like it at all. "What are you doing?" she demanded.

"I was hoping," put in Tom, "he would get dressed."

"Exactly." But Seth's voice held no humor.

He was withdrawing, that's what he was doing. Jamie could feel it, when she needed him badly.

Seth slid off the bed and escaped the room. Escaped her.

"The clothes are in the bathroom," she called unnecessarily.

She let out a breath of relief when Seth returned, even if he hovered in the doorway.

"We need to call the police." His voice was brittle.

"Wait." Jamie wanted to discuss how they would present what had happened to the police.

Before she could say more, Trey spoke. "I'll be in charge of this investigation, as it crosses state lines. His money-laundering occurred in Georgia, his death here."

"You?" asked Jamie. "How can you be in charge?"

"He's FBI, Jamie." Cynthia's pride was evident and Jamie understood why Cynthia had entered the FBI herself.

Seth's hope was tentative, but there. "*You* will ask me questions?"

"That's right," said Trey.

"Will you arrest me?"

"No." For the first time, a ghost of a smile hovered on Trey's face. "Not necessary."

Seth let out a huge ball of breath and Jamie felt shaky with joy. She moved to the edge of the bed to reach for Seth but he was too busy staring at Trey. Who stared back.

The moment lasted and Jamie had the impression there were undercurrents she couldn't fathom.

Trey broke eye contact first, rather politely. He turned and looked at Jamie.

"I think you two should go to a hotel for the night. This house has to be sealed off. And tomorrow, it should be fine for you to go to Seth's." Trey flipped open his phone and started calling in instructions.

"Or, you can come to our place." Tom looked quite pleased with how things were working out.

At Seth's sudden jerk of the head, Tom added, "And you too, Seth. After all, you're family. Cynthia's long lost cousin. She thought you looked like her father when she first met you. That's why she insisted on taking your photograph way back when."

Trey got off the phone. "I'd suggest these two go to a hotel," he drawled.

"We have space," Tom insisted. "Don't we, Cynthia?"

"For God's sakes, Tom, don't be thick. They want to be alone." Cynthia mouthed something to Tom which Seth must have caught because he looked embarrassed.

Tom held up his hands in surrender. "Up to you, Jamie."

"Yes, Jamie," repeated Seth. "Up to you."

Everyone stared at Seth and Jamie got mad. "What the hell is that supposed to mean?"

Seth looked sideways and back. "Uh, up to you, your choice. Tom's place might be familiar and comforting."

"You might be familiar and comforting," shot back Jamie. "We're going to a hotel. Together."

"Good. Pack your bags," ordered Trey. "My people will be here soon and I want you all away from here."

C3

Seth drove to the hotel in Jamie's car. The closest one being Holiday Inn, where Derek and Andreas were staying, but Jamie didn't think there was any danger of running into Andreas at midnight.

At least there better not be. Derek was supposed to have put Andreas to bed after they called at eight. Seth was about to become an important part of Andreas's life, but now was not the time to explain everything to her son. Or to Derek.

The lobby and halls were quiet. Jamie and Seth made it to their room without seeing anyone but the receptionist who checked them in. The room was clean. To prove it, the smell of disinfectant lingered. Seth opened the window to let in some fresh air.

As he turned back to her, she embraced him, clinging, and he pulled her in, holding her tight. After a long time, he released her, then oh so gently touched her bruised throat.

"In all the excitement, we didn't put ice on this. Let me go to the ice maker."

"I don't want you to leave me."

"I'm coming back," he assured her.

Nevertheless, she followed him out, too nervous to be left alone, even in a hotel room.

Once they returned, she started to talk and he silenced her with his fingers on her lips. He carefully applied the ice, wrapped in a hand towel.

The cold wasn't comfortable, but Seth's large hand on the back of her neck was. As was his proximity.

Ignoring his shushing noises, she insisted on talking, despite the ice applied to her throat.

"Your throat will hurt if you speak," he said, and it occurred to her that he was worried about what she had to say. Which meant it was even more important that they talk.

She started with a safer topic. "Why do I feel like you're restless and ready to take off? Is it because of the moon?"

He shook his head. "The moon is on the wane, actually. I'm ready to stay human for a while." His mouth curved ironically. "Especially after these last two weeks on the run."

"So?" she prompted. "What's going on? Why are you jumpy? Well, apart from the obvious. Is there more than the obvious?" She didn't want to bring Gordon Carver's murder into their hotel room.

Seth looked away, then back at her.

She waited.

"Okay." He closed his eyes, as if prepared to make a big confession.

She held her breath.

"You saw me shift," said Seth.

She smiled. "Yes. That was interesting." Amazing, but she didn't think she should stress how out of this world that process had been. Someday, under better circumstances, when Seth was comfortable, she would like to see it again. Unless he disliked the idea.

He raised his eyebrows in disbelief. "Interesting, eh?"

She nodded.

"I thought it might be too much for you."

"Meaning?" She wouldn't say more, she had to let him fill the silence, so she could find out what he needed from her.

He cleared his throat. "Look, I want to give you a chance, it's only fair, to say, uh..." He faltered.

"What?"

He gritted his teeth. "If you don't want me, I'd understand."

"Well, I wouldn't," she said hotly. "And what message am I sending you right now, anyway?" She was clutching his arm. "That I don't want you? *Need* you?"

"No. But maybe you need time to think."

"Think about what?"

"Jamie, I killed a man tonight."

"Uh, Seth? Do remember the events that led up to Gordon's death, okay? I was being strangled, our baby was in danger, a gun was pointed at my head. You saved me and the baby."

"Yes, but..."

"That's right. If someone attacks a man who is assaulting me, I'm offended." She punched him with her free hand. "Are you serious?"

"Well..." That he looked uncertain amazed her.

Her hand came up and caressed his face. "So beautiful and yet, so dumb."

"Hey," he protested, but his expression lightened. It tugged at her heart that he worried about her feelings for him on top of everything else.

"Listen to me, Seth. I love you. You saved me. I want to be with you. I even want to marry you, but I'll wait for you to ask me, if you're ever ready. If not, I'll take what you can give me, though I insist on full fatherhood for this baby of ours."

His eyes grew shiny. She removed the ice pack, which had done its work, and snuggled closer. The worst of his tension left his body.

"I think I understand," she said softly. "People keep leaving you. Your parents. Your sister. No one stays around. But I will, Seth. For better or worse, I'm Miss Dependability. So, you'll have to leave me and if you do, it will devastate me."

He hugged her more tightly, as if he could breathe her in, and they lay like that for a while. She could hear his throat working and understood that he was trying to speak.

"I'm not leaving you, Jamie. But there's something you should know."

"Okay."

An embarrassed rumble of laughter vibrated through him. "Cynthia told Tom already, so I suppose I should tell you."

"Yes, you should."

"Well." He cleared his throat. "You're my mate."

She pulled back to look at him. "Mate?" It sounded good but she wanted a definition to go with the one syllable word.

"Yeah, we're more monogamous than the average guy." His crooked smile made her fall more in love with him. She kissed the salty corner of one of his eyes and smiled back.

"That's the most wonderful thing anyone has ever said to me."

"I'm glad you're not alarmed."

"I'm curious, not alarmed. When did I become your mate?"

"Well, the process started more than ten years ago."

"Really?" She was flattered.

"Though our first night together firmed it up."

"Did it now?" For some reason, this delighted her. "Could've fooled me at the time. My ego would have been less bruised, if I'd known."

"Well, I panicked—"

She placed fingers on his mouth.

"Hush, I know. I *know*."

"And when you came knocking on my door with Tom, well, that was it."

"So, you're stuck with me? And have been for a while?"

"That's one way of putting it. I feel blessed."

"Oh, Seth." She snuggled in again, sleepy now that she felt secure. "You have the amazing ability to say just the right, wonderful things to me."

He kissed her eyelids, her nose and her mouth, lightly, and the caresses allowed her to unwind enough that much-needed sleep took her.

For a long time Seth lay beside her, watching and marveling in the presence of his mate. Then he, too, slept.

Epilogue

Jamie woke with her back warmed by Seth, his long arm draped over her side to rest on her very pregnant stomach.

"Hey," he said drowsily.

"Hey, yourself." She turned to him and they shared a deep, warm morning kiss that never failed to delight her. Seth's hand stroked her stomach. His expression turned thoughtful.

"Do you think you'll have the baby today?" he asked, as he had every morning for the past week.

"Well, Seth, like yesterday, I don't have the answer to that."

He looked sheepish. "But the due date is tomorrow."

"I could be late," she pointed out.

"Do you feel different?"

"Not really. I doubt I will until I go into labor." They had this conversation often, but Seth needed the reassurance.

"You'll do great," he declared.

She smiled. "You bet I will. I have a great childbearing body. So don't worry."

"I'm not worried."

She raised one eyebrow in doubt. "It's your first time, so you're allowed to be concerned."

It was more than concern. Seth feared losing her, as he had lost Veronica.

"Well," he said, giving himself a pep talk. "My biggest worries are in the past." His face clouded with painful memories.

"I know."

"I feared we'd lose the baby after Gordon messed with you."

"Shhh." She knew how Gordon's assault had upset Seth. "This girl's tenacious. Like her mother. She holds onto those she loves, and who love her."

They heard a door creak open and small feet were running down the hall. Moments later, Andreas flew into their room and launched himself onto their bed.

They moved apart so he could climb in between them.

"Hi, sweetie."

Andreas ignored her greeting and placed his hand on her stomach. With great concentration, he waited to feel the baby move.

"I think she's sleeping now," said Seth. "I was trying to feel her move earlier and had no luck."

"Oh." Andreas's lip stuck out, disappointed.

"I'll let you know when she wakes, okay?" Jamie was thrilled Andreas was excited to be a big brother. "Then you can say hello."

Andreas nodded.

"How about a hug," suggested Jamie. He threw his arms around her, and she held him for a moment before he squirmed away and bounded off the bed.

"I have my first T-ball game today! I'd better get dressed."

"Honey, the game doesn't start for five hours."

"Oh. Okay." Andreas looked at a loss.

Seth got out of bed. "We'll let your mother rest while we grab breakfast and throw a few balls outside. How about that?"

"Can Sanjay come over and play, too?"

"Sure. I'll give Rani a call."

"Yes!" Andreas raised his fist in the air, pumped once and disappeared to get changed.

"What is this?" Jamie imitated Andreas's newest gesture.

"Derek," explained Seth. "He pumps his fist in the air to show Andreas he's excited about whatever he's doing."

"Whatever works." She giggled. "Derek sure has changed."

Seth eyed her. "Not too much, I hope."

"Don't be ridiculous. You're the love of my life."

"I was joking."

She nodded wisely.

Andreas returned, half-dressed. "Dad says he can take me to my T-ball game today."

"I think we'll all go, honey. Then you'll go to your father's for Saturday night, as usual."

"Okay. I'm hungry." He raced off to the kitchen. Seth lingered in the doorway.

"What?" she asked.

"I'm really, really happy," he said in a low voice.

She smiled. "Soon we'll be really, really busy, but in a happy way." She blew him a kiss.

"Seth," called Andreas.

"Coming, slugger." Seth disappeared from the doorway and Jamie laid her head down again.

She dozed as the men in her life made breakfast, their voices comforting her as she rested, preparing for the days to come.

About the Author

Jorrie Spencer has written for more years than she can remember. Her first attempt was a book of butterfly poems. She's moved on since then, and her latest passion is romance and werewolves. She lives with her husband and two children in Canada and is thrilled to be published with Samhain.

To learn more about Jorrie Spencer please visit www.jorriespencer.com. Send an email to Jorrie Spencer at jorriespencer@gmail.com or join her Yahoo! group http://groups.yahoo.com/group/jorriespencer.

She also writes as Joely Skye (www.joelyskye.com).

Look for these titles by
Jorrie Spencer

Now Available

Haven
The Strength of the Pack

Coming Soon:

The Strength of the Wolf

For longer than she can remember, Veronica has been wolf.
Dreams give her a name and the image of a brother.
Memory gives her nothing and no one.

The Strength of the Wolf
© 2007 Jorrie Spencer

One late winter day, David Hardway saves a malnourished wolf from a trap and takes her in. During her time with David, the wolf finds in herself the desire to be human again.

David loves the wolf he saved, but dislikes the strange woman who asks for his help. Still, he is incapable of turning away someone in need and, despite himself, David becomes intrigued. As Veronica strives to remember why she abandoned humanity for wolfdom, David becomes determined to save her from her violent past.

But others are in danger and Veronica will have to act to protect her newfound pack.

Available now in ebook from Samhain Publishing.

Enjoy the following excerpt from The Strength of the Wolf...

Water splashed and David jerked up to sitting. The sound came again. Maybe from the loon whose lonely call had echoed about the lake earlier. But under the circumstances, he had to check it out. He reached for the tent's door.

Against the silence of the park's night, the zipper sounded loud in David's ears. He looked at Linc who slept like a log. He shut the tent back up.

Dressed only in boxers, a flashlight in one hand and a pocketknife in the other, he walked down to the shore, his bare feet on dirt and pine needles, and then on rock that rose up out of the water. He came to its edge and crouched down.

He wasn't surprised or even dismayed—though he should have been—to see Veronica swim breaststroke towards him, her hair sleek and dark with water. He thought of otters.

"Hi," she greeted him.

He nodded in acknowledgment and put his flashlight down on the rock so it didn't blind her.

She reached the rocky ledge below him and hooked her arms on it. Then looked up at him with enormous eyes and bare shoulders. He couldn't make out anything else.

He glanced back at the tent.

"The water's warm," she said and his gaze came back to rest on hers, golden in the night. "Come on in."

If she'd smiled, he would have turned away and left. But her face was quiet, watchful.

"You don't—" He stopped and cleared his throat. "This isn't necessary."

"Necessary?" She sounded puzzled.

"You don't think you have to trade for a ride home, do you?"

She shook her head mutely and he didn't know what to say.

"I like you, David." The words were soft, an admission.

He was embarrassed. He hadn't been nice. Nor did he like her, although he admired her industry. And her body.

He switched off the flashlight. "I'm not coming in, Veronica."

"Okay." She climbed out. Her body was gray against the blackness of the night and difficult to see clearly. His breath hitched.

He stood abruptly. "Look," he said with little force, and couldn't even continue that rebuff when she shivered beside him.

He no longer wanted to say no. As his blood pooled south, he tried to remember why it was important not to have sex with someone who was willing.

She stepped up beside him and reached out to clasp his hand. Her cool fingers found his wrapped around the pocketknife and she stiffened.

"A knife?" she asked as he transferred it to the other hand.

"I'm a protective uncle." A rattled uncle, he wanted to explain, but he would not give her details of the Linc debacle. So he let himself sound stupid, expecting her to laugh at him.

She just stood still, as if at a loss. "Someone used a knife on me once. Here." She took his hand and skimmed it down her side. He felt where skin was rough then smooth then rough. "I don't know why."

Aw, shit. He didn't know what to say so he held fast to her fingers, squeezing them gently as if that would reassure her. She held on.

Neither of them looked at each other.

"I shouldn't have said that. Wrong time and place, right?" The question seemed genuine and it struck him that she was oddly brave, putting herself out here like this. He should let go of her hand and return to the tent, but he couldn't release her now. Not without saying *something.*

"Was it a boyfriend?"

She hesitated. "Yes." She sounded unsure.

"I think you'd better find a better quality of boyfriend, Veronica."

"Yes. I'm going to try." Her earnest tone made him feel helpless.

"Good."

She smiled in the grayness. "You're nice, David. I'll show you where I put your sleeping bag, okay?"

He went, unable to think beyond her past violence, her delicate hand in his and his erection. Unable, really, to say no.

When they reached the sleeping bag, she released him, placed two palms on his hips, and slid her hands down, taking his boxers with them.

He woke up, then, to what was happening. This was not some stupid daydream. He was not sleepwalking. He pulled her up to face him.

"What?" Her confusion made his next words die in his mouth. Instead of saying, *look,* not that he'd thought beyond that one word, he curled a hand around the nape of her beautiful neck and kissed her.

Good, he thought rather furiously and his kiss intensified. As her mouth softened, he skimmed his hand down her smooth side, still slick with lake water, and cupped her bottom.

Her entire body tensed up.

He broke the kiss. "Veronica?"

GET IT NOW

MyBookStoreAndMore.com

GREAT EBOOKS, GREAT DEALS . . . AND MORE!

Don't wait to run to the bookstore down the street, or
waste time shopping online at one of the "big boys." Now,
all your favorite Samhain authors are all in one place—at
MyBookStoreAndMore.com. Stop by today and discover
great deals on Samhain—and a whole lot more!

Samhain
Publishing Ltd

WWW.SAMHAINPUBLISHING.COM

GREAT
CHEAP
FUN

Discover eBooks!

THE FASTEST WAY TO GET THE HOTTEST NAMES

Get your favorite authors on your favorite reader, long before they're
out in print! Ebooks from Samhain go wherever you go, and work with
whatever you carry—Palm, PDF, Mobi, and more.

 samhain
publishing ltd

WWW.SAMHAINPUBLISHING.COM